Fortune Cookie Karma

Other Five Star Titles
by L. F. Crawford:

Blaize of Glory

Fortune Cookie Karma

L. F. Crawford

Five Star • Waterville, Maine

This novel is a work of fiction. Names, characters, places and incidents are either the product of the author's imagination, or, if real, used fictitiously.

First Edition
First Printing: September 2005

Published in 2005 in conjunction with Tekno Books and Ed Gorman.

Set in 11 pt. Plantin by Liana M. Walker.

Printed in the United States on permanent paper.

Library of Congress Cataloging-in-Publication Data

Crawford, Louise.
    Fortune cookie karma / by L. F. Crawford.—1st ed.
      p. cm.
    ISBN 1-59414-311-0 (hc : alk. paper)
    1. Police—California—Los Angeles—Fiction. 2. Psychics—Crimes against—Fiction. 3. Beverly Hills (Calif.)—Fiction. 4. Fortune cookies—Fiction. 5. Serial murders—Fiction. I. Title.
    PS3553.R2865F67 2005
    813'.6—dc22   2005013394

Dedication

For my brothers, Martin and Lloyd, who inspired Murry and Billy's relationship.

Acknowledgments

Special thanks to the Beverly Hills Police Department for their assistance. Any errors or discrepancies in this work are not theirs, but the author's. For the sake of the story, I've used a medical examiner instead of a coroner, and taken some liberties with BHPD's administrative and procedural matters.

This book resulted from a vivid dream, but it would not have become a reality without the input of my writing buddies: Liz Crain, Jay MacLarty, and Gene Munger. Thanks for hanging with me all these years. Thanks to my husband for his support and understanding. It's tough to be a writer and I imagine it's tough to be married to one. Thanks also to my daughter, for all the times my mind was stuck on plot problems and she had to drag me back to the real world of school lunches and homework. I wouldn't trade away one moment with either of you.

Chapter 1

Only 10:00 a.m. and it was unusually hot for Beverly Hills, a muggy, wet heat that made Art Murry want to strip to his skivvies and clip his shield to his waistband. Most of the time he liked the job. Sometimes it sucked—like now.

Thirteen years in Hollywood, six years with BHPD, and it never got any easier. No matter how many murder scenes he'd done, it always surprised him how much a human body smelled like fresh beef. It was enough to put McDonald's out of business. Unlike a car accident or natural death, there was a different feeling at a murder. An unpleasant awareness of violence. It hung in the air like fog, clinging to every overturned chair, every blood-spattered wall, every grisly detail. And as if that weren't enough, it brought back flashes of other murder scenes, other bodies, none of which did a thing for his stomach. He wished he hadn't eaten breakfast.

"He didn't force the door," Evan Vermont said, examining the frame.

Murry liked and respected Vermont. The husky, six-foot-three crime tech's rumpled appearance contrasted sharply with his impeccable attention to detail. He was one of those guys that instinctively knew what Murry would want and expect, didn't cut corners, and made sure everything went into his reports. He was also a big-time hockey fan, so Murry often dropped a pair of tickets in Vermont's lap as a way of saying "thank you" after a rough case. A case like this one.

From where Murry stood, just inside the front door, the condo felt cavernous. A vaulted ceiling soared over the adjoining dining and living rooms, leaving a narrow, dark corridor to the two bedrooms and bathrooms. From the outside, the peak-roofed condominiums, half-hidden behind clumps of palm tree fronds, appeared smaller.

"Maybe she let him in," Vermont added.

"Or he had a key." Murry wondered if the security gate was habitually left open. They'd found it that way. The two cameras were broken, and he doubted the film would show anything. "You check the roof?" he asked.

"Yo," Vermont answered. "And the windows. None locked. Best bet is the bedroom; found some wood flakes on the sill." Vermont never assumed anything.

Obviously she'd felt safe behind a gate and living in an upper unit. Murry's walk-through had shown a rumpled bed, pale pink silk sheets and matching bedspread spilling onto matching Berber carpet—she liked pink—and a broken Tiffany lamp in the bedroom. The bronze base of the lamp, resembling the curved, twisted roots of a tree, was undamaged, but the green and violet stained-glass leaves lay in ruins. It was enough to make an antique dealer weep. He had no doubt it was genuine; the rest of the house was furnished in authentic turn-of-the-century Art Nouveau pieces. Ones he wouldn't mind owning. Bookcases and cabinets with upflowing lines rose toward the ceiling. A couch, its turquoise velvet cushions and dome-shaped back edged in intricate walnut inlay, managed to take up an entire wall. A nice pad for a ballet dancer turned part-time college professor. Very nice. Where had the money come from?

He could hear his partner, Billy, talking to the crime tech

in the bathroom, and tuned out the conversation. Quelling the sickening lurch in his belly, he turned back to the kitchen, and the victim. Time to take in the details. Olga Shostakovich: dark hair, small breasts, long legs. Nude, except for the black nylon stocking stretched over her face. The nylon looked like it had been cut from a pair of pantyhose, but so far they hadn't found the rest of the stocking. Beneath the black mesh, he could see a rectangular shadow. Her mouth had been taped shut.

She lay on her back, her head slumped to one side. Ice picks pinned her hands to the polished parquet. Her long, tapered fingers had curled in agony around the picks. He could feel his own fingers curl in response, everything in him wanting to turn away. But this was the job, what he did, and he was going to catch the son-of-a-bitch. He knew that was the only way he could get through this, to promise the tiny ballerina nailed to the floor that he would catch her killer. That her death would be avenged. He could see pale white nail polish scratched into the wood. The holes in her hands were bigger than the diameter of the picks. She'd struggled. He took a deep breath, reminding himself he'd seen worse, though he couldn't remember when.

A third pick was embedded in her chest. There was no blood, just a puffed-up wound. Two more picks skewered her insteps. Brownish blood stained her feet like some awful tan-in-a-bottle stuff. Around the body, the floor as a canvas, the perp had painted intricate curved lines of blood, extending like wings from her ankles to wrists, the total effect more like a gruesome butterfly than a crucifixion—Murry's first thought. Thinking of butterflies led him to the idea of caterpillars emerging from cocoons. Was the killer sending some kind of message about transformation?

"He took some time painting those," Vermont said.

"Yes, he did." But he wouldn't know what the elaborate ritual meant until he had the killer in cuffs. He tried to look at the corpse dispassionately, but all he could see was the lovely, dark-haired woman in the stack of Christmas photos they'd gone through. Her eyes full of happy mischief, she wore a Santa hat and looked like she had everything to live for. Happy New Year, he thought, thankful he couldn't see her face.

"Cold and blue and stuck full of holes, too . . ." Billy drawled in a fake country-music twang as he clomped into the room, patting his pockets for the pack of cigarettes he no longer carried. His off-the-wall comments usually didn't bother Murry—they were Billy's way of relieving the unbearable tension—but this time he had to bite back a snarl.

The scent of peppermint wafted from the Kid's mouth as he chomped hard and fast on his gum. Nineteen years older than Billy's twenty-three, Murry no longer smoked, chewed, or imbibed anything but an occasional glass of wine. His biggest vice was his addiction to work. Something he hadn't realized until he started dating Mary Éclair, the local medical examiner. Figuring out time to be together—just the two of them, no dead bodies—sometimes took a Houdini act. But they managed.

As though brought to life by his thoughts, Éclair slipped past Vermont and crouched over the corpse. Like wrinkles on a Shar-Pei, her loose blue-cotton top and baggy khakis bunched around her slim figure. She glanced at Murry, warmth flooding her eyes, then got down to business. "Photos done?"

Murry nodded.

Vermont ducked beneath the bright red Le Creuset pots and copper-bottomed sauté pans that hung above the island.

"Yell when you turn her over," he said, before retreating outside.

"Will do," Éclair said absently.

"Winslow's in the master bedroom dusting for prints," he called from the landing. The balding lab tech, who looked like a bearded Patrick Stewart, was working his way from the last bedroom to the kitchen.

Éclair exhaled and snapped on latex gloves. She pulled a micro-cassette recorder from her fanny pack and quickly ran through the litany of identifying herself, date, time, and location. Murry preferred his spiral notepad. He hated recorders, cell phones, video cameras, and faxes—damn machines didn't give his intuition a chance to work. More and more they intruded on his job. He liked quiet and the chance to give his brain cells time to percolate. Éclair teasingly labeled him a leftover Victorian, because he enjoyed poetry and opera and trusted himself more than anything mechanical. Damn right.

He eyed the body as Éclair noted the position of Olga's limbs. "Did she shave her pubis, or did the perp?" he asked. Neither Éclair nor the papers had mentioned that detail on the other victims.

"She did. The others weren't shaved and she's got a shadow of growth."

He jotted a note about Olga's lack of pubic hair next to his drawing of the body's position. He roughed-in the walls, forming a cross on either side, then sketched the ceiling and lights. Vermont had already measured everything in the room and made a more detailed drawing of the cabinets, island, stove, and refrigerator. Billy was mapping the condo as well, because Murry liked a second set of notes. His training was finally getting through to the Kid. Good.

Éclair stepped cautiously around one outstretched arm,

keeping her Nikes away from the bloodstains, her gaze on the hand. "Looks like she may have scratched him."

"Deep?"

"If that's his blood under her nails, I'd say yes."

He liked the idea that Olga might have surprised the guy with her strength. Only five feet and one hundred pounds, but most of it muscle. "First time for that, too?"

"Compared to the others? Yes."

Scratches could be important evidence. He eyed the body. There seemed to be more blood on the floor than on the corpse. The clothes were missing, which was consistent with the other victims. Did the killer keep them as souvenirs? Most serial killers collected trophies—something that would pay memory dividends and give the sick bastard a high. On the other hand, Olga might have slept nude, or Ice Pick might have dumped or burned her clothing. With all the hills and vegetation in the area, they might never be found.

Billy resumed his mapping of the kitchen. He paused every now and then to glance uneasily toward the body and stroke his caterpillar mustache. The mustache—thin and fair as it was—kept him from looking pre-pubescent. His favorite complaint was that he couldn't buy a brew without getting carded. Murry couldn't remember that problem.

Éclair squatted closer to the body, peering at the neck, first one side, then the other. The ragged edges of the black nylon that covered Olga's face ended just below her jaw line and made her skin look greenish white. Éclair lightly depressed the area on both sides of the neck, the skin blanching around fingerprint-sized patches of skin. Bruises could be confused with *livor mortis*, but bruised skin didn't whiten when depressed.

"Strangled first?" Billy asked hopefully.

If only she had been, Murry thought, eying the holes in

Olga's bloody hands. Two decades ago, his own fiancée, Rachel, had been murdered in a B-and-E gone wrong. In the blink of an eye, she'd been taken from him. Ever since, Murry's desire to nail bastards like Rachel's killer hadn't diminished one iota. He wanted to escort Ice Pick to the gas chamber and drop the pill himself.

"He choked her, but not to death." Éclair leaned closer to the corpse. "That's consistent with the other victims. The bruise to the jaw is not."

"She was a fighter," Murry said. Olga had well-developed calves, a dancer's strong legs, and he imagined her kicking and scratching the son-of-a-bitch before he choked her and jammed the picks through her palms. It took an act of will to shut off what she'd suffered through after that: the rape, the picks hammered through her feet, then that last, final pick to the heart. His breath was shallow and he forced himself to take a deep breath. She was beyond their help now. All he could do was the job. "Exactly what are the physical similarities between Shostakovich and the others?"

"They were all short, slender, green or blue eyes, brown hair."

That caught him off-guard. *Éclair fit that description.* But she worked with cops. The other victims were all college students or, in Olga's case, a college teacher. So why was he so damn uptight all of a sudden? Why was this case affecting him so much? He had the feeling that if startled, he'd jump out of his skin, like there was too much energy surging through his veins, searching for a way out. He shifted his weight and worked for a blank face to hide his uneasiness. He didn't want Éclair or Billy asking if he was all right. But he was afraid that maybe he wasn't. The last time he'd felt this jumpy was while shaking the hand of a Voodoo sorcerer. He'd ended up on his knees screaming, sure he'd had his hand hacked off with a machete, everyone else wondering if he were having a heart attack or nervous breakdown. No one had bought his "didn't eat my Wheaties" explanation, and the "psychic detective" label continued to dog his career. He wasn't psychic; he had hunches, intuition. And once in awhile a weird vision-flash he couldn't explain, didn't even want to attempt to explain. Those went into a lock-box in the back of his brain, where the box stayed chained and padlocked. He didn't believe in that mumbo-jumbo. He realized Éclair was watching his face. "I thought one victim was blond?" he asked.

Éclair nodded. "Dyed her hair."

"Think he knew?"

She shrugged.

"Any other similarities?"

"They were choked, staked out, crucifixion-style, then raped. In this case, I'd say he choked her into semi-consciousness, she came to, he slugged her, hammered the picks through her hands, raped her, and put picks through her feet. The last one's always through the heart."

"Jesus," Billy said.

Yes, a grim crucifixion, Murry thought. And until they caught the guy, there would be more just like it. Billy had been excited about Ice Pick leaving his latest on Beverly Hills' turf. Murry had wished the body had landed somewhere outside their six square miles. But he was determined that nothing would get screwed up on his watch. A watch that would end as soon as the head of the Ice Pick task force arrived. The man heading up the unit, LAPD Lieutenant Paul Jamison, was stuck in a pile-up behind a jack-knifed rig on the 405, leaving Murry temporarily in charge. Murry had worked with Jamison during his first couple of years at Hollywood and remembered him as driven and not very talkative. They'd lost touch over the years. Would Jamison draft Billy and

Murry into the task force? He had mixed feelings about joining a task force. Other cops didn't always like Murry's questions or his hunches. And if drafted, he'd be working late hours to play catch-up. He turned to Éclair. "Anything else different about this one?" Jamison would expect the details.

"Can't say yet."

Murry ran his hands through his hair. They'd worked together for years and he knew the drill. "You'll get back to me."

According to the newspaper, Ice Pick's timetable had gone from six months to three. Three months. Which meant they'd be lucky to have three months before the next kill. Jamison was probably blowing a gasket. "She's number five, right?" Murry asked, praying they'd catch the guy before the next call.

Billy blew a bubble and popped it between his teeth. "As far as we know. Farel's still checking with other states."

Farel was a friend of Billy's from the Academy, worked out of Hollywood, and was a member of the Ice Pick task force. Farel and BHPD Detective Ray "Latin Lover" Ramirez were working the building together. They'd already interviewed the neighbor who'd discovered the body, a Miss Marple type who had the good sense not to throw up until she'd reached her own kitchen.

Murry's cellular shrieked, and he jerked it from his pocket.

"Geez, Murry," Billy mumbled around his wad of gum, "why don't you buy your own? That's the third dinosaur they've given you this year."

"I have a bad-ass rep to maintain. Besides, I like the way it blows the wax out of my ears." He let it shriek one more time before moving into the living room. "Murry here."

"What's up?"

Captain Daniels, his boss, sounded like he'd just run five

miles up stadium stairs. The guy was in good shape, but a serial killer in Beverly Hills had him sweating. Taxpayers who paid to reside in this particular fantasy land lived under the illusion that homicides only dotted less expensive landscapes. Ice Pick had burst their bubble.

LAPD would be running the thing, making the decisions, which meant politically Daniels could pass the buck—except he would want to keep his fingers in as long as possible. And if Murry solved it, Daniels would kiss his feet.

"Looks like number five."

"Press there?"

"Yes. Uniforms are keeping them behind a perimeter."

"The ME?"

"Éclair's here."

"Okay." Semi-satisfaction. "What about Jamison?"

"Still stuck in the pile-up."

"Probably pissing up a rope, too. Okay, talk to me as soon as you get back."

"You got it." Murry slipped the cellular back into his pocket and returned to the kitchen. "The captain says hello."

Éclair hovered over the victim's feet, clearly absorbed at the sight of the ice picks' wooden handles above the victim's toes. Billy winced and stepped out to the landing.

"What am I missing?" Murry asked.

She shrugged. "Not sure." Murry knew she wouldn't say until she was certain. Maybe tonight—if they were lucky enough to hit the sack at the same time. His sack this week. Hers next. Not a bad arrangement. It spread the workload between both places and staved off taking each other for granted. Not that he could ever imagine taking her for granted. He wasn't about to lose a woman who made him want to out-sing his Pavarotti-famous brother.

He watched her depress the skin along the side of the

arms. The dependent areas, where the blood pooled, looked reddish-purple. Despite the pressure of her fingers, the skin remained discolored. "Fixed *livor mortis?*" he asked. Important for determining if a body had been moved.

"You thinking of changing jobs?"

"Education via osmosis." Through the window, he watched Billy bum a cigarette from Vermont, light it, and inhale to his toenails. So much for the Kid's latest health-kick.

"Hey, Vermont," Éclair called.

Vermont and Billy ambled in, Billy almost as green as Olga. Éclair's gloves snapped as she pulled a second pair over the first. "Let's remove the ice picks, bag the hands and feet, then turn her over."

Vermont donned gloves and carefully gripped the ice pick that skewered Olga's right hand. He gave it a tug, then another. "These things are hammered in."

Murry nodded at Billy. "Check with the couple downstairs. See if they heard any pounding. Maybe they thought Olga was hanging pictures."

Vermont finally jerked the first pick free of the floor. The body groaned like plywood as he gingerly eased it from her grip. Éclair placed the bloody pick into an evidence bag, slid it inside another, then marked the outside. Vermont wrenched out the second pick and handed it over, repeating the process until all five were removed.

Murry helped Éclair lift the body, heavy and stiff with rigor, the arms outspread, the legs rigid. They turned her over and laid her face-down on a sheet of plastic. His stomach clenched. The wounds in the back of her hands and feet now appeared like tiny punctures. The shoulders, buttocks, and calves looked pale.

Vermont snapped off a roll of pics while Murry and Éclair stood back. "You going to remove the nylon?" Vermont asked.

Murry noticed what looked like blood and stepped close. "No." Using the end of his ballpoint, he tried to ease the black mesh from Olga's dark hair. It stuck. "Any of the others get slugged on the back of the head, Doc?"

Éclair crouched beside him. "No."

Murry's imagination painted Olga desperately fighting for her life, not giving up until her heart stopped beating. Even though he couldn't see her face, was glad he couldn't, he could feel the violence shrouding the body. He couldn't give Shostakovich back her life, but he could make sure she got her bit of justice.

Billy ambled back in. "Hammering woke up the wife around two-twenty," he said, "but it stopped and she went back to sleep."

"Good." Murry scribbled 2:20 a.m. in his notebook. "See if you can find what he used to pound with. Maybe he slugged her with it."

Snap, snap, snap. Vermont shot more pics of the back of the ballet dancer's head.

Billy crouched, staring at Olga's head. "Maybe that slug to the jaw knocked her against something?"

Speculation. Murry wanted facts. "Where's Ramirez and Farel?"

"At the end of the street. You'd think with ten units jammed in so close, someone would have seen something."

People hardly looked out their windows anymore, Murry thought. He made a mental note to find out what had been released to the papers and what had been held back.

"I'll be with Winslow," Vermont said, heading down the hall.

"Does two to two-thirty sound right for time of death?" Murry asked Éclair. Witnesses' memories were not as reliable as forensics. Miss Marple in the condo next door had seen

Olga come home at the usual time, 6:15—alone. Olga had waved to the gray-haired widow before going inside. Evidently, they were friends and shared coffee on Saturday mornings. No coffee today.

"Two-thirty?" Éclair, busy taking a swab from the inner thigh, nodded. "I'd say she's been dead eight to twelve hours, but physical exertion can speed rigor. Could be less."

"Semen?"

A curt nod, but she didn't look happy about it.

He'd expected at least a sound of satisfaction—semen was evidence that could link Olga to Ice Pick. Obviously she didn't think this was a big break, and he wondered why. "You find semen on the other victims?" he asked.

She glanced up. "No."

Another inconsistency. Jamison wasn't going to like it. Murry's gut churned like he'd eaten too many fat-free potato chips. The protein shake he'd sucked down on the way over roiled on waves of unease. He'd never worked a serial before and he felt edgy. The whack on the back of Olga's head, the semen—suddenly Olga had a couple of question marks. Though he doubted it was a copycat, he had to consider every angle. He peeled off his gloves, then made a concerted study of a framed poster of Pavlova's ballet slippers while Éclair took the victim's rectal temperature. He waited until he heard her tapping on her calculator before asking, "Same timeframe?"

"Body temp's eighty point one."

"So, if her body temp was normal when she died, then—?" He knew she hated to be pinned down before she'd done the autopsy, but he was impatient for information.

"Then she's been dead twelve hours."

Twelve hours would put the death around two-thirty. Good. Conflicting evidence was a pain in the butt, supporting evidence, a bonus. He had a feeling he'd need all the bonuses he could get.

"But that's only a guess, Murry. I'll know more—"

"I'll take anything I can get, Doc. Every second counts, you know that."

Her gaze questioned why he was pushing her. "Every second may count, Detective, but if I cut corners and rush things, I'll pay on the witness stand. You know *that*."

"Touché." He handed his phone to Billy, who looked all too ready to watch the two of them duke it out. "Get Jamison for me, will you?"

While Billy punched in the number, Murry adopted a conciliatory tone, addressing Éclair. "You working late?" Translation: talk later?

"Yes."

Since she probably wouldn't remember to eat unless he reminded her, he offered, "Why don't I drop by with dinner?"

A half-smile. "Italian?"

"Lots of garlic," he said, hoping to mask the odor of disinfectant and death.

"I'll try to finish before midnight; either way, I can take a short break."

"Between seven and eleven?" A ballpark time was the best he could give her, and she knew it.

"I'll be hungry," she said, her lips quirking up at the corners before her gaze shifted back to the body. Back to business.

"You notice anything else different about this one?"

She hesitated. "The most obvious: one of the ice picks looks old—used—and there's no decorative scrolling on the sides. In the other cases, the wood was new: no rust, no brand, swirls etched into it."

"Swirls? Like a pattern or message?"

"Far as I know, no message has been deciphered. You'll need to talk to Jamison about that."

Murry eyed the one odd pick. "Maybe he lost one. Grabbed one here or one from his own place." He thought about that. "Do you own an ice pick?"

"No."

"Neither do I." It wasn't a common household item anymore. "Bones handling the lab work?"

"Yes."

"I'll have him go over the picks in all five cases. See what he comes up with. Maybe we'll get lucky."

Éclair humphed as though to say it shouldn't take luck.

"What about the back of the head?" he asked. "Any idea what he hit her with?"

"Murry, you know I hate this kind of theorizing—later, okay?"

He held up his hands. "Later." As long as it wasn't when they were between the sheets. Visions like this didn't lead to fun in the sack.

Billy handed Murry his phone. "Jamison just pulled up."

Murry waited on the landing, glad to be out of the condo, glad to breathe in the scent of the ocean, feel the hint of a breeze cut through the muggy air.

Jamison's carrot-red hair, dulled by strands of gray, came into view above the mob of reporters. He squeezed past the uniforms at the gate and took the stairs two at a time, his face flushed from exertion. "The boys all hate you, Murry. They don't get an opportunity like this every day."

"Like you'd give them a ticket to the show?" Murry razzed back. "Aren't you the one who used to say, 'You let one guy look, next thing you know you've got a contaminated scene'?" The last thing Murry wanted was to sit on the witness stand and explain something like that.

"You remembered." Jamison grinned and shook Murry's hand. "Long time since our Hollywood days," he said. "Thanks for holding down the fort. Where's Sundance?"

"Don't let Billy hear you. He already thinks he looks like Redford."

Jamison's friendly face sobered as he stared past Murry. "Never gets any easier." He turned away. After a pause, he said, "You stay on this, you may have to work with Tack."

Obviously, Murry's soap-opera divorce had traveled the gossip chain to LAPD.

"That a problem, Murry?"

Problem? Why should there be a problem?

Just because he fooled around with my wife and caused the divorce?

Just because I broke his jaw and almost lost my job?

Just because I made him look like a fool in the Voodoo case?

"No problem at all."

Jamison gave a nod of approval, but his gaze held the silent warning: *there better not be.* "Where's the ME?"

"Right here," Éclair said from the living room. "I can't tell you anything conclusive . . . until—"

"You finished?" Jamison interrupted.

"Yes."

"So where's the meat wagon?"

"At the curb."

"Okay. Bag her and get her out of here." His gaze shifted to Murry. "Give me a rundown."

"Vermont and Winslow are inside with Billy. Farel and Ramirez are interviewing neighbors. Two uniforms are searching the perimeter." Murry flipped his notebook to the first page. "Vermont and Winslow already bagged everything obvious—a wine glass, a half-smoked cigarette in the ashtray . . . They've dusted the bedrooms and bathrooms, but not the living room or kitchen."

"She smoke?"

"Didn't find a pack anywhere, but she might have. Some dancers smoke to keep their weight down."

"Give me a walk-through."

Murry led the way into the master bedroom. "Looks like the killer came through the front door with a key, or through this window. Vermont found a few paint flakes on the sill. Killer wore gloves."

"Anyone hear screams?"

"No. He got to her quick enough to slap tape over her mouth. She had strong legs. She must have got a kick in. Guy might have bruised balls. I'd say she scrambled from the bed, knocked the lamp off the dresser as she ran."

They moved into the hallway. Jamison gestured toward the three angled eight-by-tens on the wall. All were of Olga with other dancers. He pointed to the guy beside her in the first photo. "Mikhail Baryshnikov. She must have been good."

"Looks that way," Murry agreed.

"Let's just hope we don't get any of her famous friends breathing down our necks," Jamison said.

Sure as shit, if she was my friend I'd be breathing down some-one's neck, Murry thought. "She probably made it to the living room before he caught her." They stepped past the bookcase and overturned chair.

Farel knocked at the door to get their attention. For the latest Lakers' game, he'd shaved his head like a basketball player, but was too short to ever be mistaken for one. "A neighbor, Mrs. Emerson, says she had insomnia last night and got up around midnight to watch TV. Her blinds were open, so she went to close them and noticed a white or gray panel truck parked just outside the gate. She remembered because her neighbor usually parks his red Mazda there."

Jamison looked pleased. "Follow it up." He turned to Murry. "This could be a break. We haven't got shit on the others."

Murry bit back the impulse to tell him about the semen. Better to wait for the prelim. "What about the decorative pattern on the picks? Éclair says all the ones used on the other victims were scrolled. Same pattern?" Had the killer bought them that way?

"You mean as in mass-produced? No. It's more like the killer's taken pains to make the picks uniquely his."

"You get any hits on ice pick killings anywhere else in the country?"

"I wish."

"Hey, Murry," Billy said, standing at the bookcase, "I think I've found something."

Using the end of his pencil, Billy pointed toward a brass bookend, a replica of *The Little Mermaid*, that had been hastily shoved onto the otherwise neatly-arranged shelf. There was a dark splotch on the felt backing.

Murry leaned closer. "Looks like blood. Good job, Kid."

Grinning, Billy bagged the mermaid while Jamison lifted the other bookend, checked it, then put it back. The books ranged from biographies to literary novels. "What did the other victims like to read?" Murry asked, knowing he was playing catch-up.

Jamison's gaze skidded over the books. "Not Stegner, that's for certain. One had a bunch of paperbacks, mostly mysteries as I recall; the other was into movies. Could've put Blockbuster out of business."

"You find any common threads besides physical appearance?"

"Not yet."

"You want to join us for a quick lunch on the way back to the station?" Murry asked. "Compare notes?"

Jamison shook his head and paused on the landing. "I've got a few details to nail down."

Nail down? The turn of phrase had Murry suddenly imagining Ice Pick hammering a pick through Olga's hand. *Whack. Whack. Whack.* He could almost hear it. Almost see her scratch the bastard before he caught her hand and forced it against the floor. With an effort, Murry wrenched his thoughts back to Jamison. Something was bugging Jamison besides the usual *details.* Murry nudged Billy. "Wait for me at the car." He waited until Billy was out of sight before asking, "What's wrong?"

"Keep this to yourself?"

Murry nodded.

"Shostakovich's not just any ballet dancer murdered by a psycho." Jamison took a pipe from his pocket and stuck it between his lips, but didn't light it. "Miss the damn thing, so I chew on the stem," he explained. "She taught a couple of psychology classes at the University and claimed to be a psychic. She called me after the second murder. She wanted to help."

The press would cut them to ribbons if they got wind of this. "Said she could help or that she wanted to help?" Had Olga had information about Ice Pick?

Jamison's jaw tightened. "She offered to help. But when I pressed her—it sounded like a bunch of hocus-pocus. Nothing concrete."

Jamison's shrewd gaze was on Murry, *the* question in his eyes, the same question Murry had faced before. *Are you psychic, Murry? Do you believe? How do you explain the hat tricks you pulled to solve those other cases?*

Murry did what he always did, ignored the look and asked a question. "You told her no thanks?"

If Jamison was disappointed in their silent exchange, he masked it. "Yeah, I told her 'no thanks'—only not so polite. Dammit, I hate those frauds out there bilking people who have no sense."

Murry had the feeling Jamison's reaction was more personal. "You ever talk to one?" Murry had read a couple of books, then decided to quit while ahead.

Jamison's face colored. "Let's just say I had a run-in, in my Hollywood days. Now I feel like shit. Even if she was a fraud, I could have handled it better."

"What did she tell you?"

"She said the killer wasn't going to stop until we caught him—and she said she kept hearing the message: it's too late."

"Too late for her?" After his experience with bòkòrs and Voodoo, Murry was willing to believe damn near anything.

"That's what she thought, and she said if we didn't want her help, then she'd pursue it on her own—that she had nothing to lose."

Murry glanced toward the kitchen. *Except her life.* He was glad he wasn't the one to turn her away. "No one's going to fault you for your decision."

Jamison raised an eyebrow. "I thought she was just after a story. She'd written a book. Figured her offer was a stunt for publicity. Besides, I couldn't justify the expense of assigning someone to her with no cause and no discernable link to the victims. But that doesn't mean I feel great about it." He stowed the pipe in his pocket and started down the stairs. "I feel like I let her down."

Murry didn't know what to say. This confession seemed a genuine move toward friendship, but it made him uncomfortable. He'd thought he and Tack were friends. If he were as psychic as his coworkers' jibes implied, he wouldn't have been the last to know his partner and his wife were doing the pelvis piñata. Come to think of it, a lot of the psychic rumors had died down with his divorce. But now he was leery of getting too chummy with anyone on the job. Besides, he wasn't into hitting the bar for a beer with the guys after work. Not these days. He'd rather spend his free time with Éclair. So he shrugged off Jamison's possible overture. "If you'd put a man on her, chances are the killer would've waited until you pulled him, then killed her. We're a clean-up crew."

"So let's clean up the mess and get this guy before he does it again."

"Are we sure he's human?"

Jamison didn't crack a grin. "I'll be sure to include any tall aliens with big shoulders and short, black hair in the line-up."

"It was a joke."

He glanced toward the doorway as the two techs from the meat wagon went in. "Yeah, well, I'm not feeling very humorous, okay?"

"You said tall, wide shoulders, short hair. You got a witness?" *That* hadn't made the papers.

"A vague description from a midget janitor with Coke-bottle glasses who thinks I'm seven feet tall," Jamison said, disgusted.

Murry figured Jamison ought to start smoking again. He was taking this too personally. But then, Murry had the same problem. Maybe because he'd never planned to become a cop—until it became personal. He'd never wanted to follow in his father's footsteps. The man had worked long hours, hardly ever came home, and died on the job. But Rachel's murder had changed Murry's career, his life, everything. It didn't matter that the killer had been caught and sent up. Every slimebag Murry put behind bars gave him a sense of justice and purpose. And in an odd way, it gave him an understanding and appreciation for his father that he'd never had when his father was alive.

He looked back as they brought Olga out in a body bag. A psychic who saw her own death? What a gruesome thought.

What would he do if he knew he was going to die?

Write down clues? Yes, if he had any. He needed to search every possible place she might have left one.

Skip the country? Not a bad idea.

He glanced at the front gate and the false security it offered. Then he thought about her hands nailed to the floor. Sure as shit, he wouldn't have stuck around.

Chapter 2

Murry put his gloves back on, took a tentative step toward the kitchen, then veered down the hallway. He paused at the photographs, wondering if the perp had checked them out.

"You're done with the hall, right?" he called toward the kitchen.

"Yo," Vermont hollered back.

Taking each framed photo from the wall, Murry turned them over. In careful, neat cursive, a date was written, ranging from five to eight years ago. Too ancient to mean anything? Nothing nudged his intuition.

Billy, obviously tired of waiting at the car, stuck his head inside the door. "We staying or hitting the road?"

"I'm staying." He handed the photos to Billy. "Identify each person and have New York check out their whereabouts last night."

"How am I supposed to do that?"

"Start with Baryshnikov. They're probably all dancers. Get New York's finest on it."

Grumbling, Billy headed for the stairs. "I'll fax these over from BHPD. Be back in thirty."

Murry gave him a nod, then moved into the bedroom. "Olga Shostakovich," he said aloud, "tell me about yourself." He slid back the window, leaned out, and peered up at the

31

roof. The killer came in through the door with a key, or he must have lowered a rope or brought a ladder. A rope would have been less conspicuous, but either one would have fit into a van. If the van had anything to do with it.

The bedding was messed, but there was no blood or semen or anything to indicate violence. He'd slapped on the tape. She'd managed to run, gotten as far as the kitchen. No, the living room. That's where he'd used the bookend, hit her on the back of the head. Probably knocked her out and carried her into the kitchen.

Then she'd come to. Murry thought of the holes in her hands, and didn't think he'd feel like eating for the rest of the day, dinner date with Éclair or not.

He opened the nightstand drawer, saw a pen and a blank pad of paper. He crouched and peered under the bed, knowing Winslow had already covered the area, yet needing to check it himself.

His phone shrieked and he reared up, banging his head on the frame. Cursing, he sat up and flipped the damn thing open. "Murry here," he snarled, rubbing the back of his head. "Murry here," he repeated louder.

"Jamison's scheduled a task force meeting at one," Captain Daniels rasped into the phone. "Since we're centrally located, it'll be in our conference room. *I've* got a meeting with the Mayor." He sounded like he'd rather be dying of thirst in the Sahara. "If you get anything, let me know."

"You got it." Nothing like a little pressure. He checked the prescription bottles. Some were a couple of years old. The refill on one was due to expire. All were concurrent prescriptions from three different doctors for the same thing: Restoril. Either Olga had trouble sleeping or she was trying to keep the weight off—although if the Restoril was to counteract uppers, he would have expected to find some. He jotted the RX numbers and doctors' names in his notebook.

Her death couldn't be a coincidence. Had she discovered the killer's identity? Tried to meet with him? What prompted him to select her as his next target?

No gun, no alarm system. Why? If he feared for his life, he'd damn well take precautions. Éclair kept a Browning 9mm by her bed, and he was careful to call before coming over. He preferred his Sig, and kept it under his pillow when it wasn't hanging from his shoulder. It did the job.

He opened the closet door and eyed Olga's clothes. College student threads and five business suits, size 2. Definitely not a clotheshorse. Neither was Éclair. It took an occasion like meeting his mother and the count or a night at the opera to get her out of her baggies.

God, why was he thinking about Éclair? Irritated, he wrenched his mind back to the case. He searched through the rest of Olga's suits, then moved to the dresser, found nothing significant, and gave up. No uppers, no downers, no in-betweeners, and no clues leaping out at him. Dammit. He opened the bottom of the nightstand. Worn toe shoes and multicolored leg-warmers. The toe shoes were signed, but he couldn't read the scrawl. He took his penlight and scanned the back. Nothing. Disgusted, he sat up and studied the bookcase headboard of antique cherry wood and the uneven stack of books. "Talk to me, Olga."

Something winked from the darkness between the piles of paperbacks. He leaned across the bed and shoved them aside to expose a compact, black Olympia tape recorder. Interesting. It was switched to VCVA—voice activation—and was on. Really interesting. He popped the cassette. The label read "September 13." Yesterday. Weird. Did she leave a tape in every night? Record her dreams? He shoved the cassette back in, hit REWIND to the beginning, then hit PLAY.

Snoring. A garbled murmur. Olga asleep?

He turned the sound to maximum while he searched for more tapes. Nothing. Odd, most people kept blank tapes around or old ones to reuse.

He glanced at the nightstand, pulled out the leg-warmers and toe shoes, and felt along the sides of the shelf, then along the bottom of the drawer. Nothing. He checked behind the dresser and the other nightstand.

A sound like the rustle of fabric whispered from the tiny speaker. A moment later the bed creaked, followed by a low, ominous warning, "Don't move . . ."

A ripping sound. Duct tape?

A grunt. A thud. A crash. He glanced toward the doorway and the broken vase shards. Holy shit.

A faint click and a pause, then Vermont's voice, his conversation with Winslow loud and clear. Murry listened with half-an-ear as he searched around the bed frame and along the baseboards.

When he heard Winslow mention Éclair, he sat up.

"You get a load of the way Murry lit up when Éclair walked in?"

Winslow grunted. "How long you think they're going to pretend they aren't blowing each other over the mountain?"

"Until they waltz down the aisle," Vermont said, amusement in his tone.

"What? You don't think he'd do it again?"

"Murry?" Vermont's tone said *of course*. "The guy's a romantic. He's not the one who'll drag his feet."

Murry could feel his face turn red. His ex-wife, Scarlett, had turned his life into a soap opera and now everyone was tuned in. Shit.

"He's—" Vermont's voice broke off and Murry heard himself and Jamison. He popped the tape and dropped it into a bag, marking the outside with the date and time, thinking Vermont would be upset to learn he'd missed something— and embarrassed when he realized his conversation with Winslow had been recorded. Maybe that would teach him to keep his mouth shut.

Murry eyed the recorder. It looked new. Did Olga record anything else? If he knew, he might understand why it had been on last night. Maybe she recorded thoughts about her dreams when she woke up at night. Because she certainly hadn't expected Ice Pick—had she?

He thought about her body staked to the kitchen floor.

No. No one in their right mind would lie there waiting for that.

Chapter 3

Conrad moved to the shady, overgrown side of the house, shoved through the thick ivy that camouflaged the door, and punched in the code on the keypad. The door swung inward on well-oiled hinges and closed behind him with an automatic *click*. He paused to punch in a second code on the inside alarm, then re-shouldered his backpack and climbed the narrow stairs. A strip of lights lit the staircase up to the butterfly room.

His room. The array of frames, some large, some small, some dating back to his teens, covered two walls. He set the pack at his feet and traced his fingers over the glass above the latest addition to his collection, the endangered Callippe Silverspot. Orange with such pretty tan and brown triangular patterns at the edges, silver spots underneath. Forever preserved. He tapped on the glass, recalling how it beat its wings, trying to escape the pins. In the end it had surrendered, as they all did. His beautiful butterflies.

His mother had hated his collection, beat him when she caught him at it. *Look at the holes in their wings. You've ruined them. Use the chloroform and pin them through the body.* He pretended to comply but never did it. He liked to watch them struggle, liked to watch that sudden calm descend before they transformed into spirit and found paradise.

He grabbed the remote, pointed it at the huge plate-glass mirror, and clicked DISPLAY. The entire wall hummed and shifted inward, then slid sideways, exposing his special dressing room.

He had lined the back wall with shelves—five deep. Each shelf held ten Styrofoam heads as though fresh from the guillotine. Some sported mustaches and beards, or goatees and Elvis sideburns; others had graying hair, fiery red locks like a clown, foppish blond curls, or were bald altogether.

His costumes, uniforms, and latex body suits hung on a motorized dry-cleaners' rail. He pressed the button. With a soft *whir* the rail rotated, bringing the costumes to the front. He eyed each of the outfits, the first four rumpled and blood-spattered, the last five pristine inside their clear plastic bags, waiting their time.

Soon. He opened the backpack and took out the Civil War outfit he'd worn for Olga's transformation, replacing the blood-smeared costume on the padded hanger. As he ran his fingers across the sleeves, he recalled the titles of his mother's B-movies: *Indian Love, Indian Summer, Buckskin Baby, A Gambler's Doll, Glory at Gettysburg.* Next up, *A Cowboy's Heart.*

He could see his mother standing in the doorway to his bedroom, holding out the Indian costume, the first she'd brought home. *"I've altered this to fit you, Connie. So we can rehearse my lines together. Put it on."* At thirteen, he was surprised by her smile and the unusual attention.

Excited, but unwilling to show it, he pulled on the fringed jacket, then the pants, as she watched.

She eyed him in the costume and frowned. Her gaze clouded, turning her expression into one he recognized and feared. He could tell she was remembering some-thing bad. *"That bastard said I can't act. Like him grunting and saying, 'How' means he can."*

"Then why do you want me to—"

"Shut up! You never interrupt me. You do what I say."

"Yes, Mother."

His contrite tone hadn't stopped the tirade, but this time she didn't hit him.

"He said I was too old for the part! Said he didn't—didn't—" She started to sob. *"Hold me, Connie. Hold me and tell me you love me."*

"Yes, Mother." She smelled like talcum powder and roses, smooth and soft and yielding, nothing like he'd expected. At that moment, he would have held her for-ever.

He pushed away the rest of the memory and stroked a dark blotch on the navy wool Civil War jacket. His mother's fifth co-star had been the first to wear it. Ten lousy movies, ten co-stars, all of whom used and dumped her like yester-day's trash. She always took out her disappointment on him—her only son. Someone had to pay. He understood that.

It began with him helping her rehearse lines and playing the scenes.

"Let's take the scene a little further today, Connie." Her hands guided his, placing them on her breasts. *"That feels good, doesn't it?"*

He could feel his heart thudding against his chest, both in fear and desire. Feel her hand on his crotch, rubbing him. *"Isn't that good?"*

God, yes.

The older his mother got, the worse her young co-stars treated her, and the more she needed him to play "their" parts, to keep the fantasy roles alive after the movies were over. At least he could thank her for marrying a rich old fart who left them with millions.

With a feeling of relief, he dropped into his chair at the vanity table. Half the wall was mirrored above the table, half taken up by his computer. With the push of a button, he could transform himself. He'd found the software at a medical convention for plastic surgeons. No one had ever suspected he wasn't a genuine doctor. His mother had taught him well.

He removed the short blond crew-cut he'd worn and placed it on the waiting head. Light hair took ten years off his face. No one would connect him to the van driver in a million years. He kept his head and eyebrows shaved, and scrubbed his body rigorously before each transformation. No trace evidence, he was too smart for that.

Smiling to himself, he reached over to the jewelry chest and pressed the catch. The door clicked open, revealing ten velvet-lined drawers. He opened the first four and retrieved his trophies—two pairs of panties, a lock of hair, a red silk scarf, and one snapshot—then poured himself a half-glass of Macallan. Liquid paradise. The snifter sparkled like diamonds beneath the skylight, its thick nectar the same gleaming gold as the lock of Lucia's hair. He feathered the hair across his cheek, remembering the texture of her skin beneath his hands, the intoxicating scent of fear mixed with flowery shampoo. Other than Olga, she had been the best. *Lucia.* He swirled the cognac and took a sip, a trickle of fire licking his insides.

He put on the first costume, buckskin jacket and pants, then stepped into the guest room to the king-sized bed. At the foot, he laid the trophies in a line and knelt down. "You're with the others now, Olga." He loved seeing them all together, seeing his butterfly collection grow.

Reverently, he lifted the first pair of panties and inhaled the musky scent. *Marcia*. His first butterfly. He rubbed himself through the buckskin. *Nothing*.

He wanted to hurry, to get to Olga, but forced himself to set aside Marcia's panties for Cindi's. Her scent was weaker. Disappointing. Her face had started to blur, the memory too distant to give him a rush. He picked up the red silk scarf. *Heather*. Her lemony scent brought scintillating recollections of her lithe form joining with his as he released her from the cocoon of life. He felt a stirring in his groin.

Wishing he'd taken pictures of all his transformations, he picked up the photograph of Lucia. *Perfect*. Open to him. Bleeding for him. Her face covered, her wings painted in perfect symmetry. On her way to paradise.

Now it was time. He set aside Lucia's photo and extracted the red leotard from his backpack. He'd found it in Olga's laundry. Lying on the rumpled bed covers, he held the crotch to his face and breathed her essence. Lavender powder and sex. He paused and closed his eyes, recalling the way her eyes widened as he held the pick to her throat and stretched the tape across her mouth. She was an athlete, hard and trim. She'd fought the transformation, scratched his neck, kicked him, and nearly gotten away. The others had been too easy, he saw that now. He rubbed the bandage, absently wondering if there would be a scar. He hoped so. He imagined her beneath him, squirming and bucking. So beautiful. Now she would never grow old, never know the pain of rejection. Forever lovely and vibrant—just like the others. His gift to them.

He was hard now, like a rock. She'd resisted—he'd triumphed. A laugh bubbled up and escaped, the euphoria from his midnight excursion. He pressed the stretchy fabric to his face and inhaled again. *Sweet. So fucking sweet.* She'd been strong and her essence powerful. She'd last a long time. Maybe she'd be the last. Maybe he wouldn't need to set another butterfly free.

He sat up abruptly.

His smallest collection, four rare butterflies from South America, hung slightly off-kilter, the glass cracked.

Fucking Maria! She had been told never to touch anything in this room.

With shaking hands, he re-stashed his treasures, then hurried down the stairs to the front door. "Maria!"

He suddenly realized the Amristar carpet was no longer in the entry. The hairs on his arms prickled. "Maria!" Maybe she'd come early, moved the rug to clean the tile. Then why wasn't it back in place? He checked the alarm panel. It glowed green—everything okay. But he knew it wasn't. He strained to hear the slightest noise. Silence.

He stepped quietly to the kitchen, noticing his blue and white Moon Flask was also missing. The vase was a cheap copy of the seven-million-dollar original locked in the bank. If he'd been robbed, the insurance company would be happy about that at least. The rug was another matter.

The newspaper was lying open on the black granite counter top. He'd tossed it in the recycle bin, he was sure of it.

The bold, black headline screamed: *King of Thieves Strikes Again!*

He sank against the counter in disbelief and read the headline again. His mind insisted there had to be a mistake. But the bare floor and empty side-bar confirmed it. The asshole had violated his private domain. He slid his fingers over the smooth newsprint, then crumpled it into a ball. "You picked the wrong place this time, you bastard. I'm going to carve you—" *Oh, fuck.*

The basement. At the bottom of the stairs, he found the door ajar. Something he never allowed. He shoved it open and flicked on the overhead. Ignoring the scatter of tools, he stooped behind the bench. The safe had been drilled, the door opened, the inside picked clean.

He sat back, stunned. The bastard had gotten his picks. He might not get back the heirlooms and twenty-five grand, but he'd damn well get his picks. He slammed the door. The money and jewelry were meaningless. But it wouldn't take long for the motherfucker to figure out what he had. This so-called King of Thieves was smart enough to put two-and-two together. Would he go to the police? No, he'd see a cash-cow ready for milking.

Have to get them back! Have to get them back!

At the top of the stairs, the grandfather clock chimed, and he realized the maid was due in less than an hour.

He searched through the rest of the house, ignoring the living room, not really caring what might be missing. TV, stereo, he could replace that junk. Even his mother's so-called "modern art" collection plastered across the sunken living room walls didn't matter. Of course, the thief didn't take any of that.

In the master bedroom, clothes were strewn everywhere, as if the thief resented Armani silk and Gucci leather.

The other bedrooms appeared untouched. He went through the entire house again, needing to see it once more, to convince himself he had indeed been robbed. His thoughts felt scattered and he downed the rest of his Macallan. Fire burned to his belly and he felt better.

What should he do first?

He needed to get the place straightened.

No. The robbery could be the perfect opportunity to connect with the police. Give him a reason to drop by now and again to ask if they'd learned anything. Maybe chat about the Ice Pick Killer. Everyone liked to talk about their work.

In his office, he hurried to unlock his desk and lift out his scrapbook. More press coverage than his mother ever got. After five transformations, Lieutenant Jamison and the task force were stalled. They all had wind up their asses and no fucking brains. There was nothing to worry about. A slow smile pulled at his lips. He offered it to the massive gold-framed mirror that once belonged to Marie Antoinette. "Please come in, officer." *Perfect.*

The phone felt light and inviting in his grip as he dialed 911. "I'd like to report a burglary."

"In progress?"

"No. I came home, and—"

"You'll need to call the non-emergency line." She reeled off a number and clicked off.

Fucking cops. He punched in the number.

"Beverly Hills Police Department. This is Desk Sergeant Lowry. How may I help you?"

"I'd like to report a burglary."

"In progress?"

"No. After the fact." *Idiot.*

"Just a moment."

While he waited, he thought about his morning, standing in the crowd of reporters, watching the detectives and the medical examiner arrive. He'd recognized the ME. She'd been called to all of his butterfly transformations. She walked with the same confident stride as Olga, the same focused, intent energy in her light green eyes. Seeing her gave him a charge.

A harried voice came over the line and interrupted his thoughts. "Detective Tack."

Chapter 4

Murry handed the cassette tape to Vermont. "Call me when it's cleaned up. I want to listen to it again. Check the other side, too. I don't care if it's three a.m."

"Yo, Dance Man," Vermont said, referring to Murry's nickname. As far as the force was concerned, he was Arthur Murray, like the dance studios. Even though his last name lacked the "a," it stuck like superglue. "I live to serve," Vermont added with a grin.

"You live to chase blondes and watch hockey," Murry quipped, grinning back when Vermont gave him a good-natured one-fingered salute.

He lost his sense of humor dodging the news vultures. Slamming the passenger door of Billy's RAV4, he nearly took off an anchorwoman's hand. Air from the a/c blasted his face. Thank God for small favors. "You'd think it was July instead of January."

"Supposed to rain." Snapping his gum, Billy shifted into first. The engine rumbled unevenly.

Murry fastened his seatbelt. "Loaded up with the cheap stuff again?"

"It's not worth an extra twenty cents a gallon. We could always drive your car—"

"Don't even think it." Murry's blue Beamer was paid off

and had no dings or scratches. A miracle he didn't want to push. "You fax over the photos?"

"Yep. New York's finest are working as we speak. You interested in Chinese food?" Billy asked.

"You really want to risk it?" Murry asked, not sure he was ready for food. The Kid still ate like a teenager, packing enough in for two linebackers and not showing it anywhere.

"It's bugging me, Murry. Somebody's got to be playing a joke."

Ever since the Voodoo case, Billy had been getting fortunes of doom. If Murry was the station's psychic guru, Billy was the bad-karma king. No wonder they worked well together, Murry thought. The Kid had a fortune cookie record going, six dire fortunes in a row. Bets were going down as the odds went up. "Maybe today's your lucky day."

Billy grunted and shook his head, his expression saying there was more to his unhappiness.

"You and Gina on the outs again?" Murry guessed.

"What do you think? With this nut on the loose and that damn King of Thieves, I've had to cancel our last three dates."

"I thought she was into spontaneity?"

Billy scowled. "Not any more. She hung up on me when I said this week didn't look good." He shook his head. "Why couldn't the asshole have waited until next month?"

"He's an inconsiderate prick," Murry joked.

Billy chuckled, but it was obvious his heart wasn't in it. Maybe he was thinking of Olga Shostakovich, too. He lit a cigarette and cracked the window.

"Gum's healthier," Murry pointed out.

Billy blew a stream of smoke from his lips, pure satisfaction on his face. "Doesn't feel nearly as good. Besides, it's only my second. I'll go back on the wagon tomorrow."

Murry figured he'd done enough preaching and filled Billy in on the psychic angle and the tape recording.

"You think the recorder has anything to do with Ice Pick?" Billy mumbled, his cigarette bobbing dangerously.

"Can't imagine anyone waiting for a killer. Especially with only a recorder."

"Me either."

But his intuition said it was important. He just couldn't think how.

They went to a run-down joint in Hollywood that changed hands and names every six months, but the food stayed consistently average and the prices cheap.

The place reeked of garlic and chicken, and was half-full when they arrived. Booths lined the walls, small square tables ate up the center. They took a booth in the corner, away from the kitchen. The red leather was cracked and duct-taped and Murry wondered if the new owner would re-upholster. "You get photos of the crowd outside Olga's?" Murry asked, after they ordered.

"Yep. Just like you wanted. I'll get 'em developed tonight." His voice said he considered it a waste of time.

Murry half-agreed with him, but the killer might enjoy watching the dog-and-pony show. "So, what do you think?"

Billy winced. "Geez, Murry. I've never seen anything— God, it made me sick."

Me, too, Murry thought. "Anything else?"

Billy squirmed on the seat. "Ice Pick underestimated her."

"Underestimated her, how?"

"Her strength, her ability to fight back."

"Why do you say that?" Murry asked.

"She scratched the hell out of him. Broke a vase. Obviously she got away from him for a moment."

Murry leaned forward. "Which means?"

Billy shrugged.

"If we don't catch him, he may try a different routine with his next target," Murry said. "This guy's no dummy. He's going to adapt each time a problem comes up. He might drug his next victim or incapacitate her in some other way."

Balancing his fork like a teeter-totter on his index finger, Billy asked, "Why's he picking up the pace? He's gone from six months to three."

"Thrills aren't lasting as long," Murry said. "The cycle gets shorter as the guilt—if there is guilt—and stress build."

"So what 'ya think set the guy off? I mean, if he hasn't been doing this before now?"

Could be anything, Murry thought, wishing he had the answer. "Most of these guys fantasize this stuff but never take it further, then some new stressor hits and suddenly they need more than the fantasy to keep going."

"Jesus."

"You said it."

"Think he's got a stash of trophies somewhere?" Billy asked.

"You bet. Everything I've read says these guys like reminders. Freshens the memory. Makes it last longer."

The fork wavered on Billy's finger. "How are we ever going to figure out what he's got?"

"Probably won't until we find a suspect and recover the underwear, hair—whatever he's kept. Then it'll be important evidence." Murry gratefully sipped his ice water, wondering if the air-conditioning had gone on the blink.

Their food arrived, Billy's chicken chow mein piled beneath an egg roll. Steam rose off Murry's asparagus shrimp. Billy shoveled in half of his before Murry took his first bite. He needed to talk to the people closest to Olga, see if she said something, found something. See if something clicked. He'd have Ramirez compile a list of everyone she knew and look for crossovers to the other cases. Were the celebrity photos for show, or was she really buddies with Baryshnikov and the others? They'd been dressed in street clothes, not leotards and tights. "I wonder if Lance has heard of Olga." His opera-singing brother knew a lot of people.

"He in LA?"

"No. Germany. Back in a few days."

"Why would he know dancers?" Billy asked dubiously.

"He knows everyone in the performing arts. He's an extro-vert." An extrovert built like a tank, with a voice and tempera-ment enough to fill the Met. Murry always worried about his twin dying from a heart attack.

"He still razzin' you about being a cop?"

"All the time. He worries about *my* stress, but I'm not fifty pounds overweight."

Billy wiped a noodle from his mustache. "I still don't understand what women see in him. Éclair likes him, right?"

"Don't remind me. She's got every CD he ever made." Murry's first date with Éclair had been to see his twin sing Rodolfo in *La Bohème*.

"So, what's wrong with that?"

"You ever try keeping an erection with your brother singing in the background?"

The Kid laughed until tears rolled from his eyes, his words coming out between gasps. "You . . . should see . . . your . . . face, Murry."

Four construction guys at a nearby table were staring.

Uncertain if they'd heard, Murry adopted a poker face, wishing he hadn't said anything. "Glad I made your day."

Billy was fighting for control and, when he seemed to be

winning, Murry said, "Maybe Olga was telling fortunes to the celebs."

"Like Lance?" Billy choked on another laugh.

Annoyed, Murry gave him a hard, "Yes."

Their waiter placed the bill between them.

Billy lost the smirk, his gaze dropping to the fortune cookies. He reached toward the nearest cookie, hesitated, then snatched the one closest to Murry.

Murry grinned, picked up the other one, and snapped it open. "You first," he said.

The Kid cracked his, read it, and dropped it on the table. "I do not fucking believe this."

Murry snagged the thin strip of white paper. *Big storm brewing. Cover your head.* "Let's see . . ." He flipped to the back of his notebook. "You've gone from *Evil spirits on the loose* . . . to . . . *Enemies out to get you* . . . *Earthquakes beneath your feet* . . . *Tidal waves in your future* . . . to . . . what was the last one?"

Billy snorted. "*Watch where you step. Land mines ahead.* You aren't doing this, are you?"

Murry chuckled at the Kid's expression as he added the last two fortunes to his notebook. "I wasn't even with you when you got the first one. You told me about it, remember?"

"Don't remind me. So, what's yours?"

"*Great opportunities are coming your way.*"

Billy shook his head.

Murry dropped a twenty on the table beside the bill. Billy would catch the next one. "It's just a quirky coincidence."

"That's easy for you to say. You don't have everyone telling you it's the zombie curse."

Murry knew the guys still ribbed Billy about being poisoned by a Voodoo sorcerer. The son-of-a-bitch had almost killed the Kid, and Murry had damn near lost his head—literally—trying to save him. He tried to keep that episode also in the closed box in the back of his mind.

Jamison was in the conference room when Murry and Billy hurried in. The Lieutenant's carrot top matched last week's New Year's crepe paper decorations that still hung from the ceiling. He still looked crisp in his tailored suit and navy silk tie, and in their Hollywood days had been the time-complex type. His pointed glance at his wristwatch confirmed he still was.

Ramirez and Farel were there, along with seven other guys: one from Santa Monica, one from Hollywood where two of the victims had lived, the rest supplied by LAPD, which had the most manpower. Ten grim faces besides his and Billy's.

Murry was just thanking the gods for keeping Tack elsewhere, when the son-of-a-bitch strolled in, an *I just got laid* smile on his Pierce Brosnan mug. Tack paused beside Jamison, his voice too low for Murry to hear what he was saying. Jamison nodded and gestured toward a front row seat. What was that about?

Jamison glanced from Tack to Murry, his narrowed gaze driving home the point. *Get along, or else.*

Murry figured he should be happy Tack was stepping out on Scarlett, but it irked him. He'd rather have her stepping out on Tack, give his ex-partner a taste of the medicine Murry had choked on.

He headed to the coffee pot, aware everyone was watching as he passed Tack. Determined to let the soap opera die between him and Tack, he filled his coffee mug with what looked like mud and sat down beside Billy.

Jamison moved behind the podium. "Captain Daniels is in a meeting, so I'll run the show. Listen up."

He looked like his lunch hadn't agreed with him. Pressure from upstairs?

Jamison glanced around the room. "We have our fifth victim."

That caused a wave of murmurs. Éclair had set a record getting her prelim out.

"I've updated my people. Farel, what's the status on the van?"

Farel shook his head. "Nothing yet."

Jamison's blue eyes fixed on Murry. "I told Vermont and Éclair that Shostakovich is priority. They talk to you. You talk to me before moving on it, clear?" His tone had lost its friendly edge.

Murry nodded. "Crystal."

"Rodman, Janks, Lasky, Machado—keep working the other cases. Murry, you and Kidman stay on Shostakovich. Check her background, work associates . . . you know the drill."

The pencil snapped in Tack's hands as he shot Murry a murderous look.

Murry tried to hide his surprise. Why was Jamison giving him the case? A fresh set of eyes? "I'd like to keep my name out of the papers—in case our guy's a reader."

"Good idea," Jamison said. "Come downtown after five, and Detective Greene will fill you in on the other four. You have anything, you give it to him."

Downtown meant Parker Center on North Los Angeles Boulevard. Often called the Glass House by the detectives, the eight-story concrete-and-glass monstrosity sat by itself in the middle of a city block with parking on either side. Robbery-Homicide was on the fifth floor. Murry nodded, feeling like he'd just won the lottery. "You have a profile?"

"FBI says we're looking for someone older, educated, organized. Could be convinced he's sending his victims to heaven, or something. This guy's acting out some sort of fantasy. The more complex the fantasy, the more intelligent the offender. This guy's smart and he's not going to stop until we nail him." Jamison directed his answer at everyone before his gaze settled on Murry. "I'll send you a copy." He asked the four from LAPD for a quick rundown, the gist being that they were re-interviewing everyone connected to the first victims, looking for something they might have missed. Translation: after eighteen months, they had zip. Jamison wound down with, "This is a team effort. Work together. You talk to each other—no one outside the task force." His gaze shifted from face to face. "Got it?"

Murry joined the chorus: "Yes."

"Okay. Unless somebody's got anything else, that's it."

Billy leaned over, the blast of peppermint vying with the odor of nicotine. "The King struck again. This morning. Tack caught it."

Then what, Murry wondered, was Tack doing here? He and Billy had been working another case, a rash of burglaries in the area. The thief was experienced enough to get past security cameras, patrols, and the general nosiness of neighbors. Which had left Murry with a missing-items list a mile long and a billion gripes from a bunch of very rich homeowners. So far, nothing had turned up on the burglar, except the heat. Because the guy was hitting the richest of the upperclass, the media had dubbed him, "The King of Thieves." Now, if only the King would dump something they could track. Murry had been reviewing fence reports until his eyes crossed. *Nada. Nada. Nada.*

Olga's murder would get him out from under the case, he told himself, but he hated to leave it open. Most thieves were snatch-and-grabs, not pros. This guy was good. And careful.

And Murry wanted the collar.

As Jamison stepped from behind the podium, Murry caught his eye. "Who'll be taking the King of Thieves?"

The lieutenant gestured toward Tack. "Steve's taking it. Daniels said you're to give him all your notes and anything not in the case file."

Instinct and intuition didn't fit in a case file, Murry thought, gratified that Tack wasn't being assigned to Ice Pick. Tack didn't have an intuitive bone in his body and Murry doubted his ex-partner was smart enough to catch this character. Murry grinned to himself. With Tack on the case, it would still be open by the time Ice Pick was behind bars. He hurried from the room, anxious to move on Olga.

Tack caught him in the hall.

"Everything's in the case file on my desk," Murry said.

"A hundred bucks says I collar the King before you get a whiff of Shostakovich's killer."

Murry couldn't resist the opportunity to shove another goose egg down Tack's throat. "Why not a thousand?" After the Voodoo case, Tack's career had nosedived while Murry's had sailed across some pretty waters that included a handshake from the Mayor and a pay raise.

Tack scowled, his eyes shifting toward Billy. "No problem." He adjusted his slacks. "The wife and I could use a night on the town."

Was the guy looking for another broken jaw? Or trying to get Murry busted back to traffic detail? Not about to take a swing, Murry couldn't resist a verbal poke. "What I hear, you don't need a night on the town, you need a sex therapist."

"Boy was he smokin'!" Billy said as he climbed into his RAV4.

Angry at himself for opening his mouth—it just kept the

soap opera running—Murry buckled his seat belt.

Billy chuckled all the way to UCLA, where Olga had taught psychology.

"A psychic psychologist," Billy said, as Murry led him through the maze of hallways to the teachers' offices. "What d' ya think she taught?" Billy rambled on, "Mind-reading for better test scores?"

"More likely Psych one-oh-one," Murry said, not in the mood for jokes.

"Didn't you go here?"

"Twenty-odd years ago, yes." Murry's work had brought him here a couple of times since, but never to the psych department. He felt a sense of *déjà vu* and wondered where he'd have ended up, if he had gone for his Ph.D. and hadn't switched to criminal law. Behind one of these desks? He might even have known Olga.

"Twenty years! Geez, you're old enough to be my dad."

Murry usually liked Billy's razzing, but his run-in with Tack had left him irritable. "Thank God I'm not. Having you as a partner is bad enough; I can't imagine how your parents survived."

Hurt flashed in Billy's eyes. "Neither can I," he muttered as he jammed a cigarette between his teeth and lit up.

Too late, Murry remembered Billy had no family. "Sorry," he said. An aunt had raised the Kid, and he didn't like to talk about it. Murry worked for a conciliatory tone. "Olga have any relatives?"

Billy exhaled, his movements stiff, tense. "Parents emigrated from Russia when she was still in diapers. Died when she was three. Foster parents adopted her. Had a lot of dough. Deceased about five years. Plane wreck." Another deep breath and he started to relax.

Should he ask Billy about his aunt, or focus on the case?

All Murry knew was that the Kid's parents had died when he was in first grade, and he'd moved from LA to the Midwest. A move the Kid equivocated to Dorothy going back to Kansas after her adventures in Oz. She might have wanted to go back, but the Kid sure didn't.

Deciding to leave the personal question for another time, Murry said, "Might explain the expensive condo." He loosened his tie, wishing he could shuck it. "This heat's a killer." He looked at Billy and recognized the Kid's too-blasé expression. "Something odd about the parents' death?"

"Only if you believe that psychic garbage. Olga had a premonition. She was supposed to go with her parents on the flight, but canceled."

"How d' you learn that?" Murry said, lacing his tone with admiration.

"Olga's neighbor. Ramirez says the old biddy has a mouth on her like Lucille Ball. Said Olga blamed herself for her parents' death because she couldn't convince them to cancel their flight."

Psychic ability or coincidence? Did it matter? At this point, he didn't see how. But he hated this psychic stuff. He trusted his intuition, but that's all it was.

Billy's gaze drifted to a pretty co-ed in a mini-skirt bending over the drinking fountain.

"How long was she a teacher here?" Murry asked.

Billy straightened his tie, then glanced at Murry. "Uh, two years."

Accustomed to Billy's on-the-prowl antics, Murry gave him an elbow. "Keep your eyes on the job."

"Hey, a guy's gotta live."

"Is that what you tell Gina?"

"Since she's not talking to me, that's not an issue," Billy muttered. Nevertheless, his gaze swung back toward the row of office doors. "Here we are." He rapped on the door to Dr. Carol Upland's office, then stepped aside to let Murry go first. He got a blast of ice-cold air. The woman had the place cooled down to igloo temperatures.

Upland, the psych department head, appeared to be about Murry's age, and her bulk reminded him of his brother. It completely filled the leather chair behind her desk. Despite the frigid temperature, her brightly-flowered dress and blue jacket were wilted by the heat, while her dark hair frizzed wildly around her flushed face. According to the class schedule pasted on her door, she taught Statistical Analysis. She glanced up from an open file. "Yes?"

"Dr. Upland?"

"Yes."

"I'm Detective Murry and this is Detective Kidman." Murry leaned over the desk to give the woman a brief hand-shake. Her damp palm made him wish he hadn't.

"Ma'am," Billy said politely, his gaze skidding from the professor to the piles of paper overwhelming her desk.

"Please, sit down. I've got an hour before my next class." Her tone said she'd like them to take as little of it as possible. Her nasal voice probably drove her students up the wall.

Billy sank into the faded-blue overstuffed chair in the corner, careful not to hit his head on the overflowing book-shelf. Murry closed the office door and claimed the edge of a high-backed wooden chair. It squeaked beneath his 180 pounds.

"My house is being remodeled and I've had to store some of my books and things here until after Presidents' Day. Thank God, it's only two more weeks. I can't stand the clutter."

Murry had the feeling she was quite at home in clutter and talked out of anxiety. He pulled out his notebook, jotted her name alongside the date and time, then asked, "You told Detective Kidman you only knew Olga Shostakovich as an acquaintance?"

"Yes. I can't believe . . . she was murdered." She made a show of wringing her hands.

Upland might look like a huge marshmallow, Murry thought, but there was an X-Acto blade inside. "Do you know if she was close to any of your colleagues?"

Upland pressed her fingertips together in a thoughtful pose that Murry was certain was just that—a pose. "Perhaps Dr. Jones. Kevin Jones. I saw them together a time or two. Other than that . . ." She shrugged.

"Together—romantically?"

Her eyes glittered with animosity. "I couldn't say."

He'd jabbed a sore spot of some kind. Adopting a persuasive tone, he said, "You must have some idea."

She didn't soften. "Sorry. No."

Billy jumped in. "What classes did she teach?"

"Parapsychology One and Two."

"Parapsychology?" Billy matched her skeptical tone.

"Yes. I'm sorry she's dead. Really. But it was all a bunch of hocus-pocus. She'd written a best-selling book that impressed the dean, or she never would have been hired."

Murry glanced at Billy. "A best-selling book?" He jotted a note to himself.

"*Read the Future, Change Your Life*. I guess this will show the dean what a fool he was."

"Fool?" Murry prodded.

"She was supposed to be psychic, Detective."

"Psychic ability isn't an exact science, is it?" he asked, disliking her more, even though she was giving voice to his own thoughts.

"She proved that."

Billy offered her a smile. "Did Dr. Shostakovich show any signs of tension, or say anything to indicate she was in some kind of trouble?"

Upland cocked her head to one side, the rolls of flab on her chin, neck, and shoulder running together. "She missed her class, last Tuesday. . . . Called at the last minute, saying she had car trouble, and asked me to post a cancellation note on the door."

"Was that unusual," Billy asked, "her canceling a class?"

"Very."

"But you didn't believe her story about car trouble?"

"Let's just say that when Kevin canceled *his* class, I was suspicious. When she came in Thursday, I asked about her car. She gave me a blank look, then sputtered some nonsense about a battery connection."

Murry asked her a few more questions, jotted the answers, then stood. "Do you have a copy of Kevin Jones's classes?"

She opened a folder, took out two sheets of paper, and handed them across the desk. "Detective Kidman asked for a list of Olga's students. I thought you might want to talk to Kevin, so I copied his schedule as well."

Murry mustered a smile. "Very efficient. Thank you."

In the hall, Billy asked, "What's your crystal ball show?"

"We know Olga had at least one enemy on the faculty."

Billy chomped on a new piece of gum. "Yep, but . . . I don't see . . . her doing Olga. I mean—"

Olga was raped. "Neither do I," Murry muttered. "Can't see her climbing through a window, can you?"

Billy laughed.

"Besides, the voice on the tape was deep, male. But Upland knows more than she's saying. Why don't you drop by and talk to her again, after we check out Doctor Jones?"

"Why me?"

"Because I'm the senior partner," Murry said. "And she liked you."

Billy choked on his gum. "Liked me? No way!"

"Don't worry, I doubt you'll have to jump in the sack to wrestle more information out of her. Just show those dimples and pretend you're smart."

"Oooh, you say the nicest things."

Dr. Jones wasn't in his office and his classes were canceled, so said the note on the door. Murry yanked out his cellular and jabbed in the man's home number.

Click. "I'm unavailable at the moment. Leave a message at the beep."

Murry did. "Guess that's going to wait, too. Why don't you give me a lift back to the station? I'll go have a little chat with Greene at LAPD, and you come back here. Get addresses and phone numbers for all her students . . . and Dr. Jones's students. Start on them. Talk to Upland again, too."

Billy nodded, jammed a cigarette between his teeth, lit it, then slid in behind the driver's wheel. "So what've we got?"

"Not much. Let me try Éclair." He punched in her number.

"You two gettin' serious?" Billy asked.

"No," Murry said automatically, although the idea of playing house with Éclair sounded pretty good. So what if she'd gone through a nasty divorce? That didn't mean she wouldn't marry him—if he asked. A big IF.

Éclair's assistant answered, said she was unavailable, and took a message. Murry dialed Vermont.

He answered on the first ring, grumbling, "Yo, I'm working as fast as I can, dammit!"

So much for quick.

Eric Greene, a pale, blond thirty-five-ish cop at LAPD, was seated behind one of a half-dozen desks in Ice Pick's case room, his ID clipped lopsidedly to his jacket lapel. Janks and Machado, looking rather shaggy, like a shower and shave hadn't been on their minds for days, were on the phone. They glanced up, nodded, then refocused on their conversations.

Greene stood. "Detective Murry?"

Because of the white hair, Murry mentally dubbed him Snowflake. "That's me."

"Welcome to the Glass House."

Despite the nickname, nothing about Parker Center seemed the least bit fragile.

"Jamison told me you'd come by. Said to show you the case files." His tone said he didn't expect much from Murry. He led Murry to a credenza behind the first desk and opened it, exposing several black binders overflowing with paperwork. "You read it here. If you need to copy something, talk to me first. You got any ideas, things to add, talk to me."

Was the guy peeved at someone new being added to the team, or just a prick in general? Murry gave him a thumbs-up, sat down, and hefted the first binder onto the desk.

Four hours later, eyes gritty, mouth tasting like burnt coffee, and stomach well past empty, he closed the first binder. Greene had done a lousy job on the case file. It was a disorganized mess.

One odd thing was an old key found on Marcia White's key ring. Described as belonging to an antique desk. But White didn't have an antique desk, nor did she ever own one. It had been dropped as a dead end. Murry wanted to know where it came from. Questions and thoughts were now jotted in Murry's notebook. Had Ice Pick been involved in law enforcement, or did he watch the Discovery Channel? No prints, no blood—other than the victim's—no semen. According to Éclair, Olga had semen present. He jotted a question about the others, then shoved the binder back on the shelf. LAPD had nothing on Marcia White's killer. The guy was smart and careful. If they ever caught him, they'd have to get a confession.

He stood to stretch his lower back.

Snowflake Greene appeared at the edge of the desk. "Find anything?"

He shrugged. "No." He sat back down and Greene left. The other two cops had been replaced by a more energetic pair of detectives, who were on the phones, pursuing the lead about the van. A needle in a haystack. Yet a needle was better than nothing—which is about what he'd gleaned from the first victim's case file.

Murry studied the outside of the other binder, Cindi Ford, steeled himself for more gruesome crucifixion photos and black nylon-covered faces, and opened it. He took the crime scene photos from both binders and placed them side-by-side. The violence seemed to leap out of the photos. Like getting static shock, the first look was the worst, then it was just business. Both victims were staked out, just like Olga. All on wood floors. Did the killer know that ahead of time? He did a quick scan of the next two victims' case files, pulled the crime scene photos, and put the four sets side-by-side. He studied the photos until they burned into his retinas. The black nylon over each victim's head was identical, same with the electrical tape over the mouth, which implied the killer brought both with him. Ice picks all appeared the same: same wood—mahogany—scrollwork on the handles, but no identifying marks. Didn't match anything available on the market. Except the odd pick used on Olga. It had been manufactured in the 1930s. Eyes smarting, he replaced everything and closed both binders. He glanced around. No sign of Greene.

He decided to look everything over again in the morning, then read the FBI profile. By then he'd have a copy of the prelim report on Olga and the crime scene photos. He shoved away from his desk. He might actually fetch take-out and join Éclair by 9:30. Surprise, surprise. He was halfway to the restaurant before he remembered what day it was. The anniversary of his father's murder.

Despite the hour, he drove out to Forest Lawn, parked, used the key he wasn't supposed to have, and climbed the green marker-covered hill to his father's grave. This was a ritual he and his brother had shared since high school. Only with Lance out of town and Ice Pick running amok in Beverly Hills, Murry had forgotten.

During daylight, the cemetery was more like a park, complete with a small man-made lake, ducks, and geese, the rolling hills adorned with miniature copies of buildings like Westminster Abbey and statues like Michelangelo's David. But standing beside his father's marker, the road and nearest lamplight twenty feet away, darkness spilling across the manicured lawn toward the light like a feathery pool, he felt uneasy rather than peaceful in the solitude of the dead. Hard to believe he'd almost lost his head to the whisk of a machete inside the Abbey. Hard not to believe in inexplicable, otherworldly things while standing in the midst of rolling hills filled with bones and ash, with his father's presence keen like a knife-edge in the quiet. Not quite approving, not quite disapproving. Or maybe it was the sensation that he'd missed his father more in death than in life. Maybe that was the way it was for everyone. You didn't know what you had until it was gone. After the shock and the tears, their mother and the Murry house had become almost a refuge of silence—no more parental fights over forcing Lance to play sports, no more fatherly rages about how his mother spoiled them with piano and voice lessons. They were freed from fatherly expectations, but not quite free from the guilt.

"You made it." Lance's voice shot Murry to his feet, before he realized he'd been sitting on the grass.

Murry brushed off his backside. "Thought you were in Germany."

Lance grew close enough for Murry to see a grin. "I was. Arrived an hour ago. Came straight from the airport. Thought you might be here."

"One of your feelings?" Murry asked in a semi-teasing tone. Lance had "feelings" about Murry, seemed to know when Murry was in trouble, seemed to think he should come running like his namesake, Sir Lancelot. As the elder twin, Murry was constantly telling his overweight, know-it-all knight that Sir Arthur didn't need rescuing. But tonight, he was glad to see his brother, glad to dispel the uneasiness he'd picked up at Shostakovich's, glad to forget for a few moments what Ice Pick did to women.

Lance was surprisingly light on his feet, with his Pavarotti-type build. He closed the gap between them and gave Murry a bear-hug. He always gave Murry a bear-hug, no matter who was around, which was embarrassing at work. Not so much around Éclair—Lance bear-hugged her, too—his unique stamp of approval. Scarlett had never received more than a formal handshake from Lance, not even at Murry's wedding, when they'd quit speaking to each other. Lance had disliked her on sight. She didn't sing, didn't like opera, didn't like Murry's commitment to his work, although Murry had thought his brother was jealous at the time. He'd thought a lot of stupid things, when it came to Scarlett. The divorce and

Éclair had helped mend the rift. Murry hugged his brother back. "You pack the house in Frankfurt?" he asked.

Lance waved a theatrical hand in the air. "Of course."

They both sat down on the cold, damp grass, stared at the lake on the other side of the road, listened to the crickets and the distant sound of cars, all the night sounds, and didn't need to say anything to know what the other was feeling. Pride in their family. In the father they had lost. Pride in each other. They sat like that for twenty minutes, until Murry's eyelids drooped. Then they both shoved to their feet and headed wordlessly down the hill to the road and on down to the wrought-iron fence.

At Murry's car, Lance stood beneath the light, his dark hair almost white in the glow. "I'll be in Seattle, then Portland, the next few days. Then Boston, Philadelphia, New York, and DC. Be home in a couple of weeks. Why don't you and Mary join me when I get back?"

Murry slid behind the wheel. "Sounds good. I'll ask her to pencil you in."

"Ciao."

Murry watched Lance retreat to his Lexus. "See you when you get back," he called.

Lance looked like he wanted to say something else, but he didn't. He climbed behind the wheel.

Murry followed his twin out of the lot. Only as he lost sight of the taillights did he identify the sound in his brother's voice. He'd sounded lonely.

The man with a million screaming female fans lonely? Murry smiled at the notion and chalked it up to fatigue. Lance loved the limelight, the fans, the music. Lived for it. He'd never once expressed wanting something different. Christ, Murry thought, this entire day has me spooked. Not a good sign. Not a good sign at all.

Chapter 5

The cop who took the phone report asked Conrad to send a missing items list to his insurance company and a copy to the station. He didn't sound too interested when the list didn't include the crown jewels of Russia.

Still, I have a name, a connection, a reason to call the station or drop by. He wanted to get a closer look at the place and the detectives working Olga's case.

He remembered the outside of BHPD as looking like a Catholic church, minus the gold cross on top of the dome. The dome towered above smooth Aztec lines and arches that circled the outside of the building and the inner plaza. Palm trees were everywhere, vying with the turquoise banisters, balconies, and tiles for attention. It looked like anything but a police department. He hoped it meant that the cops inside were a little smarter than the ones investigating Marcia and the others. Smart enough to catch subtle touches, like the different pick he'd used on Olga.

He compiled a list of stolen items and dropped it in the mail. Returning from the mailbox, he studied the manicured lawn and neatly-shaped shrubs that framed the front walkway, then glanced over at his neighbors' yards, which were equally well maintained. Could the thief be connected to a gardening service? Landscapers? Security? None of the other houses on the street had been hit. Why his?

Had the guy somehow known he would be gone that night? Pondering the puzzle, he retreated to his office, booted up his computer, printed a map of the area, then began pulling up all the newspaper stories, from the first robbery to his own. On a spreadsheet, he listed the people hit, their addresses, items taken, and the dates of the robberies. From that list came another data search and another list. If there was a pattern, he didn't see it.

He fell asleep in his chair, waking abruptly after nightfall with a hard-on—and the medical examiner's face etched behind his eyes.

Chapter 6

It was after eleven when Murry pulled in beside Éclair's black BMW. Out of habit, he scanned the well-lit, practically empty parking lot. He recognized two of three cars: one belonged to a tech, one to Éclair's assistant. But who, he wondered, owned the black foreign job in the corner? It looked like it came off the Indy 500.

As he locked his Beamer and juggled the Italian take-out, he felt his nape hairs starting to do their little warning dance. Something about the harsh, white glow of the overhead light made him feel like a target. He scanned the lot again. No movement, no sound but the distant freeway. Shrugging off his uneasiness, he hurried inside and up to Éclair's office. There, a vanilla-scented candle struggled to mask the unmistakable meat-locker odor. She'd cleared a space on the cluttered desk. Stomach rumbling, he arranged four cartons, two plates, and assorted bits of plastic-ware around the small flame. While Éclair washed up, he glanced out the window. Behind the tinted windows of the foreign car, the bright orange light of a cigarette flared. That unpleasant sensation prickled him again.

He was halfway down the hall, just as Éclair rounded the corner. "Murry, where—"

"Be right back," he called over his shoulder. "Forgot

something." He arrived outside just in time to see the flash of taillights as the sports car vanished down the street. He felt foolish, yet unsettled. Penlight in hand, he jogged across the blacktop to where the car had been parked. He wished he'd checked it out immediately, or at least gotten a plate number. He peered up at the three-story building—stucco and glass. Éclair's silhouette showed clearly through the window. The best view of her office was precisely this spot. Nah, he decided, dismissing his uneasiness. Olga and all her psychic mumbo-jumbo had his imagination working overtime. He hurried back upstairs.

Éclair was spooning ravioli next to a serving of chicken Marsala with button mushrooms. She popped one into her mouth and moaned with orgasmic intensity, then handed him a plate.

He shoveled in a couple of bites, his thoughts churning. "Who else is working late?"

"Just Sue and Marty." Éclair took a bite, and moaned again. "This is wonderful. There's enough garlic to scare off a vampire. Why the dash outside?"

He shrugged. "Just a feeling. Probably nothing."

"A feeling about what?"

"A car in the lot. Looked expensive, and I didn't recognize it."

"So?"

He shrugged again. He didn't want to bring up the cemetery, his father, Lance, or the strange uneasiness he'd felt all day.

"Doctors park here sometimes—easier to find a space. You know how the hospital lot gets."

Across the street, the hospital, a 1950s dinosaur whose color was a mistaken attempt at adobe peach, was an overcrowded eyesore. He nodded and tried to shove down further speculation, at least until the meal was over. Doctors did use the lot. That car was certainly a doctor's ride, not a mugger's, not unless it was stolen. But who'd sit in front of an ME's office in a stolen car? People usually avoided reminders of death, and this place was a constant reminder. Determined to enjoy the moment, he lifted his wine glass. "To time well spent."

Éclair smiled, echoed his sentiment, and took a sip. "This from your private stock?" she asked over the rim.

"Only the best from my brother, and who better to share it with?"

"Smooth talker." Her cheeks flushed with pleasure. "I had a great time with your family over New Year's. Even singing Mimi's lines with your mother was fun."

This was the third time she'd mentioned the family holiday get-together and her opera-singing debut—a family tradition—and suddenly he knew he wanted her there every year. Working to hide the marriage proposal running through his brain, he said, "You have a great voice." Her voice was what had prompted him to ask her out. He loved it. Loved her. So did his family.

"But my Italian's not so great."

"Neither is mine. You know what? We ought to take a vacation when this is over. Go on a cruise to Italy. Get some practice."

She cocked her head at him. "In all the years I've known you, you've taken one vacation, and that was last year, after we started dating, and I twisted your arm to go with me to Mexico."

"And I had a great time," he admitted. "So why not do it again?"

"Because it's only been nine months since then." She gave him a suspicious look. "What are you up to?"

"Nothing," he said truthfully, although the idea of surprising Éclair with a cruise to paradise and a proposal sounded good all of a sudden. They could meet up with his mother and Lance for a dinner with Lance's opera buddies. Éclair would love that surprise. And they'd have some uninterrupted time together. He glanced at his watch. Almost one. "You finished?"

"Yes. You want to know about Olga Shostakovich?"

"Absolutely not! I was thinking about racing you back to my place for a quickie on the dining room table."

Her lips curled up. "I prefer bear rugs."

"I can arrange that." His mind shifted back to work. "But now that you mention it, what did you get on Shostakovich? Jamison and Greene'll want an update ASAP."

"Is Greene that guy from LAPD with the freaky white hair and eerie blue eyes?"

"You got a thing for Snowflake?" Murry asked. Éclair didn't usually describe people like that.

"Snowflake, huh? Hate to think what you call me when I'm not around."

He grinned. "So, you hot for him or what?"

"I like to keep you on your toes, Murry."

"And?"

"He's been calling since this afternoon, stopped by twice. A real pain in the backside."

"A lot of heat on the Ice Pick cases." He hesitated, but had to say, "I know you got the prelim off to Jamison. Anything you can tell me?"

"The way she was killed, the order of the pick wounds, the rape, were all consistent with the first four. But not the head wound, the bruised jaw, and the semen."

A sudden image of Olga's body pinned to the floor sent Murry's appetite plummeting. "Let's table this until morning. I'd like to enjoy what's left of tonight."

"I thought you cops have one thing on your minds when you hit the sack."

Murry chuckled. "Oh, Billy does. He makes me feel ancient sometimes." He let his gaze linger appreciatively. "But you make me feel like a teenager."

She gave him a wry grin. "Still want to try the dining room table?"

"Long as you're on the bottom," he said. "This is the land of equality, Doc."

Murry's alarm blasted like a shotgun. Éclair barely stirred. He rolled over and switched off the noise. Mary's backside tempted him to play spoons a little longer, but the case beckoned, and he raced for the shower.

By the time he hit the kitchen, Éclair was under the steamy spray, singing something from *Madame Butterfly*. She had a voice sweet as whipped cream.

Reluctantly, he tuned her out and opened the FBI profile on Ice Pick. A careful read produced nothing new. Jamison had hit the high points. Nothing else stood out.

By the time he reached his cubicle at BHPD, it was 7:15, his cell phone was screaming, his desk phone was clanging, the voice mail light was glaring like a one-eyed demon, and Billy was standing beside his desk ready to burst. "Jesus." Murry snatched the receiver from the cradle. "Murry here."

"Detective Art Murry?"

Murry sank into his chair, inexplicable prickles dancing up his spine. "That's me. Who's this?"

Click.

"Hello?" Murry stared at the phone, then dropped it back in place. "Weird."

Billy fidgeted by the desk. "Kevin Jones called back this

morning. I'm on my way to talk with him. Unless you have something else you'd rather have me do."

"Huh? No. Where's he live?"

"Westwood."

O. J. Simpson territory. Sprawling, ranch-style homes on huge estates with endless driveways and decorative but efficient fences that implied *keep out* without posting the actual words. "I'll follow you over. Just give me a sec." He handed Billy the profile on Ice Pick. "Read this tonight. Let me know if you have any brilliant thoughts." Billy set the file on his desk.

Murry fast-forwarded through his messages, listening to Bones at the lab: *"The nylon appears to be the same type and make as those used on the previous victims. Same with the tape. The ice pick hammered through one of Number Five's feet was different than the rest. I'm sending over a report this morning."*

Click.

Vermont's voice. *"There's not a whole lot I can tell you about the cassette, Murry. You can hear the guy give her a warning and slap on the duct tape. Maybe if we get a suspect we can match the voice, but with only one word recorded it's a long shot. I'll send over a report."*

"Wonder if she has other tapes?" Murry asked, as he followed Billy downstairs to the parking lot.

Billy popped his trunk, retrieved a shoe box, and shook it. "These were in her office."

Murry wanted to kick himself. He'd been in such a hurry to check the case files, he'd forgotten about her office. "How many are there?"

"Twenty-three."

"You listen to 'em yet?"

"Give me a break. I've been talking to Upland and to Olga's students." Before Murry could ask what time Billy knocked off, Billy asked with a smirk, "Guess who Olga shared an office with?" Billy's unlit cigarette bobbed with his words.

"Kevin Jones?"

"Bull's-eye." His match flaring, he sucked nicotine, a look of bliss washing over his face.

"Quit inhaling and tell me what you have."

Billy slammed the trunk closed and climbed behind the wheel, an eyebrow lifting as Murry slid in the passenger's side. "Thought you were taking your own ride," he said.

"Changed my mind. We can talk on the way over, and drop by Olga's office on the way back. We did get Dr. Jones's permission to search the office, didn't we?"

Billy gave him a two-fingered salute. "Yes, sir."

"Anything else you're just dying to tell me?"

"Gina has forgiven me and I'm a happy dude."

"About the case, Kid."

"Not yet. New York's identified all the people in the photos. You were right. They're all dancers. They talked to Baryshnikov first. Hasn't left New York in months and has a zillion witnesses to his whereabouts during all the murders."

Not a surprise, Murry thought.

"They've taken statements and gotten alibis from all the rest but two. Of the two, one is out of town at the moment, supposedly dancing in a show in Miami. The other is in the hospital, unconscious. Got hit by a taxi last night. Had luggage and was obviously coming from the airport. They're talking to his parents and friends, and checking to see where he'd been. But they don't think he's Ice Pick. Doesn't come close to the profile."

Murry didn't expect anything to come of photos that dated, but you never knew.

"Ramirez is cross-checking all Olga's and Jones's students. Comparing a list against LAPD's computer printout of the known associates of the other victims."

"Any of them own a van?"

"They're checking that angle, too. So far, no dice."

"How many students are we talking about?"

Billy cracked the window and exhaled. "About one hundred eighty a semester, but we're going back six months prior to the first killing, just in case."

"Go back further. A couple years."

"A couple—" Billy's cigarette dipped dangerously, spilling ash. Swearing, he tossed the smoke out the window. "This a psychic hunch from your gray-celled hotline?" he asked, brushing the flakes from his khaki slacks.

"No, it's another long shot. Maybe Ice Pick took Olga's class and decided he was a reincarnated killer."

"Or maybe he sees her on the street, thinks, hey, she rings my bells, and none of this psychic crap or her students has anything to do with it."

Murry shrugged. "Either way, a—"

". . . cop's gotta do what he's gotta do."

"You got it, Quick Draw. Farel talk to Olga's doctors yet? Check them against the others?"

"As we speak."

Murry's cellular shrieked. "Murry here."

Farel's excited voice came back. "We might have something. One of Olga's prescriptions was filled at the same pharmacy as Cindi Ford's."

"Same doctor?"

"Yeah."

"Run down his whereabouts and get back to me." Murry disconnected and updated Billy.

"Think they all had the same doctor or pharmacist one time or another?"

Murry punched in Jamison's number. "Let's find out."

Jamison picked up and Murry gave him an update. "Let me check. Hold on."

Murry flipped open Éclair's prelim report and scanned it until Jamison came back. "They all had different doctors. Who's following up the pharmacy connection?"

"Farel."

"Okay. Have him check out the docs who wrote the scrips, and the pharmacists and employees that work there—everything." He paused, as though interrupted by someone, then said, "You have any thoughts after looking through the files?"

"A couple," Murry admitted. "Guy's smart and careful. Except with Olga. Maybe she put up a fight he wasn't expecting. He left semen traces. Nail scrapings from her right hand show tissue and blood—not hers."

"Sounds like she rattled his cage. Good. We get a suspect, we'll have something to tie him in. Anything else?"

"Anyone check the floors?" He'd planned on checking that himself, but Jamison sounded hungry.

"Floors?"

"All the victims had wood floors, right?"

Jamison's "yes" came slow, as though his thoughts were tracking Murry's.

"Tough to hammer ice picks into cement. Either he's been inside or he's damn lucky."

"You thinking he installs cable or phones or does some kind of construction?"

"Possible."

"I'll get some uniforms on it," Jamison promised before disconnecting.

Billy pulled the car to a stop along the curb of a row of well-maintained wood and stucco houses, all with shake roofs, all painted various shades of beige or brown. A proliferation of rose bushes adorned most of the yards. Jones lived on the more affordable side of Westwood. "You think the killer might be a contractor or a repairman?" Billy asked.

"I think he knows ice picks don't hammer into concrete. Let's go chat with Olga's office partner."

Dr. Kevin Jones had the red-rimmed eyes of a hung-over bloodhound. His body swam in an overlarge T-shirt with a faded Deadhead logo and baggy acid-washed jeans. His bare toes were speckled with brown hair, the same color as the mop on his head—the same color as his eyes.

"I'm Detective Murry; this is my partner, Detective Kidman." Jones's flabby handshake preceded their entry into a smoky living room dark as a mausoleum. Murry was tempted to pull out his penlight.

"Mind if I turn on the lights?" Billy didn't wait for an answer, but switched on a row of recessed bulbs.

Jones grimaced. "I told Detective Kidman this morning was not a good time, but he was particularly insistent. What is it that can't wait until after the goddamn funeral?" He spoke with a slight drawl that probably only surfaced when he was stressed.

"Olga's murderer," Murry said in a brutal tone. "We'd like to catch him before he kills again."

"Ah, Jesus." He sank into a leather recliner, not noticing the paperback until he'd sat on it. He dropped it on the floor, resumed his seat, and rubbed his eyes. "I—I just wanted to be alone today, that's all. Olga . . . the funeral . . . they won't release . . ." He waved his hand in an irritated gesture. "You all know this, why am I telling you? You do this every day." The last was tinged with bitterness.

Billy picked up the pack of cigarettes. "Mind if I bum one?" he asked.

Jones waved his hand in a distracted assent.

Murry retrieved the paperback, curious what this tortured soul liked to read.

"You a crime buff?" he asked, studying the cover.

"It was Olga's. She read all of Anne Rule's books."

"We didn't notice any of Rule's books at her place," Murry said, watching Jones's expression. A lot of serial killers liked reading true crime. Of course, a lot of other people did, too.

"She didn't keep them. She traded them at the used bookstore. This is the only one she kept—so I could read it." His Adam's apple bobbed and his voice rasped. "I never finished it. Doesn't matter now." He closed his eyes as though dismissing them.

"Did she ask you to read it for a specific reason?" Murry asked.

He stared past Murry as though caught in a memory, then said, "No."

"You sure?" The guy was hiding something.

"We often traded books. If this one was special, she didn't say why." He crossed his arms, eyed Billy's lit cigarette, but didn't reach for the pack. "How much longer . . ."

Murry tried to adopt a sympathetic tone. "Just a few more questions. I understand your grief at losing a colleague, but—"

"Colleague?" His brown eyes blazed open. "She is—we were—lovers."

Murry settled himself on the edge of the couch. If this guy was the killer, he'd eat green eggs and ham. But Jones knew more than he was saying, all the same. "Then you might know . . ." He purposely let the sentence dangle.

"Know what?"

"Why Olga shaved her pubic hair?"

Jones's body contracted, tight with tension. "She's dead. How can this—"

"We need to know if the killer shaved her," Murry lied. Éclair had been definite—Olga had shaved days earlier. Jones didn't like the question, though, and that interested Murry. Was he embarrassed on Olga's behalf, or was it something else?

"She—she shaved because of dancing."

"But she retired ten years ago."

"She still . . . she did ballet at her gym. Said she liked dancing for herself."

Murry jotted in his notebook. It cleared up the pubic hair question and fit Éclair's report. Jones's anxiety could be attributed to talking to police. Cops tended to make even law-abiding citizens uptight. Still, he was unsatisfied with Jones's answer, though he wasn't sure why. He thought of the photographs in her hallway. "Did she keep in touch with her dance buddies?"

Jones shook his head. "Not that I know of."

"There was a photo of her with Baryshnikov. Were they friends?"

He frowned. "Acquaintances. She was in the chorus of one of his ballets, I think. That was years ago. What does it matter now?"

"Just covering all the bases," Murry said.

Billy paced the room, studying the dusty photos and art prints on the walls. A far cry from Olga's expensive and tidy condo. "What do you teach?" Billy asked from the corner, drawing Jones's gaze.

"Abnormal Psych and Psych History." He ran his fingers through his hair, messing it worse. Murry suspected women might find the gesture attractive. He had the look of an arrogant poet who loved misery.

"How long were you seeing each other?" Murry asked, one part of his brain still wrestling with why Jones's answer about the pubic hair bothered him. He pushed it to the back of his mind. Trying to force it wouldn't work.

"Is this necessary?"

Murry nodded. " 'Fraid so."

Jones's gaze swung toward the couch. "I don't . . . nine months, a year."

"You don't remember when you started dating?" Billy asked with a slight tone of doubt.

Jones's voice scratched with irritation. "It was around Easter, because I invited her to have some coffee after a staff party. She looked bored. I certainly was, so I asked if she'd like to share a cup. We'd talked before—outside her class or mine—in our office. But she'd seemed distant and determined to remain so."

"She explain the change of heart?" Murry asked.

"She'd recently broken up with someone, she said."

"She give you a name?"

He shook his head. "Just said it was over."

"Another teacher?"

Jones's drawl became more pronounced. "I don't know. When she didn't want to talk about something, that was it. She didn't talk."

Billy unwrapped a stick of gum. "So she took you up on the coffee. Then what?"

"We went to a couple of movies. Dinner . . . you know."

"Jumped into bed."

"We had a relationship, Detective." He checked his watch.

Murry asked, "What can you tell us about the last two weeks? Was she acting strangely? Did she say she was in danger?"

Jones glared from Murry to Billy, his gaze settling between them. "Of course she was acting strangely. She was afraid." He swore under his breath. "She wanted to help, you know. You turned her away. You all don't believe in this stuff."

"Believe in what?" Murry worked to sound like he didn't know what the man was talking about.

"Psychic ability. Precognition. Whatever." He gestured with one hand, as though they were too far down the gene pool to understand.

Murry played along with Jones's presumption. "Precognition—what's that?"

Jones's brow lifted. "It's when you see the future, Detective."

Murry scratched his head. "You saying she saw her own death?"

Jones's mouth formed a scornful line. "No. After that second woman . . . Cindi something . . . was killed, Olga started having nightmares. She recorded them. Thought they might help her learn the killer's identity."

"Did they?"

"No. Just frightened her."

Murry asked, "What were the nightmares about?"

"About Heather Gristham's and Lucia Carlson's murders."

"Did she record her dreams on the cassettes we found in her office?"

"How would I know?"

Murry wondered if the man was trying to be evasive or was merely annoyed at the intrusion on his grief. "Just answer the question, please."

Wearing a surly expression, he said, "If you found the cassettes in her office, then they're hers. Since she recorded her dreams, that's probably what's on them, but I wouldn't know without listening to them, would I?"

Murry shot Billy a look. Those tapes might be a goldmine. He wanted to hear what they had to say, before handing them off to Greene. He wanted Billy to hear them, too. "Had you listened to them?"

Jones shifted uncomfortably in the chair. "She told me about them."

"Did she give you any specifics?"

"She said the killer wasn't going to stop until he was caught. She said she could be next."

That could have come right out of Rule's book. "What made her think that?"

"A feeling she had." His voice grew defensive. "That's what she said."

"But she wasn't sure?"

"Psychic ability is not an exact science, Detective."

Almost verbatim what he'd said to Upland, but that commonality didn't make Murry like the guy. He ignored the scathing tone. "So she was uncertain, but afraid."

"That's what I said."

"Did she tell you why she dreamed about the last two murders and not the others?"

"She thought she might have met them, that maybe they'd been in one of her classes, so they had some kind of connection." He spoke with a tone of doubt.

Murry jotted down the information, wondering if it would lead somewhere. They had a list of Olga's students. "Billy, call the University and see if they have a list of anyone who signed up for Olga's classes, then dropped." Billy stepped into the kitchen and flipped open his cellular.

Murry looked at Jones. "What about Cindi Ford? Did Olga know her?"

"Who?"

"The second victim. She used the same pharmacy."

"She did? First I heard about it."

"Did you know Olga had several prescriptions for Restoril?"

"I know she took sleeping pills when I didn't stay over."

"How often was that?"

He shrugged, forced casualness in his tone. "She didn't like me staying nights before her classes. Said I kept her up too late. So I usually spent Tuesdays and Thursdays, sometimes Saturday."

Again Murry wasn't sure if it was *cop* anxiety or if the man was hiding something. Murry jotted a note to ask Éclair about a toxicology screen. "What about this Friday—around midnight?" Murry asked, wondering if Jones had an alibi.

His face paled to a chalky whiteness, making his unshaved jaw appear jet black. "Is that when she—" His hand found the arm rest. If it was an act, it was a damn good one. "I—I play sax in a jazz band. We were playing at The Bulldog. Broke up around—around one, I think. I came home and hit the hay."

Murry jotted it down, noting Jones's hesitation and how his voice had risen when he'd stated the time. "Any neighbors see you come home?"

"I don't know." He blinked at Murry with an expression of disbelief. "Do I need an alibi?"

"We have to eliminate every possibility, Dr. Jones," Murry said apologetically. "That's our job." He made a show of reading his notebook and flipping through several pages. "You both missed class last Tuesday. Why?"

Jones made an exasperated sound. "She had car problems. She asked me to follow her to the garage and give her a lift to work. By the time we left the garage, she had a migraine and wanted me to take her home. There was no way for me to make my class. I canceled."

Murry offered a skeptical look. "Dr. Upland seemed to believe you two canceled so you could play between the sheets."

A hot flush washed up Jones's neck. "Upland's a dyke who hates men and had the hots for Olga. She didn't take kindly to Olga's rebuffs."

"Didn't take kindly, how?" Billy asked, stepping back into the room.

Jones made an impatient sound and glanced at his watch. "She spread rumors about Olga being a lesbian. When Olga and I started dating, it left egg on her face. Then she started checking on Olga's classes. Believe me, Olga heard about it if she was a second late. Or if she bent the rules to help a student, Upland was on her case."

Billy leaned against the wall. "What rules?"

"Sometimes a student wanted an extended deadline for finals. Olga would give it to them. Upland had a fit." He mimicked Upland's nasal voice, " 'There's a reason these rules are in place, Olga.' "

"So Upland was doing her best to make Olga's job difficult?" Murry asked sympathetically.

"Every way she could." He looked pointedly at his watch. "If there's nothing else . . ."

He led them toward the door while Murry debated how hard to push, and when. He noticed the decal on the window. "You have an alarm?"

"Doesn't everybody?" Jones tugged open the door.

"Olga didn't," Murry said. "You ever talk to her about it?"

"Yes, dammit, I told her to get one. But she thought those stupid security cameras and the gate were enough. I mean, hey, she lived in Beverly Hills."

For a moment, Murry flashed on his fiancée's apartment. If she'd had an alarm. . . . Twenty years and he still wished he'd made her get one.

"Awfully obliging," Billy observed when they were back in the RAV4.

Murry glanced out at the manicured lawn and neatly trimmed hedges that bordered Jones's home. "Guy thinks we're idiots, let him. You pocketed a cigarette butt for the lab?" He could feel the heat wafting through the windshield. Another scorcher on the way.

"And the cellophane from the pack. But why didn't we just ask for them?"

"Because I don't want him calling a lawyer. Have Winslow lift his prints, compare them to any found in Olga's apartment, have Bones compare the saliva on the cigarette. See if he's even in the mix."

Billy jammed a smoke between his teeth, lit it, and inhaled. "You think he did it?"

"Roll your window down. Probably not, but he's holding back. That cigarette butt we found at her apartment could be his. She wasn't the type to leave dirty ashtrays lying around. I want every word he said checked out. If Olga had a previous boyfriend, or girlfriend, I want to know."

"Girlfriend?"

"No assumptions, Kid. You remember any photos of him in her place? Any of her in his?"

"Nope," Billy said.

"See what you can dig up on him. Maybe he's got another girlfriend or two. Maybe they cheated on each other."

"Who has time?" Billy grumbled, as though he wouldn't mind having more than one girlfriend.

Murry thought one was plenty. "What kind of car does Jones drive?"

"Black Celica." Smoke floated above Billy's head.

Thankful it was cool enough outside to roll his window down, Murry did, even though he knew it was pointless. He'd still reek like a tar pit when he got out. "Thought you were just gonna smoke *a couple* yesterday," he said sarcastically.

"I was—until you sent me back to talk to Upland, who—by the way—was not thrilled to see me again. I can believe she's a dyke."

"Why? Because she didn't swoon over your dimples? She tell you anything?"

"Nope. Just pointed me toward Olga's office."

"What about the list of drop students?"

"Nothing yet. It'll be faxed to BHPD. I'll check it after I talk to Ramirez."

"I'll take half the tapes, you take the other half; we'll trade in the morning."

"Guess that means I'm not sleeping with Gina."

"Thought she dumped your sorry ass," Murry said unsympathetically, before recalling that Billy had said she'd forgiven him. He'd be lucky to see Éclair in passing, let alone in bed.

"I showed up on her doorstep with flowers, and gave her the killer smile."

Murry laughed. "Éclair would've dumped them on my head and slammed the door."

"So what'd it take to crawl back into her good graces?"

"How would I know?"

"Geez, Murry, you've got to've pissed off Éclair at least once. Give."

The Kid wasn't going to quit, Murry could tell by his tone. He shrugged. "I'd show up with my brother's latest opera CD, a bottle of expensive wine, and swear on a stack of Bibles, no phone calls."

Billy rolled his eyes. "I hear that. Gina's beginning to hate the phone."

"Don't we all," Murry said. No, Éclair was not going to be happy. The one time they could talk, connect, was in bed, and he'd be pulling a very late night to get caught up on Ice Pick. They had a standing agreement that if one of them worked late, he/she would sleep in his/her own bed. Two crabby people from lack of sleep only served to create relationship problems.

Billy dropped him in front of BHPD, and he punched in Éclair's number as he headed for the garage.

Her voice mail clicked on.

"This is Art. I'll be working late." Translation: I can't get together tonight. "Call me if you have anything significant on Olga. Otherwise, I'll talk to you tomorrow. Maybe we can connect for lunch?"

Fat chance of that, he thought. Just thinking of the long day ahead made him want to crawl in bed and sleep for a week.

Chapter 7

Mary, Mary, quite contrary. That was how he thought of his beautiful new butterfly. She hadn't come home last night. At least not before 2:00 a.m., when he'd finally packed it in.

He'd downed a few drinks and slept in late, then speculated over coffee: Was the cop he'd seen in the parking lot her boyfriend? He'd recognized Detective Murry from Olga's place. His sidekick, a blond kid, looked fresh out of high school and was appropriately called Kidman. Another dumb dick. Where did they find these losers?

"The dumb dicks club," he dubbed them aloud. "I left you two perfectly clear messages: the extra key on the key ring after Marcia's transformation, and the seventy-year-old ice pick I used for Olga's. You still don't get it."

He flipped through the paper, reading about Olga. As usual, they didn't understand. Stupid reporters. Just like the dumb dick cops. They didn't get it. These women were *chosen*. Lucky. Blessed.

He rinsed out his coffee cup, set it on the counter, and retreated to the bedroom to enjoy his trophies again.

Soon, he'd have something of Mary Éclair's to keep.

He'd considered sneaking into her place, but it was too soon. Olga was too fresh, alive, in his mind. He didn't want to waste that. He had plenty of time to learn more about Mary.

Was she getting fucked by the cop? Was she a workaholic? He'd know soon enough.

He studied the Polaroid he'd taken of Olga's transformation. Unlike Marcia's, this photo didn't excite him, it irritated him. The symmetry was off. Afraid the neighbor might have heard the chair topple and Olga's body hit the floor before he dragged her into the kitchen, he'd rushed the rest. Now what he imagined behind the black nylon wasn't an expression of surrender but instead the kind of sneer his mother might have worn.

You're a lousy artist.

You'll never amount to anything.

You'll never create anything of value.

You're like all men: disgusting, dirty, perverted.

His mother's words crowded his mind until he remembered her death. Then he grinned. The cops had never tied *that* back to him. It had been a simple stab-and-grab. The famous Georgia LaFleur hadn't even recognized her own son or seen the pick coming.

He took a lighter and held the flame underneath the photo of Olga until it burned black, then dropped it into an urn. *Goodbye, Mother.*

He chose his favorite navy blue suit, and accessorized it with a Louis Vuitton tie and his gold Cartier cufflinks. He gathered his photos of the stolen property and headed for the police station. Time to play with the idiots.

Chapter 8

At his desk, Murry sat back to listen to his voice mail while he waited for Billy. Another heat wave was predicted, and Murry prayed for an ocean breeze. Wearing his shirt stuck to his back made him irritable.

"Murry, zilch so far on the pharmacist angle, but I'll keep digging." A promising lead was turning to shit. Farel sounded appropriately depressed.

Next message.

Winslow. *"Hey Murry, lifted a thumbprint off the cellophane. Matches one lifted from the medicine cabinet in Olga's bathroom. No other usable prints. Check my report. Should hit your desk this afternoon."*

Next message.

Bones, the master of the lab. *"Not enough saliva on the butt. Get me another one. And tell Jamison I'm working as fast as I can."*

The heat must be red-hot, if Jamison was bugging Bones.

Next message.

Éclair's voice. *"Murry, I checked the scrapings from under Shostakovich's fingernails, right hand. Contents contain blood. Doesn't match the victim. Give me a call when you have a minute."*

For personal reasons or because she'd found something

else? He reached for the phone, then stopped as Bones's voice came on a second time.

"Hey there Murry, found an unusual fiber in Shostakovich's room, on the bedspread."

Something the killer left behind, or another lead that wouldn't pan out?

"Looks like silk. Doesn't match anything in her condo. Could be from some kind of a rug—not sure."

Murry punched in Bones's number. "Silk?"

"You got it. Sending it to another lab."

"Not a fiber from a shirt or jacket?"

"Not sure, that or a rug."

Who the hell had a silk rug—if it was from a rug? Who the hell wore silk on a killing spree, come to that? "You talking, like a rare rug? The kind you might hang on a wall or put behind glass?"

"Could be. I'll beam you when I know more."

"Beam me the killer while you're at it."

Bones, a die-hard Trekkie, ha-ha'd and signed off.

Murry left a message for Farel about the fiber, then punched in Éclair's number. "You called?"

"I'm sending over a report, but thought you should know. The blood under her fingernails and the semen are not from the same person."

"Two assailants?"

"I'm not saying that. Only giving you the facts. Oh, and no drugs. Nothing in her system."

No Restoril. Jones said she took a sleeping pill when he didn't stay over. Interesting. He glanced at some of the questions he'd jotted down after reviewing the other case files. "A condom lubricant was found in the other victims. Find any?"

"Yes."

If the blood under the nails came from Ice Pick, the semen

could have come from Jones. He was the obvious candidate, but that didn't make it fact. Not yet. "Ever identify a condom brand?" he asked.

"Yes. It's an expensive one. I'll highlight it in the report."

"He raped her before she died, right?" He'd forgotten to ask earlier. Or maybe he hadn't wanted to hear the answer.

Éclair's voice tightened. "Yes. Consistent with the others."

Murry thought of the semen, then of Dr. Kevin Jones. "Thanks, Doc." He replaced the phone, looked up and saw Billy coming through the door, and waved him over. "Éclair says Olga hadn't taken any medication. The blood under her nails is from a different person than our sperm donor. We need to talk to Jones again. See if he visited Olga the night she was killed." He gathered the reports and stuffed them into his briefcase.

"I called him this morning to ask for alibis in relation to the other murders," Billy said with a smug smile. "He wasn't too keen on talking, but told me he was in Maui when White was murdered—attending his parents' sixtieth anniversary. Shared a room with his uncle. Uncle lives in Las Vegas. I called the locals, asked 'em to get a statement from the uncle, but haven't received a call back yet."

"So if Jones is involved, we have two options. One, he's Ice Pick and his alibi won't hold, and someone else was screwing Olga. Two, Jones screwed her and left, then Ice Pick showed up. What did his colleagues and students have to say about him?"

"Arrogant asshole who pretends to be a nice guy. Girls think he's cute. Can be nice. He likes women. Picks 'em up at The Bulldog after gigs. But the only name anyone knew was Olga."

What did Olga see in him? Murry wondered. "Fool around with students?"

"No hanky-panky on campus. At least no one admitted to it."

"What about the bottle? Been his best friend for long?"

"Nope. No one ever saw him drink more than a beer or two. Nothing in his background except a parking ticket."

"Good job, Kid."

Billy grinned as he unwrapped a stick of Doublemint gum. "If he was with Olga the night she died and he's not Ice Pick, why d' he hold back?"

Murry shrugged. "Afraid. Guilty. A hundred reasons. You check on the drop list?"

"Got a partial, A through F. Glitch in their computer system. I'm to get the rest by tonight, maybe."

"You stressed how important this is?"

"Yep. They have someone doing it manually, which may take two days. But if the system comes up, we'll have it to-night."

"I hate computers. They're like driving a car with no gas gauge. Never know if it's going to run or sputter to an abrupt halt."

"Here's the tapes," Billy said, extending a manila enve-lope. Murry traded him for the batch he'd reviewed. He'd taken notes, but Olga hadn't analyzed her dreams, merely said what she'd been dreaming about and went back to sleep. Nothing seemed relevant to Ice Pick, and most were two or three years old. "Anything on yours?"

"Flagged the most recent one with red tape. Dated eigh-teen months ago. Olga says she saw Ice Pick in her dream. His back anyway. He had dark hair, medium build, and was stalking a woman. She was afraid it might be her, but thought it could just have easily been his last victim.

Jesus God. Why didn't she catch the first plane out? Murry wanted to know in the worst way.

"Dark hair and medium build fits Jones," Billy said.

"Fits lots of people."

"Yep, but she wasn't dating Jones when she had the dream. Maybe that's why she *started* dating him."

"Creepy. But interesting. Good thought, Kid." That might explain her interest. Of course, a guy torn up over his girlfriend's murder had a right to look a little shaggy. If the whole thing wasn't an act.

"So whatta we got?" Billy asked.

Murry shut his briefcase with a snap. "Blood under her nails from one person. Sperm from another. A missing van that could belong to Ice Pick but hasn't been found. A pharmacy link between Ford and Olga. A silk fiber that could be from a rug—possibly expensive. Olga go anywhere she might have picked it up on her clothes or shoes?"

Billy flipped open his Palm Pilot.

"The battery dies on that thing, you'll wish you'd used paper."

"Saves trees," Billy fired back. "Friday. Olga spent the morning in her office, picked up a sandwich for lunch, back to her office, worked until three-thirty, went to the gym, arrived home at the usual time. Six-fifteen. I'd say no. Want me to call Vermont, have him check the locations?"

"I'll do it." Murry left Vermont a message, then turned back to Billy. "New York get back to you yet?"

Billy tapped his palm several times, read for a second, then looked up. "Hospital dude flew in from England. Was dancing in a show there. He's out of the picture. The other one, a woman, they're still trying to contact in Miami. But a woman—"

"Doesn't fit the profile. And since Olga had semen in her,

93

and Ice Pick raped his victims, she's way out of the ballpark," Murry finished, not really surprised that the photos hadn't led anywhere. He doubted the killer would have left them hanging on the wall if they had. "There's another angle we need to follow. Our boy might have had advance knowledge of the victim's place—the type of flooring."

"How?"

"Could work for a flooring company. That could tie in to the rug fiber. Farel's on it."

"What else we got?"

"Semen not present on any of the victims—except Olga. And a boyfriend who recently left his thumbprint and cigarette butt in her apartment."

"So?"

"There were only a couple of tissues in her garbage. No dust on anything. The watermarks on the counter tops indicated they'd been wiped. The woman liked things tidy." Murry pointed toward the quarter-inch pile of stapled papers on Billy's desk. "What've you got there?"

Billy flipped through the pile. "Cindi Ford and Lucia Carlson both attended the University. Took some night classes. Two years ago, Ford dropped Olga's parapsychology class. Carlson dropped it last year."

"What about White and Gristham? One and three."

"Nothing yet."

"You check 'em against Jones's classes?"

"I'm waiting for the list, check 'em all at once."

"Okay. We find a link between the victims and the University, we have something."

"What now?"

"We check out Jones's alibi at The Bulldog. Talk to the other musicians, talk to the bartender, waitresses, you know the drill. Then we hammer him."

"You really think he might have been with Olga the night she died?"

"Unless Olga had another lover."

"You think he might be Ice Pick?" Billy asked.

"Ice Pick uses a condom."

"Could have broken?"

"I'm not buying it. You see any scratches on Jones?"

"She could've got him on the back or someplace easily covered."

"No. She's beneath him, struggling, right?"

Billy nodded.

"She'd go for the hands, arms, face. I'd like to think Jones is our guy. But I don't."

"That's an awfully big assumption, Murry. Your crystal ball working on this one?"

Unwilling to admit his intuition was doing exactly that, and wanting to avoid the title *Psychic Detective,* Murry tapped the top of his head. "This one is, Kid."

They ran down two musicians from The Bulldog. Jones left after the last set, but neither could remember exactly when. One recalled him making a phone call around ten. Neither recalled seeing him after that. Both figured he had a woman on the line. Could have been Olga, could have been someone else.

"Let's see what we shake loose," Murry said, rapping on Jones's door. If he looked bad the day before, he now looked worse, like a tragic poet on a bender. His mop of brown hair was clumped together like dreadlocks, his unshaved jaw dark with a two-day beard. The odor of unwashed body and booze almost made Murry gag.

Jones squinted at them through bloodshot eyes. "Now what do you all want?"

"We need some more information," Billy said.

"I told you everything I know." He started to shut the door.

Murry caught the door with his foot. "We can talk here or downtown."

Face a furious red, Jones stepped back and headed into his cave-like living room. A haze of smoke hung below the wood-beamed ceiling. He sent a tiny bottle rolling across the carpet with his toe, retrieved it, and carefully set it back into one of several groupings of airplane liquor bottles arranged on either side of his recliner. He sank back against the dark leather.

Murry offered him a congenial smile. "Looks like you have a system going."

"My tea-toting aunt was always bringing me these little airline bottles," Jones slurred. "Left me a collection." He reached down and snagged an unopened miniature Jack Daniels. "Finished the round ones first, then the square ones. Amber ones next." He twisted off the cap and tipped the bottle, swallowing nonstop. He gagged and coughed, then finally cleared his throat, tears in the corners of his eyes. "Christ, how can anyone drink this crap?" He set the bottle beside a similar one—the beginning of a new group—then reached toward the overflowing ashtray and lifted a butt to his mouth.

Murry's eyes stung. "Friday night, The Bulldog. What time you leave?"

"One."

"One?"

"S'right."

"Sure it wasn't earlier?" Billy asked, drawing Jones's gaze.

"Yes."

"Everyone we talked to says you left around ten," Murry said. "After making a phone call."

His bloodshot eyes narrowed. "They're mistaken. I didn't

make a phone call and I didn't leave until one." His voice wavered.

"Can anyone verify that?" Murry asked.

"Don't know."

Murry glanced at the neatly arranged bottles on the floor. This guy was anal all right. "Several people saw you make the call. Who to, Doctor?"

His mouth tightened into an obstinate line.

"Mind explaining how you left a cigarette butt at Olga's, if you didn't go there?"

"I—" His mouth snapped shut, and Murry imagined Jones's thoughts racing at mach speed through his intoxicated brain and getting lost.

"Care to tell us exactly where you went after leaving The Bulldog?"

His fingers clenched the armrests. "Home—I came home."

Murry softened his tone to a warning. "We're going to get the truth. You hold back—it's called obstructing justice and we throw you in jail."

Jones rubbed out his cigarette. "I have nothing to say. I still feel like shit and have another two hundred flights to drink. *In private.*"

Billy pulled out an evidence bag and shook some butts from the ashtray into the bag. "Mind if we take these?"

"Yes!" He looked from Billy to Murry, his expression that of a trapped animal.

"We can get a warrant and come back," Murry said, "but the search might not be so pleasant."

His gaze narrowed with fury. "Take whatever, and get out."

"Thanks for your cooperation," Murry said. "Mind if I use your bathroom?"

Jones shrugged.

Murry headed down the hall, made a quick search for condoms, but came up empty.

Billy threw a curious look at Murry as they climbed into the car. "Why didn't you ask if he was screwing around on Olga, or ask him why she didn't take a sleeping pill that night?"

"Saving ammunition."

"Think he still believes we're idiots?"

"In the words of the Carpenters, *we've only just begun* to rattle his cage."

"The who?"

"Forget it."

Billy wore a grin all the way back to the station. After pulling to a stop, he held up the evidence bag. "I'll drop these at the lab."

"Double-check Olga's schedule," Murry said. "What she covered in class, if she had any guest speakers, if they took field trips, whatever you can think of. I'll call Ramirez and have him talk to Ford and Carlson's parents again. See if they recognize the other victims, or friends of the victims, like Jones. I'll also have him cross-check the names of everyone who used the pharmacy in the last two years."

"He's gonna love that."

"Yes, he's—" Two men were passing by his side of the car and his nape hairs began dancing the old two-step warning. He recognized the back of Tack's head as Tack matched strides with a dark-haired guy in a three-thousand-dollar suit. Italian shoes. Loaded. Another victim of the King? Gold sparkled at the man's wrists—old-fashioned double-sided links. As the man's left arm swung back, Murry glimpsed a very expensive wristwatch, one he was sure he'd seen in a *New Yorker* ad. The suit disappeared around the corner as Tack climbed into a new fire-engine red Viper. The asshole only had his Lexus a couple years, now this. Was Scarlett footing the bill? Tack roared past and squealed through a yellow light.

Murry realized Billy was speaking. "Rewind."

Billy snapped his bubble gum with a loud pop. "I asked if you wanna meet later."

"Depends. Page me when you've got everything on Olga's classes."

"Could be midnight."

"You get something, you call." Murry climbed out of the car, then leaned back in. "I'm going to update the captain, then Jamison, then review the case files again. Tell Bones to compare the saliva on Jones's cigarettes against the blood and semen. Tell him I want the results yesterday."

"If either one matches, we going to haul him in?"

"For questioning."

"No arrest?"

"Not unless he confesses. We'll only end up doing a bunch of work for nothing. He's a jerk, but I don't think he's our guy." He knew any kind of arrest on this case would look good after five murders, and no one from the captain up to the Mayor would care if Jones's name or career got torpedoed. But a bum arrest would only alleviate the heat a short time, dumping it on the DA, and then subsequently back on the rest of the task force—the evidence collectors and case builders for the State. If Jones's saliva matched the blood under Olga's nails, he'd take a new job.

After updating the captain, Murry met Jamison at Parker Center. A police memorial stood on the front lawn, a black granite fountain surrounded by a black granite base engraved with the names of police officers who had lost their lives while serving the City. The building, named after Chief Parker, an eight-story concrete hive of cop activity in downtown LA, was a zoo that morning, with arrests in progress, people swearing out statements, detectives going in and out. Murry filled Jamison in on the latest details.

He looked pleased. "You think Jones is Ice Pick?"

Murry wasn't ready to give a black-and-white yes or no. "Jones has an alibi for Ford's murder—uncorroborated at the moment. If he didn't do her, it's not him."

"So you think he was there the night Olga died, but he's not our boy?"

Murry nodded.

Jamison looked unconvinced. "You get a chance to look around his place when you were inside?"

"Just the living room and bathroom. Didn't find any condoms."

"Bring him in for questioning. Double-check his alibi for Ford."

"Might be better to wait for the lab comparison. Hit him with everything."

"Soon as you get the results, bring him in. If he gives you any flack, read him his rights. If his alibi falls apart, keep him."

Murry eyed Jamison, disliking the order, and searching for a way to stall. "Jones has a rep as a womanizer. Not a trait I'd associate with our guy. If the interrogation isn't conclusive, I want to let him go."

"Conclusive as in what? A confession?"

"Yes."

Jamison shook his head. "No. He loses his alibi and the butt is his, *and* it matches the semen or the blood, arrest him. For all we know, he could be working with someone else."

Murry had considered the possibility of two men, but once again his intuition told him no. "Give me a few more days."

Jamison gave Murry a hard look. "All right, two more

days, Murry. If you don't have a better lead by then, arrest him." He walked away muttering, "Get the fucking Mayor off my back."

Murry's pager startled him awake. He sat up, groggy and uncertain where he was. The case file beneath his head came into focus, along with Greene's desk. Jesus, he'd nodded off. The pager buzzed again. He checked the number, then reached for the phone. "It's me, Kid. What's up?"

"Not my dick," Billy said, "that's for sure."

Murry squinted at his watch. After midnight. The two guys in back on the phones probably never even noticed he was sawing z's. "You got something?"

"Bones called. Said you weren't answering your cellular or page. Don't worry, I won't tell him you were asleep. Got a match—the semen and saliva. Not the blood." He sounded disappointed. "Same guy. Jones."

So she didn't scratch Jones. "It's progress, Kid. Pick me up and let's go wake the good professor."

Jones answered the door in his shorts, black silk. His bloodshot gaze turned to angry slits of recognition. "This is harassment, goddammit. I'm going—"

Murry interrupted, reading Jones his rights.

"Wait a minute! What are you—you can't—" He stepped back as Billy advanced.

Murry said, "Get dressed, professor."

"What questions? What is this about? Are you arresting me?" His tone said this couldn't be happening to him.

Murry didn't answer. They followed Jones into his bedroom and waited while he yanked on jeans and a shirt, then slipped into a pair of Birkenstocks.

By the time they reached the station, Jones was demanding his attorney. Murry said smoothly, "No need for a lawyer. We just need to clear up some discrepancies; then we can all go home and go to bed."

Billy yawned dramatically. "Want some coffee?" he asked as Murry opened an interrogation room and settled Jones on one side of a small table.

"Long as it hasn't been baking all day." Murry set his chair directly across from Jones. "Like a cup, professor?"

Jones was rubbing his eyes, his dazed disbelief funneling into anger. "What is so goddamned important you couldn't wait until morning like any reasonable human being?"

Billy set up the video camera, switched it on, then left. Murry opened his briefcase and pulled out a copy of the lab report. He held it up. "We got the semen test back. You were with Olga the night she died. Care to explain that?"

Panic sparked in Jones's eyes. "I don't know what you're talking about." Not an accomplished liar.

"You had a little sex, then smoked a cigarette. We know that. But what happened after? You find out she's seeing someone else?"

He came halfway out of his chair. "She was not seeing someone else!"

Murry kept on. "Maybe you lost your temper, got in a fight, slugged her too hard. Or maybe you are Ice Pick, maybe that's why you started dating her. Play with her awhile—see just how good her psychic abilities were."

Jones looked flabbergasted. "You're saying—"

Billy came back with the coffee, set down both cups, then sank into an adjoining chair.

Murry leaned forward. "Doesn't look good, Doc. You dated Olga; you knew Ford and Carlson, too. They took your Abnormal Psych class."

"I teach two hundred students a semester! Do you actually

think I remember them?" His drawl became more pronounced as his tone rose. "I was in Hawaii when Ford was
killed. I told that to Detective Kidman."

Murry lifted an eyebrow. "So, maybe you had a fight,
slugged her too hard. Decided to blame her death on Ice Pick.
Is that how it went?"

Jones shook his head, his mouth working, no words
coming out.

Murry didn't believe Jones was Ice Pick or that Olga was a
copycat killing, but he had to be certain. He stood up and
leaned over the table. "You were there, weren't you?
Thought it would be nice to stop by for a quickie after your
gig."

Jones continued to shake his head.

"Come on, let's clean this up. Don't be embarrassed. So
you had a fight. Things turned bad, you slugged her. Hey, it
happens. But don't go taking a murder one rap because you
had a fight, Doctor."

Jones patted his shirt pocket for the pack of cigarettes that
wasn't there.

Billy offered one of his. "We know you were there," Billy
said in a friendly, help-us-out voice.

Jones's hand shook.

Murry backed off in a show of disgust.

Billy reached over and lit Jones's cigarette. "We just want
an explanation. Then we can all go home."

Jones shook his head. "No way. I tell you I was there, you
try to pin Ice Pick on me. I'm not an idiot."

No, but he was overtired, over-stressed, and had over-im-
bibed. Murry knew this was their best shot.

"My partner wants to close the Ice Pick case and get some
shut-eye," Billy said. "Me, I'm in no hurry. You have an alibi
for Cindi Ford's death. So far, it's holding up. But you were

with Olga the night she died and that muddies the water. We need to know when you arrived, when you left, any details of who you saw, what you noticed. You could help us catch the guy, Doc. You could be a hero."

The tip of Jones's smoke flamed red. "Olga tried to be a hero and look what happened." His voice cracked. "Christ."

"A hero—how?" Billy asked.

"By trying to figure out who the Ice Pick Killer was! I told her to let the police handle it. But they didn't want her help." A sound of what might have been misery escaped his lips.

For the first time, Murry thought Jones might have really cared about Olga.

"I didn't believe she could help. Didn't believe in any of her psychic mumbo-jumbo." He glared at Billy. "You want a hero? It isn't me."

Murry stepped forward and slapped a crime scene photo on the table. This was the one part of his job that he really hated. "Take a look at what he did to her. You going to let him get away with that? Or is this your handiwork?"

Jones averted his gaze. Murry waited. Sooner or later, they all caved. Like a mouse attracted to a trap full of cheese, Jones couldn't resist. He finally looked down at the photo. His jaw dropped and the blood left his face. "Christ Almighty." He heaved alcohol and stomach acid onto the table, the stench filling the room. Then he started to sob, holding his abdomen, his head down.

Billy glanced toward Murry, and Murry motioned for him to wait until Jones came up for air. In the interim, Murry got some paper towels, blotted the photo, and cleaned off the table.

Finally the sobbing subsided.

Billy offered Jones another smoke. "Help us."

Murry held up the damp photo. "Before he kills again."

"Before—" Jones inhaled, his eyes suddenly alert. Nothing like a slasher photo to sober a guy up.

Murry dropped the photo in the trash. "I'm sorry you had to see that, Doc. What Ice Pick does to women . . ."

"Help us," Billy repeated more urgently.

"All right! All right!" He sagged against his chair. "I left The Bulldog as soon as the gig ended. I'd said I'd stay and party, but Olga paged me and begged me to come over. The guys were drinking. I didn't think they'd care."

Or notice, Murry thought. "Any specific reason she wanted you over?"

"She wouldn't talk on the phone. When I got there, she said she thought someone had been in her place."

Murry waited—knew there was more coming.

"This was like the fourth time she had one of her *feelings* and asked me to search the house." He sucked on the cigarette like his lungs were starved for nicotine.

"Find anything?"

"No. I don't know. I only pretended to look. I never bought the psychic crap, so I didn't—" His words died in a strangled pause.

"You say this happened three times prior to that night?"

"Yes."

"Did you only pretend to search the other times?" Murry asked, working to keep his tone free of judgment.

Jones shook his head. "No. I searched the place every time but . . . the last." Guilt and anguish laced his words.

Murry's heart raced. "Were things ever disturbed? Missing?"

"No. She said everything seemed to be there, but not exactly as she remembered. The woman was a fanatic. Knew where every damn thing was."

"Then what happened?" Murry asked.

"I told her to give it a rest, that her imagination was running wild over the Ice Pick murders. That pissed her off. I finally got her to calm down. Then she talked about calling the cops, but what could they do?" His gaze reproached Murry.

"What happened next?"

"We made love, and—" His gaze skidded away. "I went home."

"Did she ask you to stay?" Murry guessed.

He finished off the cigarette, but didn't reach for another. "I should've stayed, but I thought it was all a game she was playing to make me believe. We'd had fights about it before."

The haze of smoke burned Murry's eyes. "Did she know you were screwing around on her?"

"What—? You mean the one-nighters after gigs? They meant nothing. They were nobodies."

Murry wondered if those *nobodies* would agree. "So you didn't fight about that?"

"No."

"What time did you leave The Bulldog?"

"Around nine, nine-thirty."

"How long did it take you to get to her place?"

"I don't—" His eyebrows drew together. "Fifteen, twenty minutes. Traffic was light."

"You notice any cars parked outside the gate when you arrived?"

"Cars?" His gaze clouded. He shook his head and shrugged. "There was a van. It was still there when I left."

Murry hid his excitement. "What color?"

"White, gray, beige, something like that."

"Anyone behind the wheel?"

Jones shrugged.

"You notice the plate?" Billy asked.

"Christ. I don't have a photographic memory." He

frowned and glanced toward the back wall. After a moment, he said, "You know . . . there was something. The number began with a one. I remember thinking he was a number one prick for taking the last space on that side of the street, squeezing the car in front so tight he'd never get out."

"Notice any parking tags, bumper stickers, things like that?" Murry asked.

"No."

Murry waited until Jones lit up again. "What happened after you parked?"

"I walked up to her condo and knocked. She answered. I've told you this before."

"You didn't have a key?"

"No. She liked her privacy. Didn't want anyone to just walk in."

"You have any idea if she was seeing someone else?"

"She barely had time to see me."

"You dated for over nine months, but she wouldn't give you a key. You were screwing around, but you didn't wonder if it went both ways?"

"No." He sounded affronted at the idea.

"Did she have a key to your place?"

He rubbed his eyes. "No."

"Why not?"

"Tit for tat. She wasn't going to give me hers, I sure as hell wasn't giving her mine."

"You said you made love. In bed?"

He frowned. "On the couch."

"You didn't go into her room?"

He shook his head. "No. Except the bathroom. To get some aspirin."

That would explain his fingerprint on the mirror. Murry

had him run through everything again, up through the time he left.

"I left around eleven-thirty, midnight."

"See anyone?"

He looked past Murry's shoulder toward the wall. "No. It was quiet."

"But the van was still there?"

"How many times do I have to say it? Yes."

Billy leaned forward, "And you didn't see anyone?"

"No. No one. I got in my car and drove home. Next thing I know Olga's photo is splashed all over the news and you guys are calling me." He shoved back from the table. "I've told you everything I can remember."

"Why didn't you tell us this the first time we paid a visit?" Murry asked.

"I didn't want to end up in the papers, looking like a scumbag." He hesitated. "I didn't believe her. I didn't search the place. I didn't stay. But I searched three times before and found nothing." The last came out a whisper of anguish and fatigue.

Murry nodded at Billy. "Officer Kidman will type out a statement for you to sign, then take you home."

Jamison might be pissed he'd let Jones go, but the man's alibi for Ford was still good, and the blood under Olga's nails was not from Kevin Jones.

Chapter 9

Murry didn't remember what time he hit the sack, only that his alarm's loud beep woke him too soon. He stopped at a drive-through for coffee and an almond croissant, hoping the caffeine would keep his eyelids from drooping. Day three promised to be as long as, or longer than, day two.

He drove straight to LAPD for an early-morning meeting. Jamison had already viewed the tape and read Jones's statement. Ramirez, Farel, and the five LAPD dicks on the task force were already seated when Murry arrived. Auble from Santa Monica and Canelli from Hollywood were getting coffee in the back. Billy, standing in the front between Jamison and "Snowflake" Greene, looked relieved when Murry walked in.

Murry nodded a greeting and claimed a chair in the second row. Billy took the seat behind him. Murry leaned back and whispered, "What's up?"

"Later," Billy said.

Jamison cleared his throat. The bags under his eyes had bags. "We have an update on number five, people. Olga's boyfriend admits he was with her the night she died. Claims he left around eleven-thirty. Farel and Ramirez, you talk to the neighbors again. See if anyone noticed his arrival or departure." Jamison's steel blue eyes swung toward Murry.

"What kind of car does he drive?"

"Black Celica. New model."

Jamison nodded approval. "We have more info on the van outside her condo. Boyfriend noticed it had a number one in the plate. First number. Lasky, Auble, Canelli, and Seranella, review the other cases, talk to everyone again, see if anyone noticed a light-colored van. I want that thing found." A wave of grim nods. "The pharmacy angle hasn't checked out, but keep on it, Farel. Rodman, Janks, Machado, go through all the victims' receipts, check stubs, whatever you can find, see if any of them had any kind of house repair or interior decorating done in the two years prior to their death. Any kind of work that might get Ice Pick into the house. See if any of the floors were new or refinished."

Rodman's eyebrows rose. "The floors?"

"Ice Pick hammers those things into the floor. Seems like he must have prior knowledge of the floors before he gets there."

That or he's one lucky bastard, Murry thought.

Jamison looked at him. "Murry and Kidman will keep a tag on Jones, follow-up on the other teachers, and students, see if any of them own a van, and coordinate with me."

Greene's gaze suddenly narrowed.

Uh-oh, Snowflake didn't like that. Too bad.

Murry waited until they were outside before asking, "What kind of squeeze-play were Greene and Jamison putting on you?"

"Greene is chapped because we didn't call him in on the interrogation. I told him you'd already talked to Jamison. I think Jamison's smoked at Greene."

"Well, you should have seen his casebook. A shitty job."

"Yep. Anyway, Greene started grilling me on procedure,

like I don't know my ass from a hole in the ground. Jamison walks up, starts saying what a great job we did." Billy's eyes lit up. "Implied that if we wanted to see a lot more action—transfer to LAPD—he'd be supportive."

"*If* we wrap up this case," Murry added, wondering if the Kid was bored. LAPD had a lousy rep with the public, but no question he'd be busy working in the Glass House. In Beverly Hills, one murder a decade was newsworthy. Most of the time he spent tracking thefts or assaults—usually drunk party-goers. In his younger days, he'd enjoyed working Hollywood and would have jumped at a chance to join LAPD, to further his crusade against the bad guys. After twenty years, he still blamed himself for dropping Rachel off at her apartment and not going inside with her. They both had finals the next day and she'd told him to go home. He'd never dreamed she'd interrupt a robbery. Get shot. The police had caught the guy. But she had died on the operating table.

Now he had Éclair in his life, and time away from the job gave them more time together. BHPD was less stressful, cops died from natural causes, and the accommodations were first-rate. "Make less money," he pointed out, not about to move.

Billy shoved two sticks of gum into his mouth. Peppermint. Murry almost missed the smell when the Kid wasn't around. And he was just getting up to speed as a partner. What if Billy decided to go it alone? Did Murry want to go through that again?

"Money isn't everything," Billy said.

Murry raised an eyebrow.

"If you go, I go," Billy said. "We're a team."

Surprised, Murry grunted, "Thanks for the loyalty, Kid."

Billy gave him a cocky grin. "So, where we headed?"

"Olga's condo first, office second. You've gone through

her place with her friend from downstairs?"

"The old lady. Yep. Couldn't tell if anything was missing."

"It was a long shot. Chances are he took panties, a lock of hair, something too personal to be missed."

"What're we going back for?"

"The tapes. Six months' worth don't just disappear."

"Maybe she taped over 'em."

"Then we'd have the most recent tapes and not the ones from two years ago. You check on field trips and special speakers for her classes?"

"She had a couple of authors come in last year to talk about their books. And she took her students to the Psychic Faire every year. That's it."

"The Psychic Faire? As in tarot cards and palm-readers?"

"As in kooks and crazies," Billy said. "Hundreds of 'em. With your crystal ball, you'll feel right at home, Murry."

"Is that it? Just a bunch of fortune-tellers?"

Billy rolled his eyes. "There's book vendors, New Age vendors—they sell anything from sage and sea salt to crystals and rocks." He flipped open his Palm. "Let's see, there's booths on healing, massage, acupuncture, acupressure—you name it, it's there."

Covering something like that would be a nightmare. "When is it held?"

"Varies. Last year it was February."

"Contact whoever's in charge of selling space, booths, whatever, and find out who participated. Go back three years."

Billy groaned.

"You get anything on the drop lists?"

"Back seat."

As he reached for the stack of printouts, Murry's back

twinged. He hadn't been to the gym in four days. He needed to stay on his routine, or his back would do more than twang the next time he played Casanova with Éclair. He scanned the list. Billy had highlighted Ford and Carlson's names. He flipped through more pages. Bingo. Gristham had taken Jones's Psych One and dropped. He flipped to the W's. "Shit. No White."

He flipped more pages, but nothing jumped. "Why didn't you tell Jamison about the Gristham, Ford, and Carlson connection? Four out of five's a start."

"A lot of people go to college. Figured we should keep a card up our sleeve, show it to Jamison when we have a better hand."

"You taking up poker?"

Billy barked a laugh. "Gina has. I've canceled so many Fridays, she's able to make the poker party with her coworkers."

"She any good?"

He groaned. "Always loses. She blows fifty bucks a week on the lottery, too. We could go to Hawaii on what she blows in six months."

"You planning a vacation?" Billy hadn't taken one since they'd started working together. Unless he counted his hospital stay as one.

"Anything to get out of cleaning the apartment."

The few times Murry had been inside Billy's apartment, he'd had to step over fast-food land mines. "You moving?"

"Nope."

"Got a relative coming to visit?" The words were out before he could yank them back, but maybe the Kid did have some obscure relatives coming to visit.

Billy got quiet. He pulled into Olga's parking space and set the brake. "Only relative I had was my aunt." His voice took on a nostalgic tone. "Used to say, 'You can do anything you've a mind to, Sonny.' Sounded like Granny on the 'Beverly Hillbillies.' Found some of her stuff when I was cleaning the spare room."

First time he'd ever talked about his aunt.

Anticipating Murry's question, he added, "Died right after I graduated from the Academy. I kept promising to go back and see her, kept finding reasons not to." He shook his head. "Then it was too late."

"I'm sorry."

"Yep. Me, too."

At the awkward silence, Murry asked in an upbeat tone, "So who's the visitor?"

Billy shrugged. "Gina's moving in."

"Whoa. When did that happen?"

"It's just a short-term thing. She's freaked about Ice Pick and feels safer with me."

Murry didn't point out that women had a way of turning short-term into long-term. The Kid needed to learn.

Billy switched gears, as though he'd reached his max of personal talk. "Photos in the manila envelope are the ones I took of the crowd outside Olga's."

"Notice anything or anyone unusual?"

"Besides the guy holding a bloody ice pick?"

"Smart ass. Just for that, you can do the photos at Olga's funeral."

Billy's smirk disappeared.

No one liked picture-taking detail. It was invasive, and mourners hated the intrusion. He'd park Billy out of the way and have him use a telephoto lens. "And when you see the guy with the picks, make sure the camera's in focus."

"Maybe you should have someone else do the pics. I'm not so great with a camera."

"Then this will be a good learning opportunity."

Billy swore under his breath.

Murry left the crowd photos on the seat. He'd check them later. He didn't hold much hope they'd show anything. Snowflake hadn't bothered to photograph the crowds outside the other crime scenes. But maybe, after the funeral, a comparison would show something. Right now, they had other bait to fillet.

He left Billy at Olga's kitchen table, cellular plastered to his ear as he tried to reach the head honcho of the Psychic Faire. Glad to leave the bloodstains behind, Murry stepped down the hallway. For a second, the hallway shimmered, like he'd stepped through the twilight zone. For a second, he saw a naked woman spread-eagled and nailed to the floor, her head covered with black nylon. Blood dripped from her palms. More blood was smeared on her thighs. One leg twitched and he realized the picks hadn't been hammered through her feet yet—or her chest. She was still alive. He blinked and the flash was gone, but his skin suddenly felt ice-rink cold. None of the victims had been staked in a hallway. Christ, was Ice Pick doing another one already?

Murry shook off the chill. *It's just my fucking imagination.* So why did he feel like the lockbox in the back of his brain was ready to slide out into the light and spring open? He glanced again at the photo of Olga and Baryshnikov. Then at some of the others. Nothing eerie about them. Nothing weird. The hallway was just a hallway.

He stopped in the doorway to her bedroom, imagining her evening. Jones comes by, pretends to search, has sex, and leaves.

He thought about the tape recording, the soft, "Don't move." The window had recently been opened and closed. If Olga opened the window earlier and closed it before going to bed, Ice Pick could have been inside when Jones arrived.

Billy appeared in the doorway. "Actually got someone about the Faire. Weird old gal, had a voice like a gravel pit. Once she verifies my credentials, she'll send me lists for the past five years. She said most of the same people participate every year. She *loved* Olga. Olga apparently always paid to have her students' fortunes read."

Murry checked the closet, wondering where Olga might have stashed the used tapes. "You set up an interview?"

"We'll see her at the Faire."

He checked the nightstands again. "If we don't have the guy by February, we might as well chuck the case over to Tack."

"The Faire starts Friday. Runs through Sunday."

Murry glanced up. "Thought you said it was in February."

"Obviously your crystal ball needs a tune-up. This year they decided January was better."

Murry scanned the room. "Where the hell are those tapes?"

"Winslow wouldn't have missed them," Billy said. "Maybe Ice Pick took 'em."

"No. He'd have taken the one in the recorder." He eyed the kid. "Feel like getting your fortune told?"

Billy groaned. "I've sworn off fortune cookies. Hell, I'm so spooked, I've sworn off Chinese food."

"Then how about a psychic reading? You can ask about the fortunes, or where the tapes are stashed."

"Why not just ask who Ice Pick is, while we're at it?" Billy grumbled.

"Good idea."

"Good idea?" Billy followed him outside. "You're kidding, right?"

"I'll take information anywhere I find it." Murry glanced

toward the street, imagining the van, Ice Pick behind the wheel, waiting to make his move—then Jones raps on the door and he has to wait. Wait or kill Jones. But that wasn't his game. He had a ritual—staking them out, raping them. And he had a reason for it. Maybe he was exorcizing demons. Maybe he was killing his mother. Whatever it was, boyfriends or bystanders didn't figure in. Of course, the van might have nothing to do with Ice Pick at all. Except that serial killers seemed to have a preference for vans. Plenty of room for a ladder, rape-kit, rope, anything a handy-dandy killer might need.

His cellular shrieked. Ramirez's voice came over, badly distorted.

"You behind a mountain or what?" Murry asked. "Can barely hear you."

"It's this damn humidity, I swear. Wish it would rain, wash a few more mansions off the cliffs, and get cool again. Any better?"

"Much. What's up?"

Ramirez's voice rose a notch. "Talked to all the parents again, showed them photos of the other victims. Got one hit. White worked part-time as a waitress in Hollywood. So did Ford. White's parents recognized Ford as one of her co-workers."

"How the hell did Greene miss that?"

"Sloppy work. Although Ford only worked with her briefly," Ramirez allowed. "White quit the Johnny Rocket's job after a month. Went to work for an antique dealer. Then she was murdered."

"Check the restaurant and the coworkers. See if anyone has a rap sheet. I assume Greene checked out the antique dealer?"

"Only one half-assed phone call. I talked to her this

morning. She's a sweet old *abuela*. Been in the business a long time. *Nada*."

Murry remembered the key on White's key ring and asked Ramirez to see if the antique dealer could identify the key; then he clicked off. "Ford and White worked at the Johnny Rocket's in Hollywood—briefly. Dammit, there's too many threads."

"So which one do we follow?"

"I still want those tapes. You notice any at Jones's place?" His brain was nudging him. He'd been in Jones's bedroom when the man got dressed. He should have taken a closer look there.

"Nope."

"Let's ask."

This time Jones opened the door before they knocked. He'd showered and shaved and had keys in his hand. He swore when he saw them coming up the walk. With an irritated wave, he stepped back and gestured them inside. "I cannot even begin to fathom what brings you here," he said, his attitude back in spades.

Murry pulled a micro-cassette from his pocket. "Recognize this?"

Jones swallowed. "A tape. So?"

"You told us Olga taped her dreams. There's some tapes missing. Someone told us you had them."

His face reddened and Murry swore at himself for not hammering Jones harder the night before. "Where are they? And don't even think about lying. I'm one lie away from slapping you with obstruction of justice."

Jones's gaze skidded toward the hall. "In the bedroom. I was going to turn them in. I just wanted to listen to them first."

"Why? She tape your sex games?"

Another flush said he'd hit the nail on the head.

"S-and-M?"

"No!" He looked horrified at the thought. "What we shared together was private—"

"*Was*," Murry interrupted, heading down the hall. He suddenly realized what his brain had been trying to tell him during their first interview. "You shaved Olga's pubic hair when you had sex, didn't you?"

Jones's mouth flapped like he wanted to lie, but didn't quite have the balls. "S—sometimes. But not that night. I told you the truth. Everything."

"You erase anything?"

"No!"

Murry stood aside while Jones pulled a shoe box from under the bed.

"This all of them?"

"Yes," Jones snapped.

Murry gave him the one-eye. "You know, Doc, I've given you a break. My captain wants your ass downtown. Me—I don't think you're guilty of anything other than stupidity. But you don't realize how serious this is. You hold anything back—anything at all—and you're going to see 'Professor Suspected in Ice Pick Killings' spread across every newspaper in the state. I'll make a show of dragging you outside and slapping on the cuffs. Your neighbors will never look at you the same. Neither will your students. Know what I mean?"

Jones seemed to shrink, his bravado obliterated by fear.

"Learn anything from the tapes?" Billy asked, offering Jones a cigarette, then lighting one himself.

Jones opened the shoe box and extracted a tape from the thirty dumped inside. It had a rubber band around it. "This is the only one that made any sense."

"What's on it?" Murry asked, reading Thursday's date on the tape. Ice Pick had killed her two days later.

"Something about Ice Pick and the Psychic Faire."

Chapter 10

Conrad turned off the alarm in the entry and went straight to his desk. The visit to the station had been a huge disappointment. The only good moment was at the end. Just as Tack screeched by, he'd noticed Detectives Murry and Kidman. No love lost there.

Detective Tack. Tackless asshole, more like it. The man had escorted him around, trying to appear friendly and dedicated, while assuring him they were closing in on the thief. All lies. Then the cop had the audacity to show off a photo of his wife, "All my love, Scarlett," scrawled in the bottom corner.

He'd nodded and smiled as Tack babbled about her being a fashion model, then idly wondered how she'd look in a black stocking and butterfly wings.

The phone rang and he reached across the desk to answer. "Hello?"

"Conrad James the third?"

For some reason, he knew immediately who it was. "Yes." He activated his scrambler, just in case the bastard tried to tape the conversation.

"You know who this is?" the man asked.

Conrad imagined the King of Thieves puffed up with pride like a blowfish, one in need of a sharp spear. "Elvis?" he drawled in the tone of a man talking to a distant relative he'd just as soon not talk to again.

"No, asshole, it's Robin Hood. It's time to take from the rich and give to the poor." When Conrad didn't respond, he added, "I've got something you lost. You want 'em back or not?"

"I haven't lost anything."

"If that's a joke, I'm not laughing."

"I wasn't aware you wanted to be entertained."

"Don't play games with me. I've read about those women, you sick bastard. You want the picks, you pay."

Conrad clenched the phone. The man didn't understand and never would about his gift to those women. The King might be a good thief, but he was a spiritual moron. He didn't deserve a transformation. He deserved to die. "I told you, Elvis, they aren't mine. I was holding them for a—"

"Cut the crap. You live alone. You keep the basement locked tighter than Fort Knox. You think I didn't notice the metal shop and woodworking stuff? You sick fuck."

Until now the guy had spoken with careful precision. But *sick fuck* had a drawl to it that Conrad recognized. African-American or Black, Spade, Smoke, Watermelon, Jarhead, whatever. Names he'd never paid much attention to now crowded his mind. *You're dead.* "I don't—"

"Shut up and listen."

Conrad waited, furious to have to listen to this nigger talk down to him.

"I want half a million in hundreds. Not sequential."

Half a mil! He'd been gathering cash since the break-in, anticipating this, but rage engulfed him. He swallowed it back. "That kind of cash would take weeks to accumulate. It's out of the question."

"A guy who keeps twenty-five grand lying around can

scrape together a few hundred. It's a lot cheaper than an attorney's fees."

"Regardless of what you believe, I've been authorized to offer a hundred-thousand-dollar finder's fee." He forced a note of disinterest into his tone. "If that's unacceptable, then do what you must. As I said before: they aren't mine."

"Right, and I'm the Sheriff of Nottingham. Four hundred. That's cheap for what you've done, and a whole lot better than death row."

"Two hundred."

"Three. Take it, or hang up the goddamn phone."

He heard the *this is the end of the line* in the King's voice. "Three hundred," he agreed.

"Glad we're finally on the same wavelength, Conrad. Put the money in a briefcase. I'll call tomorrow, tell you when and where we'll meet."

Conrad's thoughts raced. He needed those picks back, but he also had to make sure the bastard didn't walk away. Olga's funeral was tomorrow. He couldn't miss that. And Saturday, the Psychic Faire. "I'll have to have the money transferred. It will take a few days to put together."

"Bullshit. Tomorrow night."

"That's too fast. Hauling it out of my bank will draw attention. Monday."

"I'm betting you've been stashing cash since the robbery. But I'll be generous, like my namesake. You have 'til Saturday night."

"Where do we meet?"

"I'll call you tomorrow. Once you confirm you have the cash, you'll get instructions."

"No. I won't be available tomorrow, and I'm not going through with this if it's not a public place. A safe place."

Silence.

He decided to take a chance, play it out. "Or you can hang up," he added, nails digging into his palm.

The hesitation on the other end of the phone told him he'd surprised the bastard. "I'm not some woman you can knock down and crucify to get your rocks off," the King said, his well-modulated tone losing some of its precision. "You don't call the shots here, creep. You got that?"

His hand shaking, Conrad set the receiver into the cradle. He found himself holding his breath.

The phone rang almost immediately. He let it ring three times before finally lifting it.

"All right, you fucking pervert, here's your instructions. You deviate from them in any way, and you'll be cell mates with Charles Manson."

Now he knew just how greedy the son-of-a-bitch was.

"Go to The Five Forty Five on Rodeo. Nine o'clock Saturday night. The place'll be packed. You'll have a reservation."

"No, don't use my name."

"What name do you want the reservation under?"

He instinctively said his mother's stage name. "LaFleur." He spelled it, all the while wondering how the King knew he could get a table.

"Park two blocks south in the lot next to Bank of America, space twenty-four. There are three lots; make sure you're in the right one. If you don't show, if you screw up in any way, I'll be sending a package to the cops with your return address." *Click.*

No, he thought, *you'll never get the chance.*

No tourist joint, The Five Forty Five catered to the ultra-wealthy of Beverly Hills. The kind of people that spent seven hundred bucks on Gucci dog bowls and wouldn't think twice about dropping a hundred grand on Rodeo Drive. He'd eaten there a couple of times. He wondered about the parking space. What was the significance? Did the bastard think he was stupid enough to leave the money in his car, so the King could steal it?

He punched star-six-nine and waited through ten rings before giving up. He called the operator. "I just received an obscene phone call and want to trace the number. I hit star sixty-nine, and there's no answer. Can you tell me what number the call was made from?"

It took a few minutes, but he finally got, "It's from a pay phone, sir. At the Santa Monica Pier."

Time for a reconnaissance. He changed into a fresh linen suit, dark blue and unassuming. It matched the new color of his van, which had gone from light green to yellow to beige, and now midnight blue. A dab of spirit-gum above his lip gave him a mustache. He pressed on a goatee. Distinguished, like a professor.

It only took seven minutes to hit Rodeo. The Five Forty Five was squeezed between a clothing store and the Little Fingers Bakery. Two blocks down, a Mom-and-Pop market and a storefront Bank of America flanked the specified parking lot. Every space in the lot was taken, a blue Camaro in number twenty-four. He pulled up in front of the bank and strolled inside to the information desk, where an elderly woman was handling the phones, their lights blinking furiously. She glanced up. "May I help you?"

He smiled. "I'd like to rent a space in the parking lot next door. Who do I talk to?"

She picked up the phone, and a minute later a junior executive stood before him with a how-can-I-please-you look.

Conrad explained what he wanted.

"We rent the spaces for our employees," he said, his tone apologetic. "However, you might check with the owner of

The Five Forty Five. He rents the other seven spaces. And Little Fingers Bakery shares the adjacent lot with three other stores. They might be able to help you."

He wasn't interested in the other lots. Who did the King know at The Five Forty Five? Was there a link between the restaurant and the robberies? Was that how he'd been targeted? He cut through the alley to the restaurant, stepped down into the trellised patio covered with honeysuckle vines that bordered the street, and walked past the empty tables to the front entrance. The humidity had driven everyone inside. He glanced around at the framed Toulouse-Lautrec posters, liking the way they fit in with the black, red, and white decor.

The maître d' jumped to attention, smoothing the jacket of his tux. Over the soft hum of conversation, words like *botox* and *collagen* surfaced. Beverly Hills—plastic surgery capital of the world. "Table for one, sir?"

Conrad checked his watch. "I'm meeting someone. Could I see a menu?" He accepted the ornate black and gold menu, pretending to peruse the list of appetizers. When the maître d' stepped away, he set it aside. Remembering there was an exit and restrooms to the left, he moved in the opposite direction toward the kitchen, wanting to get a better feel for the layout. He glanced back, surprised to see double doors that opened into a separate dining area and at least one room beyond.

So far, he hadn't seen one black employee, but knew there had to be a connection between this place and the robberies. He continued down the hallway and pushed through a swinging door into a world of stainless steel and the clatter of pots and pans.

"Where's my salmon?"

"Waiting on my shrimp salad."

"Eighty-six the pumpkin soup."

Oddly, as conspicuous as he should have felt, the chaos made him feel nearly invisible. The scent of wine and garlic wafted around him. Beyond all the action, he saw the door to a huge refrigerator, and near that, what appeared to be a door into the alley. At least three ways out of the building then.

A waiter paused in his rush for the kitchen door. "May I help you, sir?"

He gave him a blank stare. "The restroom?"

The waiter shoved the swinging door open and held it with his foot. "Down this hall—at the other end, sir."

"Thank you." He ambled to the restroom, went in, came out, noted the emergency bar on the exit door to his left, and headed back to the entry. If anyone went out that way, they'd trigger the alarm. He walked around to the back, slowing his pace as he passed another door, not the one from the kitchen. This one exited at the rear corner of the restaurant—the corner furthest from the parking lot and probably a hundred yards from the alley. A private exit. Not for deliveries. Those would be made at the kitchen entry off the alley. For what then? Did it matter? He imagined someone like his mother escaping out that door while reporters hung out in front, hoping for a snapshot of the producer's wealthy widow. She'd become a recluse after that—with only Conrad for company.

But what was the King's connection to this place? Had he told anyone about the picks? The thought sent a chill down his back. He would have to find out. But first he had to get them back. And what about the parking spot? Why twenty-four?

He returned to his van, grabbed his notepad, and sketched a diagram of the restaurant. He knew the King would have a plan. The trick would be to turn his greed against him.

He jotted down the plate numbers of all the cars in the lot, taking special note of the blue Camaro and wondering if it had any connection to the King. At six o'clock, the last of the sun disappeared behind the line of buildings. Within fifteen minutes, most of the bank employees had left, leaving only spots twenty-two through thirty filled.

Whap! Whap! Whap! A police officer peered at him through the passenger window, a baton in one hand, the other resting on the top of his holster.

In a heartbeat, Conrad's pulse rate shot to two hundred. For a moment his breath stopped. His hand shook as he rolled down the window. How had he screwed up? He was wearing a disguise, they couldn't know. But the hammering in his chest didn't slow.

"Mind if I ask what you're doing here?"

He opened his mouth, but nothing came out. A sickening sense of panic sank his stomach to his knees. Had the King set him up?

The cop's gaze flickered toward the B of A.

He thinks I'm casing the bank. He lifted the clipboard, showing the sketch of the restaurant. "Just finishing a sketch before I visit the client. Should have finished it yesterday, but . . ." He gave him a *you know how it is* shrug, praying the words "kitchen," "hallway," and "bathroom" scrawled on the paper would make it obvious he wasn't in the "banking" business.

The cop nodded. "Sorry, but you need to move on. Only one-hour parking along here."

"No problem, officer." His pulse still thudding in his ears, he drove two blocks down and parked. For an instant, he'd thought they had him. Saw a long row of bars flash before his eyes.

He took several long breaths. But instead of feeling calm, a terrible hollow sensation expanded in his gut, familiar, yet unexpected. It was a black void, demanding satiation. He tried to ignore it, to distract himself with the people passing by.

But it only got worse. *Have to, have to, have to, have to . . .* He fumbled to unlock the glove box and reached for Olga's leotard, the stretchy fabric cool against his palm. Soothing. He rubbed it across his cheek, then buried his face in it. Only a hint of lavender remained.

Not enough, not enough, not enough . . .

Chapter 11

The red light on Murry's kitchen phone was blinking furiously as he walked in. Dying for some shut-eye, he hesitated, then reluctantly pressed PLAY.

"Dammit, Murry, would you leave your cellular on? It's Mary. It's after two. I'm home, and . . . I think someone's been in the house. I've locked the doors, and I have my gun, so call before you walk in."

Murry glanced at the kitchen clock and punched in her number. "It's Art. I'm on my way. You okay?"

"I'm fine," she said, though her voice sounded shaky. "I think it's just a case of nerves. Everything's fine. I searched the place. Everything's fine. You don't need to come. Get some rest."

"To hell with that. I'll be there in twenty. Don't shoot me, okay?" That got a small laugh, but he wasn't joking. She was scared, even if she didn't admit it. And Éclair didn't scare easily.

He rang the doorbell to let her know he'd arrived, then used his key. She was in his arms before he took a step. The uncomfortable weight of her 9mm touched his back as her hug tightened. "Hope you got the safety on?" he murmured.

"Yes."

"Good. Wouldn't want a bullet in my backside."

She chuckled, sounding more like herself. "I wouldn't either." She stepped back. "Thanks for coming."

"You check the closets, under the bed?"

She raised an eyebrow at him. "Yes."

He glanced around. Nothing appeared to be missing. "What spooked you?"

She turned and studied the room, then shook her head. "I just felt uneasy when I came in. I've been working so many hours, my imagination's on overtime."

But he knew she wasn't the type to have an overactive imagination. Not with her job. "Get a security system installed. Tomorrow."

"If someone wants to rob the place, a security system isn't going to stop them." She held up her gun. "That's why I have this."

"But it'll make someone think twice. And if you're asleep, it'll wake you up, so you can use that."

She argued all the way to bed, but by morning agreed to make the call. Relieved, Murry told her about Olga's tape over coffee and eggs.

"So you think Ice Pick might be connected to the Psychic Faire?" She sounded doubtful.

"It's possible. I have a feeling about that damn Faire—or maybe it's just because of Olga's tape." He shrugged, feeling as though the answer lay buried in his brain cells. "The guy could be targeting victims anywhere, but it's odd three of the five victims have a connection to the Faire. If only I could find something on White or Ford."

"I thought Ford dropped Olga's class or something."

"She did. *Before* the Faire."

"Then maybe she went to the Faire on her own. If she signed up for Olga's class, she must have had an interest. Do you know why she dropped it?"

"No." Murry jotted himself a note to find out.

"But White knew Ford from work, right?"

"Yes, but Ford's parents didn't remember them ever getting together. They recognized White from their visits to the restaurant—that's it."

"Was White interested in psychic phenomena? Maybe she went on her own."

"Maybe." Murry called Billy and asked him to question White and Ford's parents about their daughters' interests and whether they knew if the two women attended the Faire. He waited while Éclair ran a brush through her hair and dabbed on lip gloss, then walked her to the car. "When's the security guy coming?"

"Three o'clock. He'll do a schematic, and if he gets the bid, he promised to install it later this week."

He leaned through her window for a quick kiss, liking the scent of her hair, the way her lips softened beneath his, her quirky smile as he straightened. "Good."

Murry couldn't stop himself from cruising by Tack's desk and checking out the King of Thieves file. Other than an interview with the latest victim, and some calls to local pawn shops, nothing seemed to have gotten done. Did Tack expect the King to dump a sixty-thousand-dollar rug at a pawn shop? Murry suspected the guy had a high-class antique dealer who didn't mind a few shady deals on the side. The fence didn't have to be local, could be anywhere in the US. Murry had given Billy the task of searching the web for possibilities, and the Kid had laughed. "Where 'm I supposed to look? Fence-dot-com. No matter how hot, I buy what you got?"

Recalling his chagrin, Murry knew he needed to get more

familiar with computers, but he hated the damn things. He glanced through the growing list of stolen items. If the King had a buyer, the guy must be rolling in dough.

"What the hell are you doing?" Tack snarled.

Shit. Murry closed the file and turned. "Just the guy I was looking for. Thought I'd left something out of the file."

Disbelief flared in Tack's eyes. His fingers curled.

Do it. I'd love to break your jaw a second time.

"You have to stick your nose in everything, don't you? Be the big shot?"

Murry offered a wounded look. "I was just trying to help." He headed down the aisle. Tack trailed him all the way to his desk. The bastard never learned. "Got something to say, Tack?"

"Stay out of my case. And away from my wife!"

"Your wife?" Where the hell did that come from? Was Scarlett on the prowl? "I've had the goods, you can keep 'em."

Tack's face mottled.

"As for your case," Murry added, "I just wanted to help."

The door to the division swung open and Captain Daniels poked his head in. "Murry, in my office." He sounded pissed.

Tack grinned as Murry shoved past. Daniels said nothing until the door closed, then he slapped a stack of phone messages on his desk. "Reporters are calling about Kevin Jones. Wondering why we hauled him in for questioning. Wondering if he's a suspect. I can't duck 'em forever. We tip 'em off, they owe us. We sit on this, we'll look like lame-brains on the front page of every paper in the state."

"I've questioned Jones and I have serious doubts."

"Doubts? The guy's got no alibi for any of the murders but one, and that's a family member."

Murry opened his mouth to respond, but Daniels continued, "Jamison says we're looking for an educated killer. Organized, careful, smart. Sounds like Jones to me. Pick him up and lean on 'em. Hard."

"Jamison gave me two days to come up with something." He explained about the tape and the Faire.

Daniels shook his head. "These guys are always looking for victims, Murry. The victims are a physical type. He's not going to return to the same place every year to find the perfect target."

"You said yourself this guy's a planner. If the Faire is part of his fantasy, it's exactly what he'd do," Murry argued.

"Thin," Daniels said. "Very thin."

"Thin, but Jones isn't a sure thing. He's not even a contender, in my book." Murry's tie suddenly felt tight. If he was wrong, he'd be writing parking tickets again. "Why would Jones date Olga, if he was planning to kill her? We can't link him directly to the other women, only to the woman he openly admits was his girlfriend. Besides, he may fit the older and educated, but he's far from organized in his classroom or home. Organizational skills would show elsewhere besides the crime scene. His office looks like a cyclone hit it." Murry leaned over the desk. "The last thing you want is to grab the wrong guy."

Daniels gave him a narrow gaze, then cracked his lips to say something.

Murry waited.

He jerked his head toward the door. "So, get me a sure thing."

Murry retreated to his desk. Tack was gone, but Billy was there, a grin on his face.

"What?" Murry asked. "My pants unzipped?"

"White went to the Psychic Faire."

"What? Spill."

"The antique dealer has a booth every year, selling replicas of famous jewelry and antique jewel boxes. Two years ago, White manned the booth for the old lady. Three months later, she's crucified in her living room. Farel talked to the old lady last night. Called me this morning. He also asked about the antique desk key. The old lady didn't know anything about it." Anticipating Murry's next question, Billy said, "He tried you at home, but you didn't answer. He figured you were doing some night work with the autopsy queen."

The autopsy queen? That was a new one. Excited at Billy's latest discovery, Murry said, "Let's talk to Jamison." With any luck, he would approve a full-fledged stake-out of the Faire.

Chapter 12

Éclair's well-manicured Moorish-Art-Deco-fantasy neighborhood was virtually deserted. Conrad's working-class van stood out. Not that it mattered. Not now. He ambled up the walk, eyeing the huge picture window and balcony, the front patio entry, and red tile steps leading to the door. The place was nice, upper-middle-class, but nothing he'd look at twice. He followed the tiled steps into the shadow of a long veil of pink and yellow roses crawling up the patio trellis and hanging overhead. He liked roses. His gaze settled on the huge, turquoise, ceramic pot outside the front door. A large, forbidding cactus had overgrown its home. Cactus and roses. Did she have a thing for prickly objects?

He knocked, feeling the same thrill he'd felt the evening before. After that run-in with the traffic cop, he'd needed a boost. Something to take his mind off the fright and off that bastard thief for the rest of the night. Mary's French doors had been ridiculously easy to open. No nosy neighbors, no dogs. It took him only a few minutes to install the phone interrupt, but he hadn't bothered to look around. The pleasure of that would come later.

For now, he was here on business. Her call to Five Star Security had been a surprise. He usually monitored calls for

weeks before intercepting a service call. The sense of right-
ness as everything flowed into place confirmed she wanted
this transformation. He was about to knock again when a
black BMW pulled into the driveway.

The driver's door popped open before the engine died.
She hurried up the walk, her tennis shoes slapping the cement. Baggy trousers and an oversized shirt hid her curves.
Silky brown hair escaped a barrette and framed her face. With
a brief flash of annoyance, she brushed it back behind one
ear. "Sorry I'm late. I'm Mary Éclair."

"Jim Conrad, Five Star Security."

She gave him a brief handshake, her grip firm and warm.

Her hands had touched the others. The thought made
his palms tingle. Careful to finger only the edges of his
phony business card, he handed it to her and followed her
inside.

"What kind of security are you looking for? Inside? Outside?"

"The works."

"Including video? We can put all the rooms in your house
on camera, or just the hallways and entry areas." He hoped
she'd go for it. He wanted his artistry on tape. He wanted the
boyfriend cop to see it. And keeping his own face from being
seen would make the transformation more challenging.

She frowned.

"We've got a special going right now. Video for the
hallway and entry is included free with any system."

"I don't like the idea of cameras on me all the time."

"They only go on when the alarm is triggered." *Usually.*

She nodded. "Okay. But I want something to let me know
if someone's broken a window, or picked the lock on the
door. That kind of thing."

He jotted a note on his clipboard. "We've got just what

you want. You have any dogs or animals that might set off motion sensors?"

"No."

"If the phone lines are cut, do you want an alternative alarm? Radio, cellular, something like that?"

"Sounds fine," she said.

"You ever sleep with the windows open?"

"Sometimes I leave the French doors open, but the screens are locked."

"You want security screens?"

"Yes."

"We can put keypads by the front and back door. Do you normally come in through the garage?"

"No, the front door. Garage door's always locked."

"Would you like a panic alarm by the nightstand?"

She nodded. "Yes. Good idea."

"Why don't I take a look around, take some measurements? I'll get back to you this afternoon with a quote."

"That'd be great." She glanced at the pager clipped to her purse. "Excuse me, I've got to make a call."

"Yes, ma'am." It amused him to act subservient. "I've got some literature in the van about our systems—in case you have questions. Be right back."

Inside the van, he grabbed his measuring tape, clipboard, and brochures. Unable to resist, he flipped open the glove box and watched the phone number she had called scroll across the tiny monitor screen. *BHPD*. Detective Murry. The cop. Smiling to himself, he closed the glove compartment and hurried inside.

He did a slow walk-through, noting the number of windows and doors and jotting down measurements. He paused in the living room to study the photo on the sideboard. The medical examiner, the cop, and the cop's famous blimp brother. The men wore tuxes, Mary Éclair an evening gown that brought out the green in her eyes. Tasteful. High class. He liked that. This would definitely be his riskiest transformation—and his most exciting. His cunning against her brains, her strength, and her boyfriend.

"Yes, the security man is here . . ."

Was she still talking to the cop?

". . . measuring windows. I took a late lunch. I will. Bye, Murry. See you tonight."

Tonight? Here? Or his place? He heard the refrigerator door open and close and resumed his walk-through, moving to the kitchen. She was at the table, eating a turkey sandwich and staring at the Palm notepad plugged into a keyboard. In-between bites, she typed, her nails clicking on the keys. Her work obviously distracted her—he intended to take advantage of that.

He pulled his measuring tape and crouched by the French doors. "Been really busy lately," he said. "What with the King of Thieves and that Ice Pick nut."

That snagged her attention.

He smiled. "Can't be too careful. Do you have any other security?"

"A gun." She took another bite, her gaze watchful.

Had he said too much? Made her suspicious? He adopted the rambling tone of a man who liked to talk. "A gun, huh? You target shoot? My wife's pretty handy with her .32."

At the mention of a wife, her expression relaxed. "I practice once in awhile."

"You have a nice place," he said as he stood up. "Love these older houses with the ornate moldings and the wood floors." He flashed another smile, gratified when she smiled back.

"Thank you." She squinted at the notepad, then resumed typing.

He lifted his clipboard, jotted the measurements for the kitchen door and window, then retraced his steps to the living room. A Lance Murry CD lay on the coffee table, more CDs stacked beside it. Perhaps he'd play Puccini during her transformation. A first. He'd never done it to music.

Taking his time, he headed down the hall, noting the perfect place for a pressure pad in the bedroom. He'd have to be clear about the specs to the subcontractor, so he didn't run into any surprises later. He was going to have to eat the cost of the video cameras as it was.

The bedroom was too frilly for his taste. Lace edging on the ivory curtains and bedspread. Very different from her mannish work attire. A cheap Oriental carpet covered most of the wood floor, and another in the living room, but the hallway gleamed, recently refinished.

A snapshot of her and the cop lay on the bureau as though she meant to frame it, but hadn't gotten around to it yet. They were standing in front of a Christmas tree. She looked pretty in black slacks and a green sweater the color of her eyes. She was leaning against the cop, a smile on her face. Conrad imagined holding her, his arms beneath her breasts, her . . .

From the living room, he heard, "Jim?"

He shoved the photo under the work order and darted into the hall. His heart was pounding like crazy. If he'd had his picks, he might have given into temptation. But that would ruin the artistry of his masterpiece. He eyed the polished hallway floor, imagining her there, her arms open, waiting . . .

"You almost through?"

He flinched and hoped she didn't notice.

"I've got an appointment at four-thirty."

"Just need to check the bathroom, then I'm finished," he said, moving past her.

She nodded. "I'll be in the kitchen."

"Five minutes," he promised. Did she keep her laundry in the bathroom? He didn't see a hamper. He followed the hall to a tiny washer/dryer area. A straw hamper stood in the corner, the lid down. After listening a moment to her footsteps in the kitchen, he flipped up the lid. Whoa—Treasure Island! No Fruit-of-the-Loom in there. He reached down through the rainbow of French lingerie and snatched a pair of hot pink satin and lace bikini panties, quickly stuffing them in the inside pocket of his jacket.

The drive home felt like hours. It tortured him to wait until he had the doors locked before pulling his prize from his pocket. Had she worn them with one of her sexy black lace bras for Murry? He read the label: *Ooh, la, la. Size 5,* then inhaled, his imagination spinning. What could be more perfect?

Chapter 13

Murry impatiently scanned the desk-filled room for Officer Anita Quintez. He turned to the Kid. "So you think this looks exciting?" He thought it looked like a bunch of overworked LAPD cops going through the day-to-day motions, praying they lived to get their pensions.

"There's a lot more action," Billy said, his eyes lit like a preacher who'd just saved an entire congregation.

Murry wasn't about to be converted. He spotted Quintez at a desk near the elevators, and nudged Billy. "There she is; let's see if she's interested."

"Hey, Murry." Lieutenant Jamison backed out of the elevator and motioned for Murry to join him. Damn, he'd hoped to talk to Quintez before Jamison.

Billy slithered over to Quintez's desk, planted himself on the edge, and gave her a killer smile.

"So, where are we?" Jamison asked.

Murry hurriedly reviewed what he had: the tenuous connection between White and Ford gave all the victims a connection to the University, and by extension the psych classes and the Faire. "I want to stake out the Faire."

Jamison shook his head. "You're talking a hundred vendors or more, five hundred to a thousand people. I can't pull everyone off their work in the hope someone will drop an ice pick from their sleeve." He pulled his pipe from his pocket and stroked it like a pet. "You're talking a major expense. One I can't justify with what you've given me."

"Four of the five victims attended the Faire," Murry said. "For all we know, Ford did too. One woman actually worked there. I thought we could set up Quintez as a vendor."

Jamison glanced toward the petite, brunette officer. Billy jumped to his feet, his grin vanishing. He gave a nod to Murry, and headed outside. Jamison fixed his blue gaze on Murry again. "There could be other connections, Murry. What about the rug fiber?"

"It's old. Probably from an Indian or Pakistani carpet. Auble and Canelli have checked out all the carpet and flooring businesses in Beverly Hills, Hollywood, and Santa Monica, and are working on LA. Nothing so far." He knew four of the guys were still digging through the victims' financial records and recording any services that required a person to enter the house. No matches yet, but they weren't finished.

"What about the ice picks?"

"Bones can't find any like them anywhere, but he's still sending out inquiries. He thinks the killer makes them, which means checking out woodworking equipment and supply places. Farel and Ramirez are on it."

"Okay. Let me know if something breaks." Jamison jabbed the elevator button.

Murry took one more shot. "Just give me Officer Quintez. She could set up a booth, talk to the other vendors, see if anyone says or does anything unusual." Farel had recommended her, said she was up to date.

Quintez, sitting two desks away, glanced up.

"You know anything about the case? Ice Pick?" Jamison asked her.

"Yes. Mid-to-late thirties. College grad, maybe a postgrad. He's patient, does his homework, brings what he needs. Always keeps his anger in check, doesn't take chances. Probably has a history of rape that may have escalated to this scenario. Or he may have fantasized this for years, then made the move when the fantasy was no longer enough. Probably Caucasian, since all the victims were."

Not only was she good-looking, but smart too.

Jamison, however, didn't appear impressed. "That's why I'm putting a tail on Jones."

Murry held his tongue. He needed more ammo for the Faire and didn't have it.

Jamison chewed on his pipe. "Who's taking photos at the funeral?"

"Billy," Murry said.

The elevator doors slid open.

"What about the Faire?" Murry asked.

"Let's deal with the funeral first. If nothing pans out, I may give you a couple of guys. Otherwise, it's the two of you." He adopted a rueful expression. "And Quintez."

"Thanks, Lieutenant." Murry turned to Quintez before Jamison could change his mind, telling her, "Talk to you later," then hurried outside, where he found Billy peering through the lens of the Nikon. It was pointed at two young women on the street corner. Both wore hip-hugger denim shorts and halter tops. Both had the long, lean Hollywood look and stood on the street corner like they were waiting to be discovered. "You got film in that?" he asked as Billy lowered the camera.

"Geez, it takes film? I thought it was one of those magic cameras. What 'ya call 'em? Oh, yeah, digital."

"Digital your ass."

They arrived late for the funeral. "You'll have to catch

them as they come out," Murry said, leaving Billy in the car. He studied the Russian Orthodox Church, gray stone, a picture of Christ centered above double doors, a huge golden dome over the central part of the building, a smaller dome over the entrance, triple crosses above both. Stairs out the back, wrought-iron fence all the way around. It looked like something from centuries past, and out of place between two modern four-story apartment buildings. A group of reporters standing on the front lawn suddenly noticed him.

"Hey!"

"Murry?"

"Hey!"

He kept his head down, ignoring the hue and cry that followed him past the guard at the gate. Damn vultures. The captain might want their favor, but Murry would rather use them for target practice. He wasn't sure who he disliked more, reporters or lawyers.

The church door clanged shut. Silence. He smelled some kind of incense, then noticed the circular structure of the room and lack of pews. Everyone was standing, lit candles in their hands. Not a large group, maybe twenty in all. The casket, open, was positioned toward the front. No one stood to the right of the priest, and Murry figured that was probably the space reserved for family. The priest, the top of his head covered, black robes hanging from his meaty frame, a dark beard masking most of his face, spoke Slavonic, Old Russian. The women, all in black also, wore scarves over their hair. Murry scrutinized everyone, wondering if the killer would show, if that were even part of the guy's shtick.

He recognized some of the faculty besides Kevin Jones, but saw no celebrities. No one stood out.

Standing by the door, he flipped through a prayer book to the *Requiem for the Dead*. When everyone blew out their candles, he set the book aside and watched until the end, when the small group filed past. Two priests ducked out the side with Kevin Jones, one in front, one straggling behind like he didn't want to face the reporters. Murry sympathized with him.

"You get everyone?" Murry asked as he slid behind the wheel.

Billy nodded and popped the disk from the Nikon and shoved in a new one. "Not many of the professors showed, did they?"

"No. Wonder why?" He glanced at the Kid. "Why don't you take another crack at them? Turn the screws a bit and see what they say."

"And when am I supposed to do that?" Billy reached for his cigarettes, caught Murry's expression, and pulled a stick of gum.

"Before tomorrow, when the Faire begins." Murry joined the line of cars.

"Thanks a lot. Another night shot."

"What's eating you?"

Billy raked his fingers through his blond hair. "Gina's driving me crazy. She moved the last of her stuff in last night, and already she's cheesed about where I drop my shoes or leave my tie. She might as well own the place."

Murry let it drop. Wasn't his job to point out that if Billy cared enough, it might be worth the effort to be a little neater.

He followed the line of cars to the church cemetery. They waited for the mourners to make their way toward the grave before Billy started snapping photos of the cars.

"Print them out and pin them up in the conference room, along with the ones you took outside Olga's place. We'll ask everyone to take a look and see if they recognize anyone from the other cases. Someone they interviewed and dismissed, maybe. Worth a shot."

Billy, reeking of peppermint and nicotine, continued the *click, click, click.* "Okey-dokey, boss."

Murry followed the last of the arrivals to the grave site, hanging back so he could watch the group. He paid special attention to every male with a medium build and dark hair.

As the first dirt clod hit the casket, he noticed a petite red-head, black scarf, black dress, tears splashing down her face. She seemed to be the only one crying. Something about her seemed familiar. The turn-out of her feet jogged his memory. The photo in Olga's hallway. When the ceremony ended, he intercepted her at the edge of the grass, introduced himself, and flashed his badge.

She gave him a shaky smile. "Galina Patrovna."

New York accent. "You a friend of Olga's?"

She rummaged into her purse, extracted a tissue, and dabbed her eyes. "Yes."

With the splash of freckles across her nose and her slim figure, he found it hard to guess her age. "You have a few minutes to talk? There's a coffee house a couple of blocks from here."

She exhaled, indecision written in the way her brows drew together, her big green eyes wary.

"Please. There's some things you might be able to help me understand."

A sigh. "A few minutes."

He walked with her to the parking lot. "You live around here?" In his peripheral vision, he saw Billy retreat. Good boy, Murry thought.

"No. New York. Actually, I'm in a show in Miami. Took two days off. I flew in today. Going back tomorrow."

Ah, now he knew who the Miami dancer had been. He

asked about her show, which she described as an off-Broadway musical.

Kevin Jones walked past. He didn't spit at Murry, but it looked like a hard decision.

Galina frowned.

"Know him?" Murry asked.

"We met once. Before he started dating Olga."

Murry hid his surprise. "Here or in New York?"

"Here. I was visiting Olga, and we dropped by her office so she could pick up some tests."

"How long ago was this?"

She hesitated. "Two years, perhaps less."

Something about her expression and the way she answered made Murry take a chance. "You and Olga—you were more than friends, weren't you?"

She scanned the parking lot. "Are we walking?"

Answer a question with a question—a cop tactic—she did it well. He gestured toward his BMW. Billy was leaning against the bumper, smoke curling out of his mouth and wafting upward. If he could have dumped the Kid for an hour, he would have, but he couldn't leave him stranded in a cemetery.

"You didn't answer my question," he said, as she removed the black scarf from her hair. He held her gaze, letting her know he wanted an answer.

"Yes, we were more than friends. And I've heard all the lines—such a waste, etcetera—so keep them to yourself."

"Believe me, I have enough of my own problems without condemning someone else's life." Murry led her to the car.

Her eyebrows rose in amusement when Billy raced around the front and opened the door.

"Galina Patrovna, meet Detective William Kidman."

"Hello." She dug inside her purse, and a cigarette appeared between her fingers.

Billy fumbled for his lighter, then held out the flame. "You from out of town?"

She inhaled, then slid onto the seat, her short black dress riding up to her crotch before she yanked it down. "Yes."

Billy looked like he'd died and gone to heaven.

Murry watched the action and chuckled. He got a kick out of Billy's attentiveness and Galina's amusement.

At the coffee house, they claimed a corner table away from the noise. Billy was still slobbering over Olga's girlfriend. Murry tossed Billy his car keys. "Print out the photos. Pick us up in an hour." He glanced at Galina. "That okay?"

She nodded.

Billy looked at her, shot a glare at Murry, then stomped off.

"I don't think your partner likes you."

"The problem is he likes you," Murry said. "He's still got all those raging hormones. They worry me."

She laughed. It died abruptly. "I didn't think I'd laugh today. Thank you."

"You can thank me by telling me about Olga."

Her gaze slid past Murry's shoulder as though enraptured with the green border print on the wall. He ordered two coffees, giving her time to collect her thoughts. "We met the year she quit dancing."

"With the New York City Ballet?"

"Yes. That last year, she was plagued by injuries. She said it was a sign—time to quit. She went back to school, got her degree, and started teaching psychology and ballet. Then her parents died and she wrote that book."

"Read the Future, Change Your Life," Murry said.

"You've read it?"

"Only heard about it. You don't happen to have a copy, do you?"

"At home. Why?"

"Because I ordered it from Amazon, but it's out of print and they're still looking for a copy. Can I borrow yours?" He handed her his business card. "I promise to return it."

"All right. But why do you want to read it?"

"I don't understand her. The minute she thought Ice Pick was coming after her, why didn't she hop the first plane out of here? I'm hoping the book can give me some insight. She had money. She didn't have to stay."

Galina studied Murry's face over the rim of her cup, her gaze assessing.

"Did she tell you about her dreams?" he asked. "About Ice Pick? Why she stayed?"

"She stayed because she believed what happens to us is in agreement with our soul purpose. Fate. There was no reason to leave."

"Did you talk to her about it?"

"About leaving? Yes. She said she was being careful, but she thought she could find him, turn him into the police, before . . ." She swallowed.

Murry leaned forward. "Find him, how?"

"In her dreams. She used them to do remote viewing."

"Remote viewing?"

"Yes. Your body is in one location, but you're able to see in another. She told herself to look for him before going to sleep."

"Did she find him?"

"She saw him from the back, not his face."

Murry jotted some notes, wondering how much more "twilight zone" this could get. "Did she have any idea who it was?"

"No."

"When was the last time you talked to her?"

She shrugged. "A week ago. Before that, not for months. Her call was a surprise."

"Why?"

"We'd split up. I came out once for a trial reconciliation. It didn't work. I didn't expect to hear from her again."

"What did she say?"

"She was very excited. Said she was close to identifying the killer. She wanted to write a new book. About psychics who helped the police solve cases."

"So she stayed because she wanted to write a book." Murry leaned forward. "And you didn't talk to her or see her again?"

"No."

"It's not your fault," he said, sensing self-blame in the way she lowered her eyes.

She gave him an appreciative ghost of a smile. "I know."

"Tell me, did Jones know about you and Olga?"

"I think he suspected. He stared at me as though I'd corrupted Olga or something."

Was Galina reading more into the meeting than was there? After all, she might have been jealous of Jones. He got her talking about Olga, how she lived, was she organized, what kind of routine she enjoyed, hoping to get a break. Nothing sparked. Finally, she pushed away from the table, a softer, more vulnerable woman than the one who'd sat down. "I feel like I've just had a therapy session," she said, "tired, but lighter somehow. Thanks."

"Just doing my job." He nodded toward the door where Billy had been lounging with the newspaper. "Our ride is here."

They dropped Galina at her hotel. They weren't even out of the parking lot when Billy said, "Man, she was one hoochie mama!"

"Hoochie what?"

151

Billy shook his head. "Hoochie mama. A hot babe."

"Yeah?"

"Yeah. Did you see those legs?"

Murry couldn't stop a laugh from escaping.

"Oh come on. Don't tell me you didn't notice."

"It's not that." Murry laughed again, "It's just that—"

"What?" Billy's mouth tightened.

"She and Olga were lovers."

Billy's jaw dropped. "You're shittin' me."

Murry raised his eyebrows. "Sorry, Kid."

Billy glanced back at the hotel. "What a waste." He repeated it three more times.

"Maybe we'll understand her better after we read Olga's book."

"We? *I've* got to read her book?"

"How long's it been since you cracked one open?"

"I'm a watcher, not a reader." Billy jammed a stick of gum in his mouth.

"Right, I forgot how observant you are."

Chapter 14

Through his kitchen window, Murry spied Billy pulling to the curb. He grabbed his keys and met the Kid at the door. Billy had dyed his hair black and was covered in leather. "What the hell are you doing? I said casual. We're going to a psychic faire, not an S-and-M club, Kid."

Billy lowered his shades. "I'm playing Keanu Reeves."

"Who?"

Billy shook his head. He studied Murry a moment and grimaced like Murry had leprosy. "*That's* what you're wearing?"

"I'm playing Arnold Palmer," Murry said.

"Who?"

Murry thought about explaining, but the twenty-year age span suddenly felt like a chasm. "Never mind." He started to close the door.

"No way you're going like that, Murry. Everybody at the Faire will know you're a cop."

"Oh, what do you suggest?"

Billy grinned and wiggled his eyebrows. "Got you just the thing." He retrieved a bag from his car.

A few minutes later, Murry studied himself in the mirror. He had to admit, he didn't look like himself. He didn't own a fringed leather jacket—nor would he ever own one—or cowboy boots. "I'm not wearing a hat," he muttered, feeling like January had turned into Halloween. "I'll sweat to death in this heat wave."

"The place is air-conditioned."

"I'm thrilled."

"You work the crowd, I'll take the vendors," he told Billy as they pushed through the double doors. A blast of cool air washed over him. The sweet, acrid scent of burning sage tweaked his nostrils. He blinked and held the door open, letting some of the smoke escape. The place smelled like a 1960s time warp.

Billy swaggered off down the long aisle, wind chimes tinkling overhead, crystals glittering like tiny suns. Soft Native American flute music floated from somewhere down the aisle. Murry spotted the two cops Jamison had reluctantly assigned. They were watching the doors—like cops. They were dressed—like cops. They had bulges under their jackets—like cops. Christ almighty, what could they be, but cops? They looked about as out of place as he felt. Especially amidst all the black and blue velvet-draped booths, the shimmering rhinestones, and dazzling jewelry displays. Fantasy and science fiction wedded to "The Outer Limits."

He attracted a few stares, but not any more than the purple-haired teenagers and the army of large caftan-covered women jingling with necklaces and wrist bangles. He half expected to see Shirley MacLaine walk by.

The next time he saw Billy, he figured he'd catch the Kid ogling derrieres, but for once the Kid's hormones were in check and he was strolling down the other side toward the New Age bookseller, talking to people, and using his million-dollar dimples. Since the crowd was seventy-five percent women, it didn't appear to be a hardship.

Murry spent the morning perusing booths, noting anyone

who fit the victim profile and how the vendors interacted with them. No one gave any of the women unwarranted attention. Of the few men who fit Ice Pick's profile, none acted suspiciously and they eventually left. What he did notice was a slim young woman in blue jeans and a faded pink tank top bumping into an elderly lady and lifting the old woman's wallet. He watched the pick-pocket work the crowd, then casually take off her coat, the pockets bulging with stolen wallets, and hand it to an older man dressed like a college professor.

Murry worked his way to the nearest Arnold Palmer cop, who gave him a slight nod of recognition. "That young lady lifted several wallets that don't belong to her and slipped them into her coat. She handed the coat to that professor-type gentleman in the tweed jacket and racing cap. Why don't you arrest them?"

He waited to see the cop move in the direction of the pick-pocket and her buddy, then moved on. By the time he came around again, a cruiser stood outside and the two thieves were cuffed and standing beside it.

On what felt like his hundredth stroll around the huge room, he decided to pay Quintez a visit. He checked his watch. Half-hour until closing. He approached her booth and fell into line. Shimmery metallic fringe hung down the sides of the booth, with "Palm Reader" across the front in shiny letters. She'd done a great job. She looked twice as good as the rest of the Elviras wandering around in skin-tight black dresses and shaggy wigs.

When he reached the front of the line, she leaned forward, showing an ample amount of glistening cleavage, and took his palm. "See anything interesting?" she asked.

"Uh—"

"Murry, my eyes are up here."

He lifted his gaze and offered a brief smile. "Just checking out the— What is that on your chest, anyway?"

"It's all about glitz," she said, tracing his life line with a long purple nail.

"Any action?"

"Had a couple of offers. One guy wants to meet for coffee after we close."

"A vendor?"

"Makes the sword and sorcery jewelry. Gray hair, pony-tail."

"Good work." Murry paid her, then ambled across the aisle to check out the guy. The man was making a sales pitch to a couple of women Éclair's age, dressed in tank tops and long crinkly skirts that looked imported from India, tiny glinting mirrors embedded in the fabric. Both women had dark hair and fit the victim profile. Pausing before a glass case of silver and gold necklaces, Murry waited and watched. They both bought a pair of delicate fairy earrings, the fairies holding a tiny crystal ball in their hands. As soon as they started away, the man turned to Murry. "Sorry to keep you waiting. What can I help you with?"

Murry pointed at the thing closest at hand, a silver dragon necklace with a red eye.

The man pulled it out of the case. "That's a ruby," he said. "The dragon's one of fifty. After that, I break the mold."

Yeah, right, Murry thought. "Been in the business long?"

The guy laughed. "Thirty years. Travel from one coast to the other. Wife usually helps, but she stayed home this trip."

The guy was slender, his straggly beard streaked gray like his hair, and looked about Murry's age. "What'd you do, start this business in grade school?"

The next thing Murry knew, he was getting a sales pitch for rejuvenating himself with nothing but juice.

The man patted his flat stomach. "Keeps me fit and strong."

Strong enough to cheat on his wife, Murry thought, or strong enough to stake women out and rape them? "You don't look a day over forty," Murry said in a challenging tone.

The vendor yanked out his wallet, flipped it open, and stabbed a long, slender finger at the birth date, 1940.

"You're over sixty?" Murry noted the guy's name, Charles Vaughn.

"Had a little help with the bags under my eyes, if you know what I mean. But the rest is real enough."

The guy was too old and too chatty to be Ice Pick, but Murry wasn't quite ready to let go.

"You come to this Faire every year?"

"Came about five years ago, then tried a couple places up north, near Mendocino. Did about the same in sales, so thought I'd try this place again this year. For a change." Vaughn held up the necklace. "So, you want it?"

He actually thought Éclair would like it, and her birthday was coming up. "How much?" He wanted to keep the guy talking.

"One-fifty."

"What if my girlfriend doesn't like it?"

"If she don't like it, you can ship it back and I'll credit your account or refund your money. I want people to feel good when they're wearing my stuff." He held out his business card. Murry felt like saying he was a cop and if the guy was lying, he'd track him down and throw his ass in jail. He hesitated, then handed over his credit card. He glanced down the aisle, hoping to spot Billy, but didn't see him. "You familiar with the other vendors, Charles?" he asked. "I imagine you all travel together."

"I know most of 'em. We don't travel together, but we

cross paths here and there. There's a few newbies, like the palm reader. I haven't seen her before." His gray eyebrows waggled. "Now there's a looker for ya."

"I'll say," Murry said, playing along, but not seeing how this guy, who couldn't be more than 120 pounds soaking wet, could tackle and overcome someone like Olga. Especially if the birth date on his license was correct. He glanced toward Quintez. "Did you get your palm read?"

The guy leaned forward and winked, but it wasn't lascivious. "Yessir. She said I have a long life line. She's meeting me after we close. I'm hoping to get her to work for me. A looker like her could sell twice as much as me."

Murry found himself liking the guy. "Good luck." Vaughn handed him the credit slip to sign and returned Murry's card. "So who would you recommend for a, uh, reading?" he asked, thinking about Olga and how she'd bought fortunes for all her students.

Vaughn shrugged. "My wife's the one into that woo-woo stuff. I tell her it's all a bunch of crap, but she don't listen. Anyway, the gypsy fortune-teller's supposed to be good, and a lady who'll let ya talk to dead relatives for a ten spot. Sophie, that's my wife, went to her last year and claims she talked to her brother."

"I thought you weren't here last year?" Murry's question came out too sharp, and he prayed the guy didn't get suspicious.

Vaughn shrugged. "Ran into her in Arizona. She's the one told us to try LA again."

Murry thanked the man, stowed the necklace in the pocket of his fringed jacket, then ambled around to the other side of the building, scanning for Billy's black hair and leather.

One of the lost-cause cops nodded as Murry approached. "You know where the restroom is?" Murry asked.

The guy pointed toward the corner.

Though he figured it wouldn't pan out, in a low voice Murry said, "Keep an eye on the jewelry vendor after closing—guy with the ponytail, gray beard. He's meeting Quintez."

After a nod from the cop, Murry turned the corner and headed down the other aisle looking for Billy. The center was closing in five minutes.

He paused outside a burgundy velvet-covered stall with a very professional-looking sign: "See What the Future Holds." A painted crystal ball emitting an aura of pale blue light glowed beside the words. Wondering if the entire exercise had been a waste of time, and knowing Jamison would be pissed if he didn't come up with something, Murry scanned the area again. Not one blasted tug on his intuition. Either Olga wasn't much of a psychic or he was missing the connection. He reached into his pocket for his cell phone, reluctant to use it. It always gave him an image of brain cells around his ear rotting away.

The stall's tent-like opening suddenly parted and Billy stepped out, saw Murry, and turned so red his dyed eyebrows looked ready to leap off his face.

Murry hid his aggravation and headed down the aisle. "So what did the old gypsy have to say?"

Billy matched Murry's pace, his expression dour. "Don't ask."

"You and Gina are getting hitched and you'll live happily ever after."

"Yep, right. That's great compared to what she really said."

"What?"

"She said we're going to catch a break on the case, but in the end it wouldn't pan out."

"You asked about the case?" Murry asked sharply.

"She knew I was a cop. Besides, you told me to, re-member?"

"It was a joke. Jesus what were you thinking?"

Billy bristled.

In a more conciliatory tone, Murry asked, "What did you say—exactly?"

"That we're working a case and need a break."

"That's all?"

"Yes!"

"And she said we'd get one, but it wouldn't lead to a collar?"

"She said we were missing the clues left by the killer." Billy's voice lowered. "I didn't tell her I was a cop, and I didn't say it was a homicide, Murry. I swear."

"I believe you." Murry's nape hairs danced like dervishes. "What else did she say?"

"She said someone close to you may die."

"You as in *me,* or *you* as in *you?"*

"You, Murry. She said, 'Someone close to your partner may die.' "

"Really?"

Billy nodded. "She gave me the creeps."

Murry read the Kid's worried expression. "Billy, in our job people die every day. She was just playing a hunch." But his mouth went dry. He'd almost lost the Kid once, because he hadn't seen what was right in front of him. He wasn't about to let that happen again. "Nothing's going to happen to you," he said roughly.

"First the zombie curse, then all these fortunes of doom. Now this." Billy's words sprayed out like the contents of a shaken soda can. "Maybe I should find a new job."

"She probably uses the same line on everyone. These

people are pros." Murry paused in his tracks and eyed Billy, thinking that in that getup no one would assume Billy was a cop. "Where's your badge?"

"In my back pocket. Why?"

"You sure you didn't tell her you were a cop?" He tried to shake off the uneasy feeling, but it stuck like super glue.

"No."

He did an about-face. Billy raced to catch up. "Where 'r you going?"

"To have my fortune told and prove it's all a line of bull." He ducked inside the tent. A single candle burned at a tiny round table, but the darkness was thick and blinding. A creaky, old voice asked with a heavy Spanish accent. "Fortune?"

He made out the black-veiled face of an old woman. She had several long silk scarves in a multitude of red hues draped around her neck and across her shoulders. Dozens of metal chains and medallions rested on an ample caftan-covered bosom that sagged onto her belly.

"How much?" he drawled like a Texan, thinking the crystal ball was probably cheap glass.

"Ten dollar."

Murry pulled a ten from his wallet, questioning his sanity. He laid the bill next to the candle. She didn't reach for it as he expected, but left it there. "So now what?" he asked, shifting on the seat, not liking the darkness.

"*Un momento, por favor.*" She cleared her throat and peered into the ball, her eyelids lowered, her lips compressed. Slowly her eyelids drooped and her mouth relaxed. "I see you watching the *televisión*. On the screen is the image of a body." She frowned. "Is *muerte*. Dead body." Her gaze broke from the crystal ball and fixed on Murry. "Someone close to you will die."

"My aunt's been ill," Murry lied, expecting her to jump on the opportunity.

She surprised him by slowly shaking her head. "No." Her salt-and-pepper eyebrows drew together. "This death is quick. Unexpected. Perhaps connected to your job."

"An oil rig accident?" He said it as though enthralled with her ability.

Again she surprised him, this time with a shrug, her chestful of necklaces jingling. She stared into the crystal, then frowned again. "That I cannot see."

She was damned good. He eyed her with dislike, recalling what Jamison said about psychic frauds ripping off the public. He started to ask more questions and stopped. What was he doing, grilling an old gypsy? He stood up feeling foolish. She was just an old lady trying to make a few bucks. "Mind if I take one of your business cards?"

"Por favor." She gestured toward the stack of cards, and he glimpsed long red-lacquered nails with tiny black flowers glued on the tips.

"Thanks."

Outside, he waited for his eyes to adjust, then read the card, "Madame Zena." The crystal ball logo was printed beneath the name. On the back was an e-mail address: Zena1@hotmail.com.

"What'd she say?" Billy asked.

"Same bit she gave you. Someone close to you will die. It's just a line she uses, Billy. She's probably sick of promising patrons they'll be rich and live happily ever after."

"So how'd she know I was a cop?"

"Lucky guess. She didn't know I was one." He eyed Billy. "She may have seen the straps of your shoulder holster, if your coat flopped open when you sat down." Murry had his gun tucked in his waistband at his back.

"Humph." Chagrin in his tone, Billy added, "Can't believe she sucked me in."

"No big deal." Murry pushed open the glass doors and stepped out into a wall of humidity.

"She tell you that bit about the donuts, too?"

"What?"

"After she said the thing about someone dying, she said she saw an image of donuts and cakes and stuff. Like those Krispy Kreme bars with the pudding in the middle. Man, I love those."

"Don't we all." Something in his brain nudged him, but he couldn't get hold of the thought. He slid his hand into his pocket and felt the necklace he'd bought for Éclair. Then he stared at Billy.

"What?"

"Did she mention éclairs?"

Billy looked thoughtful. "I don't know. I was shook up about the dying part and not listening too much to the rest."

Was he reading too much into an off-chance remark? Yet how many times had he or someone else teased Éclair about her name? Called her Dream Whip or Whipped Cream? He felt a wave of cold roll down his back, just as if he were standing in Olga's hallway.

"Where you going?" he heard Billy call from behind him.

"To talk to Madame Zena."

Billy caught up to him. "Why?"

"Because something about her really bugs me, and dammit, I want to know what."

He hurried back inside, Billy on his heels. The booth was gone. All the velvet, the table and chairs—gone. Wrong spot? He scanned the aisle.

Billy shook his head. "She sure vamoosed in a hurry."

Murry stepped to the next vendor where a middle-aged

woman was packing crystal animals into a box. "You see Madame Zena leave?"

A twinkle in her eyes, she nodded. "Never saw anybody pack up so fast. She folded everything up, including the tent, balanced it on a luggage carrier thingy, and hoofed it out the back way." She pointed toward a single door leading to the parking garage. "She was late for an appointment."

Murry headed for the exit at a jog, half of him saying he was being a fool, the other half spurring him to hurry. He shoved open the door. "You take that side, I'll take this," he told Billy. There were cars and people everywhere, but no old woman. Maybe she'd walked. He headed out to the sidewalk to check the street. People and more people, but no sign of the gypsy. She'd vanished into thin air.

"See her?" Billy asked, panting.

"No." He handed the woman's business card to Billy. "Find out everything you can. Then we'll pay her a visit."

Billy pulled out his cell phone.

Murry stared at the Kid's dark hair, sunglasses, long black leather coat, cellular pressed to his ear. "Now I know who you're talking about. The guy from *The Matrix*."

Billy rolled his eyes.

"Just don't get sucked down the wire." Murry stared some more. "Your mustache. Jesus, you shaved it off."

The Kid smirked. "Took you long enough."

Feeling foolish and sure the entire exercise was nothing but a waste of time, he said, "Takes awhile for the gray cells to work when you're over forty. Let's check out Quintez's coffee date."

Chapter 15

Conrad squeezed the steering wheel of his rented Ford with anticipation. Playing a priest at Olga's funeral had been fun. Yesterday's Faire had been fabulous. Especially talking to Kidman and Murry. What an unexpected surprise. He shouldn't have said so much, but it worked out. He'd shaken Kidman up, then reassured Murry it was all a game of smoke and mirrors. He liked that. But those thrills were minor compared to tonight. Tonight would be the *coupe de grace.*

He drove past The Five Forty Five and turned the corner. The parking lot looked like Jay Leno's garage, every car an Avalon, Lexus, or Mercedes. Space twenty-four stood open like a deadly invitation. No one in sight, but that didn't mean anything. He parked in the space and settled back in the seat. An image filled his mind, of driving an ice pick through the King's eye, of seeing the man's life fade like a TV screen going dark. He knew it wouldn't be the same as a transformation, and puzzled over why it excited him so much. Then he realized it was the power of life and death. Being one with God. Yes, that was it. In complete control. Like God. He touched up his blush, ran a comb through his wig, straightened the bow of his blouse, then pulled on his specially-designed gloves. Steel mesh reinforced the inside of the skin-colored latex. Nothing would poke through and the mesh didn't show. Perfect. He lifted the shopping bag from the floor and examined the tiny metal edge taped to the inside of the handle. Once it pricked the bastard . . . no turning back, no pardons.

Calmly, he climbed from the rental and straightened his long, broomstick skirt. With slow, feminine steps, he passed the van he'd left in the alley that afternoon. Magnetic signs on the side panels read: "Jensen's Electric." Everything just as he'd left it. Good. No one noticed service vans. Scanning for watchers, he walked slowly down the alley and turned the corner to the restaurant entrance.

Like the parking lot, the patio chairs were filled with the glitz and glitter of Beverly Hills. He recognized Sharon Stone, but not the guy with her. They were huddled together like agent and client, negotiating the next ten-million-dollar deal. A soft glow of light spilled through the glass door.

The maître d' glanced up. "Reservation, ma'am?"

"LaFleur. Nine o'clock."

"One moment." He looked down at the book. "Will Mr. LaFleur be joining you?"

"No. I'll dine alone."

The maître d' didn't appear the least bit nervous or suspicious. If the King was watching, he'd see an attractive but fading blonde carrying a Gucci shopping bag. Nothing out of the ordinary on Rodeo. One thing for certain, there would be no exchange of money until he had his picks. And then . . . no return engagements.

He scanned the area. Two black waiters in dark slacks and gold-patterned paisley vests worked the rooms like cogs in a well-oiled clock. Neither glanced his way. Maybe he'd been wrong about the caller being black.

He followed the maître d' down the hall to the rear dining area. They continued into a private room, a cozy hideaway for two with its own private door. He'd been right about that. How convenient. The man pulled out one of the two high-backed chairs. "Enjoy your evening, ma'am."

"Thank you." Sinking down onto the upholstered seat, Conrad casually dropped the bag beside his leg and adjusted the ankle-length skirt so nothing but the toes of his black pumps showed. The faint clink of dishes from the kitchen faded to quiet when the maître d' closed the door. Perfect.

It seemed to take forever for his waiter to arrive, one of the two who'd been working the front room. A frown furrowed his forehead. "I'm sorry ma'am, but this room was reserved for Mr. LaFleur."

Conrad recognized his voice instantly. His nametag read *Jamal* and he looked like Denzel Washington, but he was the King, no doubt about it. A diamond earring glinted from his ear. *My trophy. How perfect.* "I'm representing Mr. James."

The skin around Jamal's eyes tightened with displeasure.

"I assure you, everything will be handled as you in-structed." He used a lady-like tone his mother would have ap-plauded.

The tension eased slightly. "I told him any variation—"

"I assure you, everything will be handled just as you wish. Mr. James is very anxious to complete this transaction."

Jamal slowly nodded. "All right then, may I bring you a drink?"

God yes, he could have used a double martini, but didn't dare. "Club soda with a twist of lime, thank you."

"Very good, ma'am." The waiter disappeared around the gold and black wall-screen, returning a few minutes later with his drink and a basket of bread.

He studied Jamal over the edge of the menu. "Am I to eat before we conclude our business?"

"It would draw attention, if you didn't order."

"I'll have the filet mignon, black and blue."

"Bloody. You got it."

Conrad smiled. *If only you knew.*

"The bread is a specialty, ma'am. You should try it."

Conrad reached for the covered basket. His heart skipped a beat at the sight of a wood handle buried between the warm rolls. He dumped the rolls out onto the table. Only one? Where were the rest? What was the King up to? Using a napkin, he wrapped it and slipped it into the deep pocket of his full skirt. His palm itched to shove it through the King's eye. *Soon. Everything comes with patience.* Still, the excitement building in his belly surprised him. He'd never killed a man.

He checked his watch. 9:35. He took his time buttering a roll. The way the butter flattened beneath the knife made him think of how his mother would smooth make-up over his face. She applied it like a sculptor creating a work of art. A skill she used often—up until the day she died. Who would have thought a B-grade actress had such an active imagination?

Jamal returned with a beautifully-arranged plate of rice pilaf, an array of lightly sautéed vegetables, and the black-ened steak.

"Where are the others?" Conrad cut a dainty bite from the meat. Red juice oozed over the tines onto the dish. He eyed the man and waited.

Jamal slid into the other chair. "First, where's the money?"

"Close."

"Not in your car, I checked."

Conrad blinked and gestured with his hands in a flustered manner. "He said you would do that."

"I want to see it. Now."

"I must ask for the return of the other picks first."

Jamal's gaze didn't waver. "Not until I see the money."

Conrad shook his head. "There's nothing I can do. I have orders to see what I'm buying."

Jamal's mouth tightened in a scowl. "Don't go anywhere. I'll be right back." Back in less than two minutes, he was no longer dressed as a waiter, but wearing tan slacks and a beige button-down shirt. "Shift's over." He opened a small napkin-wrapped bundle, flashing the steel points, then covering them again. He dropped into the chair, laying the picks on the edge of the table like a winning hand at poker.

Conrad hefted the Gucci bag and shoved it toward Jamal.

The King grabbed the handle and dropped the bag beside his chair. He pulled his hand back, a bead of blood on the back of one finger. "Damn paper cut."

Conrad checked his watch. *Ten minutes for the toxin to kick in.* "The money's beneath the tissue. Now, if you will give me the picks, please."

"First, I make sure it's here." He carefully counted one stack, then fanned the remaining packets. His gaze narrowed. "Where's the rest?"

"That's half. The other half is outside in a van. I'm to give the driver the picks, and he'll give me the rest of the money."

"That wasn't the deal." He cleared his throat, poured a glass of water, and drank it down. He poured another and drank it, too.

It was beginning to work. Conrad reached for the picks, anxious to get the man outside.

Jamal grabbed them. "I'm going with you."

"As you wish."

Jamal snagged the shopping bag and stood up.

Conrad shoved open the private door and stepped outside, his skirt swishing around his legs, his heels clicking on the asphalt.

Jamal was already sweating like a horse. Bad sign. He

stumbled and managed to right himself.

Conrad found he was holding his breath and slowly let it out. The King had to make it to the van or the plan would fail. It was only a hundred yards, but looked farther.

Halfway across the lot, the King made a choking sound and slumped. Conrad caught him under the shoulder and propelled him forward.

A man in the parking lot climbed from his BMW. "Everything okay?"

"Help—" the King rasped.

"I am helping you," Conrad said in the kind of impatient tone a spouse would use, his pulse jumping into double-time. He shook her head at the BMW owner. "Too much celebrating."

Jamal's jaw worked but no more words came. He was rapidly becoming dead weight. Conrad worked to make it look easier than it was to hold him upright.

"Sure?" the guy persisted. "He looks in pretty bad shape."

Conrad offered an embarrassed smile. "He looks this way every night." Jesus Christ, the last thing he wanted was to be noticed. He offered a throaty chuckle as the man shifted on his feet. "It's okay. Once he sleeps it off, he'll be fine." His nerves were screaming and the van was still a good fifty feet away.

The guy shrugged and headed toward the street.

Conrad tightened his hold around the King's waist. "Come on. Just a few more steps. You can make it."

They reached the van and he propped Jamal against the side as he fumbled with the key. Finally, he got the back unlocked. *Thank fucking Christ.* After a quick glance around, he shoved the King inside and climbed in after him. 10:01. Eight minutes. The poison was working too fast.

Beneath the van's dim light, he could see the King's eyes,

open and watching, his body twitching with tiny spasms. Conrad quickly stripped off his skirt and blouse and stuffed them into an empty grocery bag. He pulled the coveralls from behind the seat and yanked them on. Glasses, hat, boots followed. Now to get rolling. He carefully maneuvered the van from the alley and headed toward the Santa Monica Highway. In the rearview mirror, he saw the King twitch, his heels hitting the van floor, the carpet dulling the sound.

"Have you ever eaten fugu?" he asked, aware that the King could still see and hear. "I wonder if you even know what it is. You might be more familiar with the term, 'Japanese puffer fish.' The fish is prepared so that the toxins offer a mildly hallucinogenic effect."

Sweat drenched the King's shirt. He managed to move his lips. His breath rattled in his chest.

"There are many similar toxins, all more efficient if introduced directly into the bloodstream. Your paper cut was no accident. Maybe you figured that out by now. Sometimes this poison kills, sometimes it merely paralyzes you for a few hours before there's a miraculous recovery." He liked the idea of giving hope, then taking it away. "You never know, you just might be one of those lucky survivors."

He should have an hour or two before the poison actually finished the guy off. Just enough time to reach his destination and have a little fun. Maybe play one of his mother's games, then one of his own.

The winding roads into the hills would be empty this time of night. Pitch black and sheer drop-offs, heavy vegetation in which you could hide an elephant. And he knew the perfect place: Topanga Canyon.

Chapter 16

Conrad killed his lights and set the brake. A sliver of moon enabled him to vaguely make out the King's form in the back, still twitching like a skewered fish. 10:49. He felt a sense of urgency, knowing the King could take his last gasp at any time.

The wind had picked up, bringing with it a wash of cool air that felt good against his face. The scent of decaying foliage wafted up out of the canyon. Despite the powder inside his gloves, his hands were sweaty. He tossed the gloves in the Gucci bag, pulled on a leather pair, then walked around to the back.

"Time to pray, Jamal." He dug his fingers beneath the man's armpits and dragged him out. Fear reeked from the man's body. It reminded Conrad sharply of the women. But with them he wanted to bury himself in that scent, know its very essence as he set them free. This time he wanted to be one with God in an entirely different way.

With a flashlight dimmed with dark cloth, he aimed the softened beam at the man's face. He opened the bundle of picks and selected one. It felt wrong in his hand. Too light. He examined it beneath the torch. Then he inspected the others. Cheap, smooth-handled, store-bought crap! There was no artistry in these, no energy, nothing.

For a moment he stood there staring at the King. "You think you can cheat me?" He gave the King a kick in the side, heard bone crunch. "You pus-licking son-of-a-bitch. Where are my picks?"

He kicked him again, repeating the question one word at a time with each kick. "Where—are—my—picks?"

Saliva and blood dribbled from the King's mouth.

Damn it, the clock was ticking. Conrad ripped the earring from the man's earlobe and stuck the bloodied diamond in his pocket. The King's head twitched.

Gripping the two-dollar pick, Conrad readjusted the flashlight. "You're gonna suffer, you double-crossing son-of-a-whore."

The King's body spasmed and pitched forward, as though hurling a final *fuck you*. Then all signs of life seeped from Jamal's eyes.

"Goddammittohell! Son-of-a-bitch!" Feeling as though someone had stolen all his trophies, he raised the pick and plunged it through the King's right eye. The tip scraped along bone. He yanked it out and plunged it into the other eye. The crunching sound reminded him of his other victims, but this lacked the excitement . . . and the release.

"You cheated me, you son-of-a-whore. Where are my picks?" He yanked the King's wallet from his pocket and crouched beside the light to read the license. LA address. He pocketed the wallet. Still holding the pick, he savagely kicked the King's body to the canyon edge and, without ceremony, gave the thief a final shove. The body rolled down the steep hill, sounding like an animal moving through the brush. When the rustling sounds stopped, he flung the pick into the darkness below, then flashed the beam down into the vegetation. Nothing.

Now what? His skin prickled unpleasantly, a silent

warning. He needed those picks.

Lying on his bed, he flipped through the King's wallet, tempted to drive to the address and search the place. One thing stopped him: a family photo. He needed to find out who else was living in the house. He held the diamond earring up toward the light, waiting to feel something. That exhilarating spark. Nothing.

How could it have gone so wrong? The King should have lived at least ten more minutes. All for nothing. Even the trophy earring had turned out to be a worthless bit of glass, not even real. He threw it across the room, then scooped up Olga's leotard and pressed it to his face. Olga's love, the transformation—it had been almost perfect.

But not quite, his inner voice whispered. *She fought hard. If you hadn't grabbed the bookend and hit her on the head, she might have escaped.*

She'd been surprisingly strong. He hadn't expected that. He threw the leotard on the floor. The next one, he vowed, would be perfect. She had to be perfect. He buried his face in Mary's red satin panties. With her, there could be no mistakes. Not one.

Chapter 17

Murry scoured the photographs that blanketed his desk—Billy's exterior shots of Olga's condo, the crowd at the funeral, and scenes from yesterday's Faire—searching for the same person at each site or something out of the ordinary. Nothing. He sent Billy back to UCLA to hit up Upland again and to question any of the faculty who knew Olga, including Kevin Jones. Meanwhile, the stack of reports looked like the Leaning Tower of Pisa. He worked all day and half the night, scanning each page, hoping for inspiration. All the victims had some kind of work done prior to their deaths, but the similarity ended there. Determined to find a pattern, he listed the dates and the type of work, intending to check each company and confirm who'd done what. And every time the phone rang, he half-expected it to be a call telling him Ice Pick had struck again. Each time he was relieved when it wasn't. But the feeling of urgency continued to grow.

He met Billy early the next morning at BHPD. Billy sank into his chair, his eyes circled with dark rings.

Murry studied his young partner. "That mustache is really looking fine."

"It's blond," he said defensively. "It'll get thicker."

"Why don't you dye it black to match your hair?"

"Ha, ha. Have you ever smelled that dye crap? Worse than

cat piss. I barely survived that stuff on my head. No way I'm putting it under my nose."

Murry gestured toward the stack of photos. "See anything?"

Billy groaned. "If any of these people are the same, I'm blind."

Me, too, Murry thought. "How'd the interviews go?" He knew the answer from Billy's frustrated expression.

"Jones accused me of harassment. Two other profs were dying to know if we thought Jones killed her. Upland accused me of patriarchal oppression. Whatever the hell that means."

"I think it translates to: 'Up yours.' "

"Whatever." Billy flipped his hair off his forehead. "If there's something there, I'm missing it."

"Relax, Kid. What'd you get on Madame Zena?"

"Zilch. I haven't been able to get anywhere. But I sent her a message, asking her to reply back."

"I thought everything was traceable in computer-land."

"She uses one of those free services. They're hell to trace. I'll keep trying, but I don't understand why you're so interested in her." His tone said he thought it a waste of his time.

"I got the feeling she knew more than she should. And she bugged out of there like a spider running from a broom."

"Everybody's in a hurry these days," Billy said distantly.

Murry realized something was eating at the Kid. "What's up? You have a gripe, tell me."

Billy glanced around. "You're always sending me off to do this and that, but you don't explain why. If I'm ever going to head up my own investigation, I need to know the whys and wherefores. Interrogating Kevin Jones—that I understand. He's the one I think we should be watching. Madame Zena's a wild-goose chase."

Heading up his own investigation? Not in BHPD, Murry

thought. It went against the Charter of the City of Beverly Hills to have more than one homicide a decade. Billy had said he wouldn't go to LAPD alone, but Murry was beginning to wonder. "Madame Zena may be a wild goose chase," Murry said. "But then again, maybe she saw something or knows something that could help. Maybe she tried to throw us a hint, then ran because she didn't want to get involved."

"You think she might know Ice Pick?" Billy's tone was doubtful.

"She brought up the murder. Makes me wonder if she had more to go on than just her skill at hustling people. Then again, maybe she's just real good at her job. Either way, I want to talk to her again." He thought about how she'd told Billy they were looking in the wrong direction. What about her vision of the dead body on the screen? What was that supposed to mean? He shook himself. He wasn't taking her too seriously, was he?

Apparently satisfied, Billy tapped the cover of Olga's book. "Anything interesting?"

"I'm not sure 'interesting' is the right word. She talks about getting flashes of information and learning how to interpret them. Sounds like plain old intuition to me."

"Well, you're the one with the crystal ball, everybody's intuition guru," Billy said, picking up the book and flipping through the pages. "You should write a book."

Murry cocked his head sideways. "I'm thinking about it. You better watch your step; you'll be in it. In the meantime, read Olga's and let me know what you think."

Billy groaned. "Haven't we got something better to follow up?" He grabbed a stack of photos and began leafing through them, then glanced up. "What about White's boss, the antique dealer? She didn't show at the Faire this year. Maybe there's a reason. We could talk to her, have her take a look at the photos. See if any of them sparks something."

A long shot, Murry thought, but he didn't want to discourage Billy's enthusiasm.

A string of bells announced their arrival. The place smelled like lemon oil and glass cleaner. Dainty figurines and china sculptures covered every flat surface. Wardrobes, chests-of-drawers, and buffets crowded shoulder-to-shoulder, of such fine grain and workmanship they almost made the prices seem reasonable. " 'Ye Olde Shoppe of Antiquities.' " Billy read the plaque on the wall. He glanced at a small rose-colored upholstered chair. "How can they charge two hundred for an old chair?"

"Some things get better with age."

Billy smirked. "You keep telling me that."

Murry scanned the room for a live body. The place looked deserted. A locked glass case ran along the rear wall, the shelves lined with glittering estate jewelry. He leaned over the case and craned his neck to see a narrow aisle disappearing into another room and beyond to an open door.

"Hello!" Not the best part of town to leave the back door open.

A tiny white-haired woman suddenly appeared from behind a huge wardrobe. "Oh!" A frail hand flew to her chest. Her other hand fumbled in the pocket of her smock, drew out a hearing aid, and settled it behind her ear.

"Hello there, young lady," Murry said. She couldn't have been a day under seventy.

Her eyes warmed slightly. "I'm old enough to be your mother." She turned to Billy, "And your grandmother. How can I help you?"

"Detectives Murry and Kidman, ma'am. We need to ask you a couple of questions."

"Detectives?" She sounded dismayed.

"That's right. And you are—?"

"Nola Brookes, the owner." She crossed her arms. "I already talked to that other detective. Rafael, Ramon, something like that."

"Detective Ramirez?"

"That's the one, yes."

"I promise not to take up too much of your time."

One gray eyebrow lifted skeptically. "That's what that other one said, and he was here for over an hour."

"Oh, Grandma, quit giving them a hard time." The teasing, feminine voice came from a young woman in a long, floral dress, her dark hair parted down the middle and falling in waves over her shoulders. She scooted in through the back door, a carton marked "fragile" in her arms.

Billy raced to take it for her.

"This is my granddaughter, Beth. She helps me around the store."

Murry gave Billy a *question-the-granddaughter* nod.

Beth unlocked a door in the hallway. Billy followed her. "You can put it in here for now." The two disappeared inside.

Murry turned to Brookes. "Where do you find all this stuff?"

"Estate sales." She frowned. "The other detective checked purchase logs, everything. I do not deal in stolen items. I told him that."

Everybody tells us that. "You sell much at the Psychic Faire?"

Her brow furrowed. "Mostly junk. Antique jewelry replicas. Nothing over a hundred dollars. Too many thieves around, ready to walk off with your profits." Before Murry could ask, she added, "Missed it this year because they changed the dates. Just frosted my buttons when I found out."

He could tell she was winding up for a tirade and hurried on, "Any young guys come in here?"

"Anyone under sixty is young to me, Detective. Most of my clients are women, forty and older. Not too many men."

"Mind taking a look at some photos? See if you recognize anyone?"

"All right, but I don't want to see those women's faces again. Especially not Marcia's. It's so awful, what happened." She shivered. "Two years and I still have nightmares. I can't believe you haven't caught that man yet."

"Believe me, we haven't given up. That's why we're here. We're still looking." He drew the packet of snapshots from his pocket. "There's nothing gruesome, I promise," he added, as he spread them out across the glass counter. Most were of the crowd outside Olga's condo and the funeral. Murry forced himself not to move a muscle, as she studied each one through the schoolmarmish glasses that hung from her neck. At the last three, her gaze shifted from one to the other two, then she frowned.

"What?"

"Nothing."

Murry peered over her shoulder. They were photos taken outside the Russian Orthodox Church. One of the old priest and Kevin Jones. One of Kevin Jones getting into his car. One of the young priest going around the corner of the building. "You hesitated. Why?"

"He reminds me of someone."

He pointed to Jones. "This one?"

"No, the priest." She jabbed the last photo. "The young one. There's something about him . . ."

A ribbon of excitement curled in Murry's stomach as he recalled how quickly the priest disappeared after the service. "What?"

Her gaze clouded a moment, then she shrugged, giving Murry an apologetic look. "I'm sorry. My memory's not as sharp as it once was."

Which meant she'd make a lousy witness, even if she did remember. "You ever attend a Russian Orthodox Church?"

She shook her head.

"No idea where you might have seen him before?"

"If I did, I'd tell you," she snapped.

He handed her his card. "If you remember anything, anything at all, call me," he said, fearing she'd sweep it away with the dust bunnies. "I know how much you want us to catch Marcia's killer. Any information could be important."

Murry waved at Billy to wrap up his conversation with the granddaughter, then met him at the car. With his shades, dark hair, and peach-fuzz mustache he reminded Murry of some geeky cartoon sidekick.

"You find out anything?" he asked as he drove toward Parker Center, suddenly remembering the task force meeting. They were going to be late.

Billy made a face like he'd bitten into a wormy apple. "She thinks getting questioned by a cop is the coolest thing that ever happened to her. Couldn't wait to get home and tell her husband."

Murry grinned. "Better luck next time, Kid. That it?"

"Yep. So what'd you get from the old lady?"

"Brookes noticed something about the young priest at Olga's funeral. While I'm at the task force meeting, you go back to the church and get his name. Check his background."

"Oh, come on, Murry, a priest?" Billy jammed a stick of gum into his mouth. "With that beard and headgear, you can hardly see those guys' faces. She's probably confused. You heard her; her memory's shot."

"Just do it, Kid."

The task force room was practically empty, the meeting obviously over. Greene glanced up, not able to keep the triumphant grin off his face. "Jamison wants you to see you. *Now.*"

Murry about-faced and headed down the hall to Jamison's office, but the lieutenant wasn't there. He flashed his most charming smile at the secretary and asked, "Any idea where he went?"

Interest flared in her eyes. "Help you if I could. But I have no idea."

Murry returned to BHPD and dug into the last of the reports. Jamison hadn't returned his calls and Daniels hadn't spoken to him. He was beginning to feel like a pariah. Tack walked by late in the afternoon, not daring to say anything but wearing a smirk. The asshole was already counting his grand, figuring Murry had hit a dead end. And if the Kid didn't come up with something on the priest, he had.

After what felt like days, Murry closed the last report and rubbed his eyes. They felt like the bottom of a gravel pit. He was squeezing a couple of eyedrops into his left eye when the phone flashed.

"Murry here."

Billy's excited voice blasted him over the line. "You won't believe this."

"Believe what? Where've you been?"

"Checking out the priest."

"It's ten-thirty. You have to fly to Moscow?"

"Just listen."

"What?"

"He's not a priest."

"What do you mean?"

"The old priest said this guy, the young priest, came in as the funeral was starting, said he was from a San Francisco congregation, wanted to ask for help with a problem. Old priest told him it would have to wait until after the funeral. Young priest said no problem, then disappeared after the funeral."

"You sure he wasn't a priest?"

"I don't know, Murry. But it's odd he'd just walk off. I thought he might know someone who attended the funeral, but no one recognized him. That's what took me so long."

Goosebumps ran up Murry's arms as he recalled the photograph. Half the man's face was shadowed by a sycamore. "You get any other photos beside that one?"

"Not of him."

"Blow that one up and start comparing it to the photos you took outside Olga's. If you find a possible match, call me. Check out where someone would get a Russian Orthodox priest costume. Maybe it was rented locally."

"Already checked. There's more costume places here in LA than in the rest of the country. Got over thirteen hundred hits on the Internet, too. He could've rented it anywhere. I asked Ramirez to help. So far, nothing."

"Keep checking. Get hold of some ecclesiastical supply companies. He might have got the costume there. Also, show that face to Upland and all the teachers, see if anybody recognizes him. Oh, and get some sleep tonight. Tomorrow's going to be a long day."

"Is that your crystal ball talking?"

"No, it's experience, Kid." His head was buzzing and he couldn't stop yawning, so he headed home, pleasantly surprised to find Mary asleep in his bed. The sheets felt cool, Mary soft and warm, and as he snuggled in close, a sense of familiar comfort washed over him. A "get married" kind of comfort that should have shot a lightning bolt of anxiety down his spine, but left him feeling peaceful and happy.

Chapter 18

The squawk of his cellular jerked him out of a sound sleep at 3:03 a.m. Jesus. Another Ice Pick victim? It was too soon for that, but he couldn't think what else it could be. He sat up, pressed the receiver to his ear, and kept his voice soft, trying not to wake Éclair.

Daniels's voice boomed, reeling off an LA address. "Pick up Kidman and get over there."

"Is it Ice Pick? He kill someone already?" Murry climbed from the bed, snagged some clothes, and trotted down the hall to dress.

"If we're lucky, he's done. Guy named Davis Jamal Kimble disappeared from work two days ago. Didn't take his car, left it parked on Rodeo. It was towed to the impound and they popped the door to get the registration. You'll never guess what they found."

"It's after three o'clock; enlighten me."

"Ice picks."

"How many?" Murry yanked on his skivvies and slacks.

"Four. Wrapped in plastic and stuck inside a paper bag."

"So why the excitement? Ice Pick uses five on his victims. For all we know, this guy could be into ice carving."

"Some young hotshot fresh out of the Academy sent them to the lab. Bones called an hour ago. They match the others."

"You're kidding." Murry pulled on his shoes and tucked in his shirt. "Kimble have a sheet?"

"B-and-E. Served two years. Been out three."

"He get physical with his victims?"

"No. Guy broke into houses, grabbed jewelry, and split. Security cameras at one of the places snapped his pic and he went down."

Ice Pick should have left a trail of dead cats, Murry thought, not simple B-and-E's.

"Jamison's on the way, along with the SWAT team." His voice rose, "We're going to nail this bastard, Murry."

"He's home?" Murry couldn't keep the surprise from his voice.

"Arrived home with his wife twenty minutes ago. Get over there."

The line went dead before Murry could ask anything else. Could it be this easy? On the drive to Billy's, he added up all the things that didn't add up. Why would Ice Pick leave his picks in the car, then abandon the car where it was bound to be towed? Why would he go home, leaving his car and the picks in the towing yard?

He pulled into Billy's complex.

The Kid was waiting. He pitched his cigarette and climbed into the car. "Holy Christ, Murry, this is unbelievable!"

"Unbelievable about sums it up." Murry disliked the ugly sensation in his gut. *Too unbelievable.*

Billy reached over to switch on the siren.

"It's three a.m., Dirty Harry. There's no traffic. Can we have some quiet?"

"What's your problem?" Billy grumbled around a stick of gum.

"It just seems awfully easy, Kid."

Billy looked ready to argue, but chomped another stick instead.

They zipped down the barren freeway. "Pull up everything you can on Kimble," Murry said.

"Kimble's at home. You're gonna see 'im in five minutes."

"Humor me."

Scowling, Billy plugged in Murry's laptop and began typing. "It'll take a few minutes to access his file."

They barreled down the off-ramp and into Kimble's neighborhood. Billy stared at the laptop. "Kimble's African-American, five-nine, one-fifty, thirty-two, married."

"Black?" Then who the hell was the bogus priest? "What do you think of that?"

"It's not exactly the profile," Billy said. "But not everything goes down the way they do in those FBI cases. Greene says—"

"Greene? Since when have you been talking to Snowflake?"

"He couldn't reach you, and called me to find out what we're working on."

"You tell him about the priest?"

"He's on the task force, Murry."

"What did he think?"

"Said it sounded like a good lead."

"You tell him anything else?"

"Like what? Other than telling me to check out the priest, you haven't told me shit."

Billy's tone took Murry by surprise. "I tell you as much as I can."

"No." The dissatisfaction in Billy's voice rose. "All you say is, 'Humor me.' Humor me about Kevin Jones. Humor me about Madame Zena. Humor me about the priest. Humor me about Kimble. Never an explanation."

The Kid's tone concerned Murry. "You thinking about going to LAPD?"

"Maybe."

"You're a good partner, Billy, but this is only your second murder investigation—"

"That's just the point, Murry. In LA, I'd get plenty of action."

"Greene tell you that?" Murry asked, trying to keep the sarcasm from his voice.

"Yep." Billy snapped the laptop shut. "Yep, he did."

Murry thought about the case and how he'd been handling things. He hadn't explained his reluctance to arrest Jones, or his certainty that the Psychic Faire had something to do with the victims, or any of his other hunches, some of which hadn't panned out. How did one explain a hunch without looking like a fool?

Before he could say any of that, he turned the corner, saw the lights flashing, and swung to the curb. Murry held up his badge at a patrolman. "Only the man and woman inside?"

The patrolman shook his head. "They don't tell me shit."

Billy nodded agreement. "I know what you mean."

Well, fry my balls, Murry thought.

The patrolman waved Murry through. "All I know is no one goes in or out that's not a cop."

Murry saw Jamison's lanky frame crouched behind a black sedan parked next door. Greene was with him. A SWAT van rolled to a stop, and a half-dozen guys swarmed to the gunmetal gray house with white shutters and trim, like ants scouting out a picnic.

Murry hurried down the sidewalk, Billy a step behind. Jamison was whispering into a hand-held radio.

"Why the SWAT team?" Murry asked, wondering why they were moving in so fast.

"Shhh. They're in position," Jamison said.

"Who's inside?" Murry asked, thinking there hadn't been time to confirm the number of people who might be living in the house.

Greene nodded. "Kimble and his wife. We're ready to go."

Murry recalled Greene's case files, the sloppy way they were put together, and watched with dismay as two guys rushed the front door. They paused barely long enough to yell, "Police," and smash it open.

A woman's scream cut through the night. One scream. No shots. A good sign.

The neighbors were getting an eyeful, Murry thought, scanning the well-lit street. Not a bad neighborhood: stucco houses in fair shape, lawns weedy but mowed. Somehow he expected either a dive or a mansion from Ice Pick, some kind of an extreme, not this. Everything about this scene tasted like coffee without sugar.

From the radio came a tinny voice. "We have them, Lieutenant."

Something in the man's voice told Murry there was something wrong.

With an apologetic note, the tinny voice continued, "Kimble's not here. We have his wife and brother. The brother lives with them."

Jamison shot Greene an eyeful of daggers. Greene reddened, a tomato capped with sour cream. Jamison looked ready to eat his radio. "They know where Kimble is?"

A pause. "No."

"Well, bring them out and Greene'll take them downtown for questioning."

With Greene momentarily out of favor, Murry had a sudden inspiration. "Why don't we let Kidman handle the interviews?"

Billy's eyebrows lifted in surprise.

Jamison nodded. "There's two of them. They can each take one."

Billy and Greene exchanged a look.

Murry watched them walk away.

Jamison turned to Murry. "You want to go inside?"

"What if Kimble's on his way home?" Murry asked, hoping to avoid any more screw-ups.

"We've staked out the perimeter." Jamison tugged his pipe from his pocket and trapped it between his teeth.

The SWAT team exited the house, surrounding a slender black woman in a pink robe and slippers. She clutched a change of clothes against her chest, her eyes darting from uniform to uniform, her expression terrified and confused at the same time. An act? Didn't look like it, but he'd been fooled before.

Another figure emerged: taller, skinnier, moving like the Tin Man in need of oil. Greene and Billy crossed the street and escorted them to Greene's cruiser.

"I'd like to talk to them later," Murry said.

Jamison nodded.

"Kimble being black bother you?" Murry asked, wondering if public pressure was making Jamison overlook the obvious.

"Profilers aren't one-hundred percent perfect. Kimble's the right age, obviously smart, careful."

So why did he sound like he was trying to convince himself? Murry gave Jamison a quick rundown about the priest.

"Let Ramirez or Farel follow it up. You stick with Kimble. If we don't find a smoking gun here, I'll eat my badge." But Jamison couldn't quite hide the worry behind his eyes. "You were right about Kevin Jones, I'll give you that, Murry. But those picks matched." Jamison gestured toward the house. "You ready?"

"Always." He felt strange going into the house without Billy.

"House looks clean," the SWAT captain said, meeting them on the porch. "One car in the garage. Belongs to the wife. Her husband left for work two days ago and never came home. Works as a waiter at The Five Forty Five."

"She file a report?"

"Naw. Sometimes he got in late, left early, and she didn't see him 'til midweek. If he came in late, he slept in the guest bedroom so he wouldn't wake her. We figured you'd want to get inside fast, so we told her to grab some clothes and change downtown."

"Think she was feeding you a line?" Murry asked.

The SWAT captain shrugged. "Hard to read."

"Good job," Jamison said. He poked his head through the door and whistled.

Murry glanced into the living room. A fifty-inch flat-screen TV dominated one wall, surrounded by black leather furniture. A black granite counter-top bar ran down another wall, with glittering Waterford tumblers inverted on a silver tray. He moved toward the hall. The white carpet felt like a cloud. No tips covered a spread like this, not even in Beverly Hills. "Where's his wife work?"

"Phone company."

"They inherit a fortune?" A huge plate glass mirror behind the couch made the room appear to go on and on.

"Don't know."

"I'll have Billy check," Murry said. He pulled his notebook, jotted a line, then pulled on gloves. "You got a list of what we're looking for?"

"Warrant's for burglary equipment, ice picks, duct tape, and black nylons."

"If he's Ice Pick, he's gonna have trophies. Also a woodworking setup to make the picks." He made a note to check for storage unit receipts.

"If he made them," Jamison said.

He made them, Murry thought. The bastard probably enjoyed every moment of creation. He'd bet his last buck they were part of the ritual. But why the odd pick stuck through Olga's foot? Was the killer trying to communicate something?

"You want the master bedroom, or the guestroom and den?" Jamison asked.

"The master." The furnishings were relatively new and expensive. He delved into the drawers first. Buried beneath Kimble's jockey shorts, he found a pair of rolled black nylons. He shook them out. One nylon foot was missing. Olga's face, covered in black nylon, flashed behind his eyes. Jesus, maybe Kimble *was* Ice Pick. Maybe he abandoned the car and left the country. *Maybe my gut's wrong.*

He bagged the nylons and moved on to the closet, where he found a black duffle bag. He finished his search, then called, "Jamison. In here."

Jamison appeared in the doorway.

Murry held up the nylons. "Found this in Kimble's stuff. The bag was in the closet." From the duffle, he extracted a handheld gadget that looked somewhat like a stud sensor. "This is a new one. Any idea what it does?"

"Oh yeah. That's for alarms. Checks for contacts." Reaching into the bag, Jamison pulled out a card key with electrodes attached. "Easy entry into any hotel room right here."

"A lot of high tech stuff," Murry said, "for breaking and entering through open windows. What you'd expect for a thief. Not for a rapist or killer."

Jamison closed the bag. "Our killer managed to get inside

the victims' homes without any signs of forced entry." *What's your problem?* his steely blue eyes asked.

"There's no duct tape, no additional picks, no trophies."

"So he stashed 'em somewhere else."

"A storage unit?" Murry thought out loud.

"Probably. You want to go through the entire house?"

"You mind?"

"Go ahead. By the time Kimble realizes we've been here, we'll have his ass. Catch up to me with whatever you find."

After two hours, Murry turned up no odd keys or anything that might lead to a storage unit, but he did find three things of interest: in Kimble's locked desk, a sheaf of clippings about "The King of Thieves;" in the wife's free-standing jewelry chest, a diamond bracelet that must have cost ten grand; and at the bottom of the duffle, a black book with notations and numbers. The top line read: *Ant. R. 60,000* and a checkmark. Beneath that, *Ant. D. Ri. 10,000* and a checkmark. Murry stuck the book in his pocket. He'd copy the pages, then send it to impound. He studied the clippings for a moment. Everything about Kimble fit the profile for the King—except for the ice picks and the nylons. He pulled his cellular, hoping to catch Billy.

"Kidman here."

"It's Murry. How's the interrogation going?"

From the hesitation, Murry imagined the Kid shaking his head. "Greene pissed off Kimble's wife, and she's yelling for Johnny Cochran. I'm supposed to hang out until the lawyer shows."

"Where's Greene?"

"With Kimble's brother while I baby-sit the wife."

"Stall the lawyer. I want to talk to her."

He disconnected before Billy could argue, and blasted downtown.

Chapter 19

Billy and Kimble's wife were in an interrogation room sipping café lattes, smoking, and chatting like two old chums. A half-empty box of Krispy Kreme donuts lay open on the table. Smart, Murry thought, wondering how Billy had stalled the lawyer. "Excuse me, Mrs. Kimble, I need to speak to Detective Kidman a moment."

In the hall, Billy spoke up before Murry could open his mouth. "I was just getting her to talk."

Murry had intended to take over the interrogation, but the Kid did look like he'd gotten her into a chatty mood. "It looks like you two are on a date. Where's Johnny the lawyer?"

Billy grinned. "At BHPD. Someone misinformed him about his client's location."

"Good." Murry pulled a sheet from his notebook. "Here's what I need. Ask her any way you like, but try to get an answer."

Billy shot him a look of appreciation. He led the way back inside and resumed his seat, Murry taking a chair in the rear, not wanting to disrupt their tête-à-tête.

"Like another latte?" Billy asked.

She shook her head. "Let's just get this over with, so I can go home." She glanced toward the door. "My lawyer here yet?"

"Not yet," Billy said. "I told 'em to page me the minute he arrives."

She pulled her jacket closed and crossed her arms. From the cut and leather piping, Murry estimated the denim pantsuit cost four or five hundred. She looked uncomfortable, but also expectant, like she knew this day was coming.

Billy scanned Murry's list of questions, then smiled. "Did your husband ever drive your car?"

"My car? No. Why?" Her puzzled frown said she didn't expect that question.

Billy ignored her "Why?"

"Did you ever drive his?"

"No. Never. He was touchy about it. You'd think the thing was alive, the way he babied it." She sounded like she wished it would get struck by lightning.

"Has your husband ever disappeared before?" Billy asked.

Her voice rose slightly. "We work odd hours. Sometimes I don't see him for a couple of days."

"So you're not worried?"

"He's probably just off . . ."

"Where?"

"Nowhere. I don't know."

She managed to make it sound halfway convincing.

"You said you didn't file a missing persons' report because you figured he'd come and gone while you were sleeping. Is that correct?"

"Yes."

"So you don't know where he's been the last two days, or even if he's been home?"

"I told you, no."

"But you think he might have gone off somewhere?"

"I don't know!"

"But you said he was probably just off somewhere. Surely you have some idea?"

"No."

Billy scratched his head. "When was the last time you saw him?"

"Before he went to work Saturday."

No hesitation. Probably true, Murry thought.

"Notice anything unusual about his behavior?"

"No. Why? Why won't you tell me what's going on?"

Billy ignored the question. "My partner says your living room looks like a theater. Man, I love movies . . . can't afford anything like what you got, though. You inherit some money?"

"Yes."

"How much?"

"I don't know. You'll have to ask Jamal. He handles all our finances."

"You seem like a smart lady," Billy said in a complimentary tone. "I'm sure you have some idea."

"No."

"And you never drove your husband's car?" Billy asked again, a hint of confusion in his tone.

"Look. I told you. No. Why won't you tell me what you want?"

"We have reason to believe your husband's missing," Billy said. "We want to find him." He pulled a pack of cigarettes from his pocket, offered her a fresh one, set the pack on the table, and lit hers. "You sure you don't know where he is?"

She stared at him stone-faced.

Aware her lawyer might show up at any moment, Murry decided it was time for the bad cop to interrupt. He shoved out of his chair, crossed to the table, and leaned over it. "Your husband's wanted for questioning in a series of murders, Mrs. Kimble. We need your help. The sooner we find him, the better. If you don't want to be implicated, you'd better cooperate."

"Murders?" Her mouth stumbled over the word. "You're crazy." She sucked down the cigarette in two long inhales. Murry narrowed his gaze until she looked away. "I don't know anything about murders. This is nuts. I want my lawyer!"

She obviously hadn't expected this. "The only way to help yourself and your husband is to tell us everything you know. You help us, we help you."

"You have any idea where your husband was January fourth?" Billy asked in his friendly, help-us-out tone.

Stone-faced silence.

"It was Friday," Murry added. "Four days after New Year's Eve."

Nothing.

"Surely you saw him when he came home?" Murry pressed. She glanced pointedly at the door, her gaze saying she was through talking.

Murry tossed the Krispy Kremes into the trash, took a photo from his jacket, and slid it across the table. "Recognize her?"

Her face paled at the headshot taken of Olga's corpse. "She dead?"

"Yes."

She shoved the photo away. "No."

"No, what?"

"Don't know her."

Billy held out the cigarettes and she waved them away.

Slowly, Murry set four more headshots on the table. "Recognize anyone?"

The skin around her eyes tightened with anxiety. Like

Kevin Jones, she couldn't resist looking. Her gaze froze on the fourth picture, a smiling headshot of Lucia Carlson. Eyes wide, she looked from Murry to Billy. "That woman. I saw her—"

Murry worked to keep his face bland.

"On the news. She was one of those . . . Ice Pick murders." She clenched her arms across her chest as though the room had suddenly dropped in temperature.

"You been following the Ice Pick stories?" Murry asked.

"No."

"But you recognized Lucia Carlson."

"From the news. Saw her photo. Rodney said she was pretty or I wouldn't have—"

"Rodney?"

"My brother-in-law. He was watching a football game."

"When was this?"

"I don't know. Last year sometime. I just remember because they talked about how pretty she was."

"Oh, your husband was there?"

"Yes."

"Anyone else?"

"No."

"No friends?"

"No."

"But he does have friends?"

She gave him a prim look. "We keep to ourselves."

"So he never brought anyone to the house?"

"No."

"Never?"

"No!"

"So what did your husband say about her?"

"Nothing. Rodney made a comment about her and Jamal agreed. It was nothing."

Murry wondered if Kimble's brother was involved. "Rodney ever get in any trouble with the cops?"

"How would I know?"

"Just answer the question."

"I don't know. Ask him." She frowned and glanced at her watch.

Murry leaned closer. "I'm asking you."

"I don't know."

"What about your husband?"

Sweat beaded on her brow. "What about him?"

"He been in trouble before?"

"You know he has, or you wouldn't be lookin' for him. But that was five years ago."

"He's been out two." Murry glanced at Billy. "Ice Pick got his first victim about that time, didn't he?"

Billy nodded. "Sure did."

She eyed Murry, her tone incredulous. "You think Jamal—"

"You know where he is?" Billy asked.

"I told you, I don't know where he is," she said slowly, emphasizing each word as though they had IQs of fifty.

Murry picked up his briefcase, opened it and pulled out the black nylons. He held them up so the missing foot showed. "See these before?"

She met his gaze head on and said through clenched teeth. "No."

"We found them hidden in your husband's underwear."

Billy leaned toward her. "Ice Pick likes to cover his victims' faces with a black stocking."

She stood up. "You're crazy. You're both crazy if you think— You're trying to pin this on Jamal! I've had enough. I want my law—"

"He told you what to say, if you were questioned,

right?" Murry asked in a hard tone.

Her gaze flew to Billy. "Yes, but—"

"But what?" Billy asked softly.

"It can't be him. He wouldn't . . . he's never done—"

"Done what?"

"Done anything like *that*."

"There are a lot of women out there who've been shocked to learn their husbands were serial killers," Billy said sympathetically.

Murry shut his case and returned to the table. "Please sit down, Mrs. Kimble. It's obvious you don't know about the murders. It's also obvious you're holding back. The only way this is going to work out is if you tell us everything you do know. Now."

When she said nothing, Billy added in a you-can-trust-me Midwestern tone, "You think a jury's going to believe you bought that entertainment system on a waiter's salary? Your husband's going down. Don't go down with him."

Uncertainty played across her face.

Murry spoke. "He told you he'd take the rap if he got caught, didn't he?"

The flicker in her dark eyes told him he'd hit the target. "That isn't the way it works, Mrs. Kimble. You lived in that home—with all that expensive stuff—you're implicated."

She sank into the chair and looked at Billy. "How long would he go in for?"

"For robbery? Three, four years, maybe," Billy said.

More like ten Murry thought, considering it was a second offense and Kimble was already on parole. And, if Kimble didn't go down for murder.

"What do I get if I help you?"

"We can talk to the DA, probably get you immunity from prosecution," Billy said.

"I don't know anything about any murders."

They had her.

"What do you know?" Billy asked.

"He wears a stocking mask when he pulls a job." She nodded toward Murry. "Those got nothing to do with Ice Pick."

"So you knew he was robbing houses?"

"Yes."

"Did he talk about it? Brag a bit?"

"He never talked about it. But there was the money, and then I found—"

"Found what?" he interrupted, thinking *trophies*.

"Newspaper clippings. About the King of Thieves."

Not what he was after. "You ask Jamal about them?"

"No. I didn't want to know."

Murry pulled the bracelet he'd taken from her jewelry chest. "Did he give you this?"

"How did you—? Yes. An early birthday present." Her voice faded to a whisper. "January sixth. Why?"

"Did he tell you where he got it?"

"He said he bought it, but . . ." There was doubt in her voice. "He didn't get home until very late that Friday. January fourth. I read about the burglary in the next day's paper."

"How late?" Billy asked.

"Two, three a.m. I didn't look at the clock, but I'd been asleep for awhile and I didn't go to bed until twelve-thirty."

"Then what happened?" Billy asked.

"He worked Saturday, took me out to dinner Sunday. Said it was for my birthday, and he was celebrating a raise at work."

"That's when he gave you the bracelet?"

She nodded. "Was it that woman's?"

"What woman?"

She glanced at the photos and pointed at Lucia Carlson.

"Why do you think it belonged to her?" Murry asked softly.

"You said this was about those murders. Thought maybe he stole it from her." She glanced from Murry to Billy. "He's not a killer. He's not a violent man. But he might have robbed her place."

Billy led her through all the same questions in different variations, but her answers no longer sounded evasive. She wanted immunity and she wanted to establish her husband was a thief, not a murderer.

"You have any idea where he fenced the stuff?" Billy asked.

She hesitated.

"I'll make sure the DA knows how helpful you've been."

Hope and doubt warred in her eyes. "He never said, but once I heard him talking on the phone and he mentioned an antique dealer."

Murry immediately thought of Nola Brookes.

"You remember the name of the place?" Billy asked.

She shook her head.

Murry spread the photos from Olga's funeral on the table. "Recognize anyone?"

She glanced at them and shrugged. "A bunch of white guys at a funeral. So what?"

"Study the faces. Are any of them familiar?"

She made a show of studying each photo. When she'd gone over them all, she gave Murry an I-told-you-so look. "Never seen any of them before."

He'd thought the priest might be a common factor, maybe a go-between for Kimble.

Billy glanced at the paper Murry had given him. "You know if he rented a storage unit?"

She hesitated. "Yes, but I don't know where. Paid cash for it. He showed me the key once on his key ring."

They hadn't found any keys, which meant Jamal probably had them with him.

Billy continued, "Did he rent it under his own name?"

"I don't know."

Billy shot Murry a look that asked, *anything else?* and Murry shook his head. The Kid had her go through the information one more time.

Finally, confusion in her tone, she said, "What do the thefts have to do with those murders? I still don't understand why—"

"Ice picks like the ones used on those women were found in your husband's car," Billy said. "You have any idea how they got there?"

"In his car?" The dazed expression returned. "No."

"Jamal's brother ever drive his car?" Billy asked.

She shook her head. "Jamal didn't let anyone drive that car but himself."

"You didn't think that was strange?"

She gave him a *get real* look.

"And you have no idea where your husband is?"

She clenched her hands in her lap. "I figured he was on the run—that he must have pulled another job. Tripped an alarm or something."

Billy's pager buzzed and he glanced at Murry. "I believe your lawyer's here, Mrs. Kimble."

Murry leaned forward. "Mrs. Kimble, do you believe your husband murdered those women?"

She shook her head. "I don't know how those picks got in his car, but he wouldn't . . . No." She sounded dead certain.

Greene was with her lawyer, and neither of them looked

happy when they saw Murry and Billy. "Mrs. Kimble's made a statement. As soon as it's ready, we'd like her to sign it," Murry said.

"I'll decide what my client will sign," the lawyer said. He was no Cochran, but he snarled like a wolf on the prowl for his next meal. He bypassed Murry and opened the door to the interrogation room.

Murry turned to Greene. "Where's Kimble's brother?"

"Down the hall."

"You learn anything?"

"Said he was laid off as a crane operator. Moved in with Kimble a couple of weeks ago. Jamal told him he was about to close a big business deal, and then they were moving to Europe."

"When did Jamal tell him that?"

Greene shrugged. "Last weekend."

After Olga's murder.

"Kimble's wife say much?" Greene asked.

Surprised that Snowflake had managed to get anything out of Kimble's brother, Murry said, "Why don't you talk to Billy? He handled it."

Greene looked at Billy.

"She knew her husband was stealing stuff," Billy said, "but says he wouldn't kill anybody."

"That's what they all say," Greene scoffed.

Murry wasn't so sure, but he kept his mouth shut until he had Billy in the car. "I want you to get a court order to examine Kimble's bank records. Then get a list of Kimble's friends. Just because he didn't bring anyone home doesn't mean he doesn't have friends—just that he didn't want his wife meeting them. Talk to the people at Folsom, too. Check on his cell mates and anybody close to him. See if any of those guys got out the same time he did, and where they are now.

Talk to his parole officer. Oh, and check out his brother, Rodney."

Billy shifted on the seat, his face obstinate.

"What?"

"You've got me checking all the right things, but—"

"What?"

"I get the feeling you don't believe he's Ice Pick. Even though we've got the picks. Why?"

"I didn't say that." Murry headed back to the freeway, traffic at a crawl. "But let me ask you this. Why would Kimble give his wife a bracelet worth ten grand, tell his brother he had a big deal about to go down, then disappear? Doesn't make sense."

"Maybe it was a goodbye present. Maybe the deal bombed and he ran."

"Ice Pick's deal is killing women. That's what he does, what he enjoys, what he thinks about. Kimble doesn't sound the type. If Kimble's Ice Pick, he didn't go anywhere willingly, Billy. He's either incapacitated or dead. By now he must realize his car's been impounded, that we might have found the picks."

"In which case, he could be halfway to China. If he's alive."

"Or watching and laughing, because he planted the picks in Kimble's car."

"You think it might be someone who knew Kimble?"

"I'm saying don't rule anything out. A lot of things don't make sense."

The Kid unwrapped a stick of peppermint gum. "Ice Pick's a sick-o. Who knows what a guy like that'll do?"

"I know one thing. If I decided to disappear, I'd do it so no one would notice. Dump the picks. Park the car where it wouldn't be discovered. Transfer every cent out of the country."

"Maybe that's what he did."

Murry pulled into the underground BHPD parking garage. "See what you can find out." Tempted to ask about Greene and LAPD, he decided to let it ride. With luck, Greene's handling of Mrs. Kimble had left a really bad taste in Billy's mouth.

Chapter 20

Conrad watched the newscast in disgust.

"The manhunt is still underway for Davis Jamal Kimble. Wanted for questioning in the robberies of several Beverly Hills homes, he may be linked to the Ice Pick killings . . ."

He turned on the lathe. The noise drowned out the newswoman's voice. The sanded wood handle felt cool and smooth, the metal tip sparked against the grinder. Perfect for Mary's transformation.

But what had the King done with the four he'd stolen? Conrad had searched his house. He'd even left the nylons, in case the cops got called in when Kimble turned up missing. He had a feeling they already had the picks. Why else would the press be speculating that he was the King? A statewide manhunt for a dead man. Morons.

Then he thought about the message from Kidman to Madame Zena. He'd been tempted to answer, but something inside threw up a warning flag every time he checked his messages. What did they suspect? Maybe he'd overplayed his hand with Murry.

His mother's voice seeped out of the dark corners of his mind. *Now you know how it feels to be a woman, Connie. Poked and prodded and told to shut up and enjoy it. This is for your own good.* He studied his palms, the scars from the needles so small and nondescript no one would notice. No one but him. *This will teach you to suffer as I've suffered.*

He closed his eyes, willing her voice away, but she only gained strength. He could feel her moving over him, kissing away his tears, stroking him, loving him. *You're so good, baby. So good. Let's fly to heaven on wings of love.*

He shuddered. He needed a release but was determined to save himself for Mary. It took all his will to shut out his mother's voice, shut out the memories. Steadying his hands, he finished the point on the first pick and picked up the second. Not long now, Mary, he promised her. Not long now.

Chapter 21

By the time the sun splashed rose pink across the eastern sky, Murry found Tack at his usual haunt, the coffee room, with a glazed donut in one hand, a cigarette in the other. He might look like Pierce Brosnan, but he smelled like an ashtray. "Hey, Tack. I need to check the inventory from the King's file." He worked for an off-hand tone. "Mind if I borrow it?"

Tack finished off the donut and wiped his hands. "Yeah, I mind." Trailing smoke, he headed back down the hall to his desk, a linebacker protecting his turf. "It's my case."

"I just need to check something."

"What's it to you?"

Tack had to make everything difficult. Murry found himself out of patience. "Would you prefer I get the captain's approval?" Tack and the captain didn't get along.

"No. No. What d'ya got?"

"Don't know yet. Maybe nothing."

Tack handed over the file, watching closely as Murry scanned through the pages. The bracelet appeared to be stolen from one Conrad James III.

Reluctantly, he opened his briefcase, took out an evidence bag, and shook out the bracelet. "Looks like this matches one of the items stolen on the fourth. Check it out for me, will you?" He hoped Tack would refuse.

Tack's eyes narrowed. "How the hell did you get it?"

Murry explained about finding the bracelet in Kimble's house.

"Kimble's the King of Thieves?"

"Maybe. If we get confirmation—"

Tack snatched the bracelet. "I'll talk to the owner, get an ID."

Damn. "Daniels wants it ASAP," Murry said, aware that Daniels didn't know about the bracelet, but that Tack would move faster if he thought the captain would notice.

Murry watched Tack saunter away and felt that uneasy stirring in his gut. Kimble might be the King but it didn't make sense that he was Ice Pick. He got on the phone and called the FBI profiler at Quantico, spilled what he'd found at Kimble's place, what Kimble's wife had said, and asked the million-dollar question, "This fit the profile?"

The man said he'd have to call back.

Murry punched in Bones's number. "You have a chance to examine the nylons?"

"I've barely had a second to park my butt," Bones snapped. "I'm working on it. Shouldn't be long." *Click.*

Murry spent the next couple of hours on the phone, checking to see if any of the victims had been robbed. Two had, but two or three years prior to their deaths. The others had never filed a complaint, so he called their relatives and asked if they knew of any unreported thefts. The universal answer was "no." He punched in Ramirez's number. "You get anything on the priest costume rentals?" he asked.

"*Nada,* Dance man. Had to quit this morning. I'm off the task force."

"What do you mean?"

"It's been cut. Most of us are back to our regular caseload."

Murry hung up and jabbed in Jamison's number, angry at being left out of the loop. When he got Jamison's voice mail, he hung up and marched into Daniels's office. "Care to enlighten me? Ramirez says the task force's been cut in half."

Daniels eyed Murry. "We've almost got the bastard and LAPD is swamped. Jamison had to cut some people loose."

"So why not me and Billy?"

"You don't have that heavy a caseload. Besides, you saved his ass when he wanted to arrest Jones. Now save your own ass and quit wasting time on that priest. Whatever problem he had, he got an answer from God during the service and didn't need to stay."

Daniels cut off Murry's protest with an impatient wave of his hand. "You've got Billy chasing geese when he should be searching for that storage unit. Tying up loose ends."

Realizing Billy had blabbed to Greene, Murry found himself working hard to speak in a calm tone. "Captain, I'm sure Kimble's the King of Thieves, but I just don't see him as Ice Pick."

"The guy's educated, the right age—"

"But the wrong race," Murry interrupted, earning a frown.

His frown turning into a scowl, Daniels hammered home each point. "Kimble had the picks. They match the picks from the other victims. He had the nylons. I just talked to Bones. The one on Olga was cut from the pair you found. He's our guy."

"The nylons matched? Bones is sure?"

"Positive. So put the final bullets in this case and quit wasting time on hunches. Hit the target, Murry."

The stocking matched. He didn't want to believe it. Maybe subconsciously he didn't want Greene to be right. Maybe that was what had him chasing phantoms.

Hit the target. He returned to his desk and read through the interview notes for the staff at The Five Forty Five.

Kimble last seen around ten.

Private party in the back room.

Woman ate alone.

Kimble disappeared.

No one noticed him leave.

Murry decided to drive over and ask a few more questions. The place was closed, but he could see a busboy setting tables. He tapped on the glass and held up his shield.

The young man opened the door. "Yes?"

Murry glanced toward a teenaged girl filling table vases with miniature yellow roses. He held up the photo of the priest. "Either of you recognize this man?"

They both shook their heads. "This about Jamal?" the busboy asked.

"Yes. You know him very well?"

Another negative head shake.

"He tight with anyone here?"

A shrug. "Don't know. You know, Alice?"

The flower girl glanced up, her face like bland pudding, zero interest. "Know what?"

"Jamal," the busboy said in an exasperated tone.

"No." She went back to adjusting the rose in the vase.

The dead ends were beginning to pile up into a permanent roadblock. "I need to check your reservations for last Saturday."

The young man handed Murry the reservation book and watched him flip through the pages.

Murry's gaze froze.

9:00 Private room—LaFleur. The handwriting for the LaFleur reservation didn't match the others. He held up the page. "You recognize the handwriting?"

"Could be Mario's. He's the maître d' most nights."

Murry checked his watch. Barely 11:00. "Know when he arrives?"

"Four-thirty."

"You have his address?"

"Uh, the manager would have that in his office."

"Is he here?"

"In the back."

"Thanks." Murry found the manager, a sixty-ish man with an air of success that made his faded blue jeans and golf shirt seem classy. From behind his functional techno metal desk he eyed the reservation book. "That's Jamal's handwriting." He stepped to the filing cabinet and pulled a file. "Here's his application. I showed it to the other detective." His tone asked why they didn't share their information.

Murry asked himself the same question every day. He made a copy of the application and reservation, gave the file back, then showed the manager the photo of the priest.

The man showed no sign of recognition. "Sorry."

Murry asked a few more questions, but other than the maître d's address, the manager knew nothing helpful.

Out of leads, knowing Billy would call if he came up with something, Murry spent three hours trying to run down the maître d' in the hopes he might get something more to go on regarding the night Kimble disappeared. The maître d', Mario Racine, worked two jobs, attended community college, and rode a bike everywhere—no car. Murry talked to several tenants of the same low-rent apartment complex and learned Mario usually returned home around two, then left again for his job at The Five Forty Five.

Around two-thirty, he saw Mario ride up, recognizing him from the manager's description: five-ten, hundred-seventy pounds, dark hair and eyes. Frowning, Mario hefted the bike to his shoulder and carried it up the stairs. "Help you?" he asked in a suspicious tone.

Murry pulled his badge. "Mario Racine?"

"Yes?"

"I have a few questions about Davis Jamal Kimble."

"I already talked to a cop at the restaurant."

"It won't take long," Murry said.

Racine led him inside a sparsely furnished, putty-colored living room, set the bike beside a sagging brown couch, and turned around. *Let's get this over with,* his face said.

Murry showed him the reservation sheet. "You have any idea why Jamal made the reservation?"

"Jamal said one of our regular customers wanted to book the room, so he'd written in the man's name while I was on break."

"A man?"

A shrug. "That's the way I remember it. Why?"

"Didn't you think it odd when a woman showed up alone?"

"Didn't matter to me. People change their plans all the time."

"Jamal said it was a regular customer. Did you recognize her?"

He shook his head.

"Did she give you her name?"

He frowned, his gaze thoughtful, then shook his head. "If she did, I don't recall. Reservation was under LaFleur—so she had to tell me that, or I wouldn't have given her the room."

"You didn't think it odd?"

"I figured her date got cold feet. She was no looker."

"What do you mean?"

"Old. Blond. Overweight. Big feet. Look, I've got to

shower and catch the bus or I'll be late for work."

Murry asked a couple more questions, but it was obvious Racine knew little. Now what? Check in with Greene and see if he'd found Kimble's storage unit? Search for the priest?

No, Daniels would kick his butt. All he had left was the reservation. Who was the woman and what did she know? All the way back to BHPD his mind chewed on the name LaFleur. An alias? Real name? Why did it bother him?

He headed straight for Tack's desk, hoping to find something in the case file that would shake loose whatever was making the back of his eyeballs itch. The file was gone. He punched in Tack's cellular number, got his voice mail, and hung up.

His own phone was ringing when he returned to his desk.

"Hey, Murry, where you been?" Billy asked. "I've got some info. Mind meeting me at Java City? I'm starving."

"Why not?"

He met Billy at an outside table. "So far I'm hitting dead ends. You get something on Kimble?"

"Yeah. Kimble had several accounts, here and in the Cayman Islands."

"How the hell did you find that out?"

The Kid grinned. "Internet connections, a little bit of hacking, the phone, a few white lies."

"What about the banks here? They cleaned out?"

"No. He had fifty-some grand spread over three banks."

Murry took the printouts, not about to ask if everything was legal. He read the entries on the foreign bank. "Sixty grand. A hundred grand. Fifty grand. If I were bailing, I wouldn't leave fifty behind." He checked the amounts listed in Kimble's notebook. The sixty grand matched an entry. The guy wasn't brilliant, writing all this down. "Any idea what the notations stand for?" he asked, wanting to get Billy involved.

Billy scanned the copies of Kimble's black book. "*Ant. R; Ant. D. Ri.* Anthill? Antiquated? Antique?" His words were muffled by a large bite of cinnamon roll.

Hearing the word "antique" shot a bolt of lightning down Murry's spine. Once more he thought about Nola Brooke's reaction to the photo of the priest. An antique dealer and a priest. What did they have in common? And where did Kimble fit? "Ice Pick used an antique pick on Olga. We also found the thread from an old rug on her bed. Maybe he's connected to an antique dealer."

"White worked for Nola Brookes. Maybe Brookes fenced Kimble's stuff and that's how Kimble met White."

"Let's lean on her and the granddaughter. See if either one recognizes Kimble's picture." If Nola Brookes or her granddaughter fenced stolen goods, he'd eat his paycheck, but he was running out of ideas.

On the way over, he gave the Kid an update on the bracelet and reservation at The Five Forty Five. "The name LaFleur mean anything to you?" he asked.

Billy stroked his mustache. "Doesn't ring any bells. LaFleur's an odd name, though."

"It's all these odd details that bother me," Murry said, thinking aloud. "A woman shows up instead of a man. A woman with big feet. The reservation's made by Kimble himself, not the maître d'. Then there's Madame Zena with her weird predictions, who vanishes before we can talk to her again. Then there's that priest at Olga's funeral. He's there, then he's gone. They may all be unrelated, but I'd like to keep digging," Murry said, then wished he hadn't. The Kid would probably blab to Greene.

Billy's gum garbled his words, "I get what you're saying, but Daniels wants us to focus on Kimble. He's not going to like any detours."

"We are focusing on Kimble. And the captain already hauled my butt across the carpet for the wild goose chases I've been sending you on." He couldn't keep the irritation from his voice. "I'm figuring you talked to Greene, he talked to Jamison and . . ."

Wearing a look of chagrin that redeemed him somewhat, Billy said, "I didn't think Greene would say anything to the captain. Sorry, Murry."

Murry was pissed, but at least the Kid owned up to it. He let it go. "I put in a call to Quantico. Figured I ought to talk to an expert."

"You called the Feds? What'd they say?"

"Guy's going to call me back. I've been reading about serial killers. They steal trophies, not antique rugs."

"So we have an exception. We're the newbies, Murry. Jamison's worked a lot of these cases. So's Greene."

Murry felt his jaw tighten. "So what's your buddy Greene say?"

"He's looking for the storage unit."

"Hope he finds it." If trophies turned up, Kimble would be the exception. If not, then he'd follow up on the LaFleur reservation and the priest.

Nola Brookes didn't recognize Kimble, and her granddaughter wasn't there. When Murry showed her the photo of the priest again, she shook her head. "He reminds me of someone . . ."

"A customer?"

"No. But maybe a relative of one of my customers. Oh, it's on the tip of my tongue, but I can't quite get it."

"Mind if we look at your customer list?"

Her mouth formed a line of resistance. "You bother my customers, they may not come back."

"Your name won't be mentioned. Promise."

"Humph." She disappeared into a tiny back office and returned minutes later with a photocopied ten-page list of names and addresses and phone numbers. "Some of these people have died or moved over the years, that's why there's an X through their names."

"I really appreciate this, ma'am," Murry said.

In the car, Billy shook his head. "Kimble had matching picks in his car, black nylons with one foot cut off, and the stolen bracelet." As soon as Billy said it, they stared at each other.

"You thinking what I'm thinking?" Murry asked.

"The bracelet was stolen the night Olga was killed," Billy said, right on track.

Murry eyed the line of palm trees and triangular green sign announcing Beverly Hills, his thoughts on January fourth. "That doesn't make sense. A guy doesn't pull a burglary, then switch hats and commit ritual murder. Maybe, just maybe, he had two gigs going, but no way he's doing both the same night. Not with the kind of planning Ice Pick does. Any chance Kimble's brother's involved?"

Billy shook his head. "His brother's got no priors, not even a parking ticket. And he was working as a crane operator in Nevada when the first three murders occurred. No way he could've pulled 'em off. Olga was murdered in the wee hours Saturday morning. Maybe Kimble hit James's place earlier, then something set him off."

Murry pulled into the parking garage, then flipped through his notebook, comparing the dates of the murders and thefts while Billy tapped his fingers on the dashboard. None of the break-ins occurred close to the date of any of the other murders. So, if he was Ice Pick, what set him off? "You get anything on his friends?"

218

Billy climbed out. "No tight friends in the joint. One of Greene's guys is tracking down his parole officer."

"Talk to Kimble's brother and Mrs. Kimble again. Hammer January fourth and fifth. See if Kimble said or did anything unusual—mentioned running into an old buddy, anything."

He returned to his desk and thought about the captain's words. *Hit the target.*

His phone buzzed and he picked it up.

"Jamison's here," Daniels said. "We need to talk."

Now what? From the sound of the captain's voice, it wasn't good.

Murry stepped into the office and closed the door. Jamison was standing near the window, Daniels leaning against his desk.

"Kimble's dead," Jamison said.

Murry hadn't expected *that*. "How? When?"

"Found the body this morning in Topanga Canyon. Dead at least two days."

"Who took the scene?" And why hadn't he been called?

"Wasn't any identification, so Santa Monica didn't think anything about it until they ran his prints. Gibbs is at the scene now."

"I'd like Éclair on it."

"Gibbs is good."

"Éclair's been on every Ice Pick murder. She's up to date on everything. She'll know if it's him."

"*If* it's him!" Jamison jammed his pipe between his teeth and clamped down.

"I'm just wondering how he ended up in the canyon," Murry said.

"Someone did us a favor," Jamison said.

"I'm sure you're right," Murry agreed, hiding his

doubts. "I still think Éclair—"

"Call her," Jamison said grudgingly. "Get her on the scene now. I want a preliminary report by tomorrow. Let's wrap this thing up."

He nodded with a twinge of regret about the overtime going Éclair's way. He wouldn't see much of her for a day or two.

Jamison pulled open the door. "Take your cell phone, Murry."

"It's in my car."

"And your pager?"

He patted his belt. *Shit.* "On my nightstand." Or was it Mary's nightstand? No wonder it'd been so quiet.

Jamison lifted an eyebrow. "I'll be downtown. Call me when you have something."

Chapter 22

Murry picked up Billy, and they zigzagged their way above Topanga Canyon. The two-lane wound like a switchback roller-coaster. Deeper in the canyon, all the jungle-like growth made it easy to imagine the area as a dinosaur's paradise a million years before. Cantilevered mansions jutted from the hills. The further they drove, the fewer the houses.

"You get anything out of Mrs. Kimble?"

"Four words: *'Talk to my lawyer.'* "

"Any thoughts on who killed Kimble and why?"

"Maybe if I knew how he died," Billy said. "Sheesh, could be anything."

"He didn't drive up there and die of a heart attack, that's for sure. Someone dumped the body."

Billy wadded several sticks of gum into his mouth. "So he pissed off someone nastier than him."

"Like who?"

"If I knew that, everyone would be callin' me for a reading and I'd be writing a bestseller like Olga."

"Oh? And what would you do then? Quit your job and go on a book tour?"

The Kid grinned, but he looked a bit green.

"You getting carsick?"

"Just overtired."

Murry slowed for a switchback, then hit the gas again, anxious to get there. "Won't be long now."

Just when Billy looked like he was about to lose his lunch, they hit the yellow tape. A uniformed officer tried to keep the traffic moving, not that there was much to see now that the body was gone. Murry swung a u-ey and parked opposite Éclair's BMW.

He tried to skirt past the reporters, but they flocked around like he was fresh carrion. "Is it true the dead man's Ice Pick?"

Someone else yelled, "What about the King of Thieves? Was he the King?"

Another voice, "Is it true he had an ice pick jabbed through one eye?"

Swatting a swarm of microphones away from his face, he said, "No shit, is that what happened? Goddamn, no one ever tells me anything."

When they realized they weren't going to get anything but sarcasm, the microphones disappeared.

Murry flashed his badge at the nearest uniform, and scanned the area. Several patrolmen were tromping through the ivy and brush at the edge of the steep canyon, calling, "Rocky," over and over. Snowflake was talking to Éclair, standing close and comfortable. Éclair was staring at the ground, oblivious to the detective's interest.

Billy beelined to Greene, while Murry questioned a patrolman he recognized. "What's going on, Al?"

"Ten-year-old boy and his dog found the body. We got the kid in the patrol car. The dog ran off."

"Why don't you have the boy call him?"

"Kid's pretty shook up. Both his parents are at work, and we're waiting for one of 'em to show."

Jesus, everyone was afraid of being sued, Murry thought.

"You been on the scene long?"

"Long enough," Al said, the greenish cast to his face saying he'd seen the body.

"How long's the ME been here?"

"Hour or so. Talked with Gibbs; then Gibbs left with the body."

"Thanks." Murry ambled over to join the threesome.

". . . never would've found the body, if not for the dog." Greene paused and nodded at Murry.

"You talk to the boy?" Murry asked.

Greene shook his head. "Just stopped for a quick look. Still checking out storage units."

Screwing off, Murry thought. He turned to Billy. "I'm not so great with kids. You wanna handle it?"

Billy snapped his gum and blew a large white bubble. "Sure."

Billy and Greene walked off, Greene saying something that had Billy chuckling.

"Just a barrel of laughs," Murry said.

"What?" Éclair asked.

"Nothing."

Billy climbed into the patrol car and settled beside the boy. Murry wandered over to the cliff edge. Patrolmen were still milling around, yelling, "Rocky," back and forth. Twenty or thirty feet down, the brush stirred.

"I'd like to watch you do the autopsy," Murry said. "Mind giving me a ride? That way I won't have to drop Billy at the station."

"No problem. How did you know I'd be doing the autopsy?" she asked. "Jamison just called me."

"I made the suggestion."

"Thanks." The tone was sarcastic but she looked pleased.

"Looks like you had a court date," he said, eyeing her expensive suit and heels.

"How—? Oh, the clothes. Don't worry I'll be back in my baggies tomorrow."

"Hey, I like this look."

"And I like comfortable."

He didn't tell her that it was nice to see her in something dressier for a change—and something that showed off her figure. "So when did you get here?"

"Gibbs called me a couple hours ago. Kimble had something sharp jabbed through his eyes. Gibbs thought it might have been an ice pick. Figured I'd be interested."

"Both eyes?"

"Yes."

Before he could ask another question, he heard a car door slam and saw Billy lifting the boy onto his shoulders, the two of them headed toward the crime scene. Billy zigzagged up to the road edge, the boy grinning. "Give him a call," Billy coaxed.

With an obedient nod, the boy yelled, "Rocky!" several times. He raised what looked like a dog whistle to his lips and blew. A small black lab bounded through the undergrowth and up onto the street, tail wagging.

Everyone froze. The dog had what looked like the end of an ice pick protruding from his mouth. Billy crouched down and set the boy on his feet. "Here, boy! Here, Rocky!" The dog advanced slowly, then lowered his head and dropped the pick near the boy's toes. The boy grabbed the dog's collar.

Éclair hurried forward. "Who would have thought?" She slipped on gloves, pinched the bloodstained handle between her thumb and index finger, and slipped the pick inside an evidence bag.

The patrolmen were struggling to keep back the mob of screaming reporters.

"That'll make the ten o'clock news," Murry observed as a

grinning Billy led the dog and its owner to the patrol car and settled them inside.

Éclair nodded. "What are the odds of that happening?"

"Million to one?" Murry speculated, giving the Kid a nod of approval. "Looks like you're a star."

The Kid's grin widened.

"Get anything from the boy?"

"Nope. The dog ran off and he went after it. Nearly stepped on Kimble's arm. Called nine-one-one."

"From where?"

"Carries a cell phone when he goes out hiking. House rule."

In Murry's day, he ran around with the promise to be home before dark. Nowadays parents would be thought negligent with that kind of loose supervision. Of course, back then there had still been some rural pockets that crime never seemed to touch. Those pockets had long since dried up, steamrolled over by waves of suburbia. What developers called *progress* and he called *sad*. He pointed toward marks in the dirt. "That where Kimble went over?"

Éclair nodded. "Only found traces of blood up on the road though, so either the killer was careful or Kimble was killed somewhere else."

Murry looked at Billy and waited for him to come up with the answer.

Excitement lit Billy's blue eyes. "Son-of-a-bitch. They had to know each other."

"Who?" Éclair asked.

"Ice Pick and Kimble."

Murry thought about the four ice picks found in Kimble's car. Had the dog found the missing one?

"Ice Pick preys on women," Éclair said. "He wouldn't bother with Kimble, unless Kimble got in his way."

"They might have been working together," Billy said. "It would explain the picks in Kimble's car and the black stocking."

"It's possible," Murry said, studying a tangle of vegetation that looked like it had eaten its way up the canyon walls and was about to start on the road. "They could have met in jail. Kimble went inside five years ago. Been out two. The first murder happened almost two years ago. Maybe they were released at the same time and, after Olga's murder, Kimble put it together and—"

"Ice Pick killed him," Éclair finished.

"I checked all of Kimble's known associates, in and out of prison, and found zilch," Billy said, scratching behind his ear and looking troubled.

Murry handed the Kid his car keys. "Check out Kimble's friends and the cons he hung with inside again. If you still get nothing . . . start checking backgrounds of the people he robbed. Maybe there's some kind of connection there. Has to be one somewhere."

"The King only hit Beverly Hills' finest. Rich and Famous, not low-life rip-offs. This one of those psychic things?" Billy razzed.

"More like desperation." Not all his hunches panned out, but enough had that he paid attention. Still, he was trying to live down the label of Psychic Detective. Checking out Kimble's victims was a long shot. He shrugged, sorry he'd said anything. "Focus on family, friends, cons."

"Later," Billy said, keys jingling as he hurried toward the car.

Murry winced when the Kid burned rubber. He glanced at Éclair. "How soon before we get a comparison between Kimble's blood and the blood found under Olga's fingernails?"

Éclair checked her watch. "A sample went to Bones. We'll know if it's the same type, secretor, nonsecretor, etcetera, anytime now. DNA will take a bit longer, ten days at least."

Murry didn't know whether to hope the blood type matched or not. What if it matched and ten days later they learned the DNA didn't? That would mean she hadn't scratched Kimble. It didn't mean Kimble hadn't been there with Ice Pick. "Thought they were speeding up the DNA process."

"They're talking about buying the 'lab on a chip' developed at Michigan University, but you know how budgets are," she said in a disgusted tone. "Hasn't happened yet."

"Borrow your phone?" he asked.

Her lips curled like she knew he'd left his in the car on purpose. "Bones isn't going to like being badgered," she said, handing it over.

"Oh, he loves hearing from me." Murry punched in the number, surprised when Bones answered on the first ring.

"Does it match?" Murry asked.

"No."

"No?" He watched Éclair's eyebrows rise. "You sure?"

"Positive. I just told Jamison and Daniels. They're not happy, so I wouldn't bug them for awhile."

"Thanks." He disconnected and looked at Éclair. "You heard it. Whoever Olga scratched, it wasn't Kimble. Mind if I take a peek at the pick?"

"Why?"

"Want to see if it looks like the others."

She shot a look toward the crowd of reporters. "I'd rather you waited until we get to the morgue."

"Understood." He turned his concentration to the crime scene. "Not much here. Just a few marks in the dirt. Looks like the dog and the boy obliterated everything."

227

"Be grateful we got a body and a pick."

"Hey, I'm grateful. Don't I sound grateful?"

"Humph." But he caught a grin as they climbed into her car.

Murry thought about the connection between Kimble and Ice Pick, more and more certain Ice Pick was a con and they were closing in.

"You look pleased with yourself," Éclair observed.

"Things are starting to add up. I can feel it."

The doors to the autopsy room slid open with a whoosh and a gust of cool air. The odor of cleanser and rotten meat hit next. Good old grade-A human, left outside to rot in warm, sunny, Southern California. Murry breathed oxygen through his teeth, hoping his olfactory nerves would hurry up and get over the worst of it.

Reflected in the stainless steel that was everywhere, his face appeared elongated and thin: 180 to 170 without dieting. Not bad. Better yet, the gray around his temples hardly showed. Never thought the morgue would improve his looks.

"You ready?" Éclair said, pulling the cover off the body.

Jesus. His stomach curled into a fetal position. A beetle crawled from a fabric tear near the corpse's balls. Small animals had gnawed the fingers up to the second knuckles and done taste-tests around the wrists and forearms. He hated to see what was under the shirt and slacks. Any moment and the acid would come gushing up his esophagus.

Since when had he grown so sensitive? Kids, he hated seeing kids, but adults in any state no longer bothered him much. He swung his gaze to the man's face. Two days in jungle-land hadn't been kind, no matter how he'd gone in. Skin the color of concrete. Flies had set up camp in the mouth and nose. But the eyes—something sharp had been shoved through both pupils.

The ice pick lay in an evidence bag at the end of the table. Éclair handed it to her assistant, Susan Newton, a tech with a star-shaped earring through her nose and a moon through one eyebrow. She looked like a punk rocker but was as efficient as a Cray supercomputer.

"Why don't I deliver that to Bones," Murry offered. "Be back before you're through."

If Éclair noticed his need for escape, she didn't let on. With a grunt of approval, she nodded.

He grabbed her keys and hurried to the car, gulping fresh air all the way across the lot and willing his stomach to settle. For the first time in a week, the humidity had dropped and a pleasant ocean breeze had rolled in for the night. He was almost to the lab when Éclair's cellular twanged a country melody that said she had a call. He flipped it open thinking she might be calling him. "Murry here."

Billy's voice rasped with fatigue. "Hey, Murry, you left your phone in the glove box. Daniels wants you to call him as soon as you get something. You at the morgue?"

"On my way to the lab, wanna give Bones the ice pick. Looks like Kimble got it through both eyes."

"Wow. Maybe he saw too much."

"Maybe he did," Murry said. "You having any luck?"

"Nothing yet. I've got three names connected to Kimble, none of them cons. Last time I talked to them, they all said the same thing: they watched a few games together, had a couple of beers once in awhile, but didn't know the guy that well. They also had alibis. I'm checking them again."

"What about inmates?"

"All the guys in the cell block with Kimble, including his roommate, are still there or got out a year after the first murder." Billy's frustration came through over the line. "I'm waiting for a call from the warden, see if there were any transfers or mix-ups in the records."

"Have Ramirez help you. Catch a nap if you need it." They'd both been working long hours since the picks were discovered in Kimble's car. "If Daniels gives you any flack about using Ray, direct him to me. Drop my car at my house and have Ray take you home." He maneuvered Éclair's car into a space in front of the lab. "Did Greene's guy ever talk to Kimble's parole officer?"

"His parole officer left on a four-day cruise with his wife. Be back tomorrow night. I told Greene I'd talk to him then."

"Since when are you working for Greene?"

"We're on the same ball team, Murry."

Then why didn't Greene know his ass from third base? Murry thought. "Okay, let me know what you get."

He disconnected, grabbed the evidence bag, and hurried inside to more stainless steel counter tops, high-tech microscopes, and analysis machines. Bones's latest trainee, a gangly guy that reminded Murry of Ichabod Crane, was perched on a steel stool while Bones snapped out questions like a drill sergeant. The young man stuttered out a response that sounded like Latin.

Bones nodded. "Good." He cocked his head at Murry, missing the relieved look on the trainee's face. "Now what?"

"Got another pick for you. Didn't want to open it until I got here." He handed Bones the bag.

Bones put on a pair of rubber gloves and lifted out the pick by the handle, carefully avoiding the blood, and shook his head. "Not the same. Look at the crimped metal ferrule around the handle. None of the others have that. And there's no scrollwork."

"What about that odd one in Olga's foot? It didn't match the others. Does it match this one?"

With a huff of surrender, Bones turned to the young man. "Write down all the similarities you see in that sample. We'll review it when I finish with Detective Murry." He led Murry to an empty counter, set the pick down, then disappeared through another door using his key card. A few minutes later, he returned with two of the picks taken from Olga. Both were smeared with brownish bloodstains, but it was obvious from the handles—one gouged and stained, the other scrolled with an intricate pattern—that neither matched the one used on Kimble.

"Kimble's pick has a rippled ferrule, probably new. This one from Olga," Bones pointed at the older pick, "there's no ferrule, and if you apply pressure to the shaft, it has some give from wear and tear."

"What about the other one?" Murry gestured toward the carved-handled pick. It had no metal edge.

"Mahogany. Matches the ones used on the other victims." Raising one eyebrow, Bones shifted his piercing blue gaze into space.

Murry's nerves jangled with excitement. "Some of the minimum security prisons teach woodworking. Ice Pick may have learned the skill inside."

Chapter 23

Conrad checked the monitor in his van, flipping from camera to camera to verify Éclair was gone, then headed up the walk. He punched in her security code, inserted his duplicate key, and shoved open the door. Easy as one, two, three.

Giddy with excitement, he worked to slow his breathing, to steady himself. This was his final check. He switched off the alarm and, as a back-up, disconnected the two cameras the alarm would trip, then stepped into the hall to adjust the camera there. It transmitted to his van. The angle had to be perfect so he could record his work.

The thought of having Mary's transformation on video so he could watch it made him wish he'd done the others this way.

He finished the preparations, glanced around one last time, and reset the alarm. Tomorrow was her birthday. And he had the perfect gift.

Chapter 24

Feeling optimistic, Murry picked up some vegetarian lasagna and headed back to the morgue. With any luck, Éclair would be finished and they could inhale garlic at his place.

She was just washing up when Murry walked in, her assistant rolling Kimble out the other set of doors. He glanced toward the covered body and everything dimmed. Time seemed to stop. An image formed so clear in his head, the details so startlingly real, it sucked the air from his lungs. The sheet disappeared and the body changed from Kimble to Éclair. Her hair was wet. He swore he could smell her lemon shampoo. Water glistened on her shoulders and bare flesh. Her face was pale and slack, eyes closed, hands open at her sides, bloody holes in both, damp blood smeared across her chest, holes in her feet. More blood stained her thighs, glimmered in her pubic hair.

Jesus Christ, no. Not her. Not Ice Pick.

His stomach churned and panic ripped through him, like he'd bungee-jumped from a bridge only to hear the cord snap and feel the ground come rushing up at his face. His legs shook. He wasn't sure if he was still standing, wasn't sure of anything, the world quiet as death stealing across a dying man's eyes. He blinked, tried to speak, blinked again, and the vision faded into Newton pushing the gurney through the door. Then he felt his stomach clench. He staggered to the nearest sink, hoping he wasn't about to screw up evidence, and vomited. Bile burned his esophagus and mouth. He sucked in air, a mistake, and vomited again.

"Murry!"

His eyes teared and he dashed water on his face, then rinsed his mouth before straightening. *It's not going to happen. It's just fatigue.* But all he could think about, when he manufactured a smile he hoped looked more reassuring than he felt, was how much he loved Éclair. If that bastard touched her . . .

"Murry?"

He managed a grunt.

"Are you all right?" Éclair had dried her hands and replaced her lab coat with a sweater. Her green eyes were tight. "What's wrong?"

"Nothing," he lied, forcing another smile, telling himself he was just overtired, that this place had finally got to him. "Let's bust out of this joint. I've got dinner in the car. Let's eat at home." The thought of eating sent a new wave of nausea through him. But the scent of oregano and Italian spices wafted over him like a fresh blanket of reality, making whatever he'd seen feel more like a bad dream. He found himself recalling the experience with the Voodoo sorcerer, the flash so vivid and real he'd thought his hand was lopped off, had seen the lump of bloody flesh in the grass. *Still have both hands. It didn't mean anything. It was just some fluke. Like now.*

But on the way to his place, he asked, "So, how's the security system working?" He managed to keep his tone casual.

She shrugged, her hand stealing into the bag and plucking out a piece of garlic bread. "I know those cameras only activate if the alarm goes off, but I feel like I'm on 'Candid Camera' all the time. Still, I'm glad for the system. It was a good idea."

"No more weird vibes that someone's been inside?"

"No," she said. "But you know what is strange—"

"What?" He spoke too quickly and worked to calm himself, to dismiss the vision he had in the lab. He'd obviously been pushing himself too hard, just like he had with that other case.

"Murry, what's wrong? Something's bothering you."

"You said something's strange?"

"About Kimble. The cause of death."

"I'd think that was obvious."

"Well, either stab wound was deep enough to kill him, but that's not what did him in."

"Oh?"

"He was poisoned."

Surprised, Murry glanced at her. "You sure?"

"Sure enough to say something. And there's something else."

"What?"

"Bones'll have to confirm it, but it looks like there's traces of make-up on Kimble's shirt. And a human hair. Blond."

Chapter 25

The next morning, Murry checked his desk but didn't find any messages from the Kid. A dead end? He got Billy's answering machine and left a "Call me," figuring Billy was catching some shut-eye.

His voice mail had one message—the Fed from Quantico. "It's very unlikely the killer and the thief are the same person, although they both appear to be highly organized . . ."

Hedging his bets? Still, it jibed with what they now knew. Kimble wasn't Ice Pick.

He called Bones about the shirt and hair.

The man sounded excited. "The make-up's a heavy foundation, the oil-based grease-paint actors use. The hair's dyed blond. It's human, but I'm betting it's from a wig. Both ends were cut, and the hair's smooth, like Asian hair, the kind most often used for wigs."

"A wig?" Murry thanked Bones and hung up, thinking about the woman Kimble had served at the restaurant. He pulled his notes on his conversation with the maître d'. *Old. Blond. Overweight. Big feet.* A man in drag?

He called Ramirez.

"*Hola,* Dance Man. You're up early."

"Hopin' for a break. Billy's not answering his phone. You got any leads?"

"*Nada*. Just finished talking to the warden at Folsom. Nothing looks good. You want me to fly up to Sacramento and talk to Kimble's old cell mate?"

Daniels wouldn't like the expense and the warden wouldn't like the implication that they didn't trust his interrogation. But the warden wasn't familiar with the Ice Pick cases. "Yes." He updated him on the make-up and possible wig hair. "See if there are any drag queens that were released around the same time as Kimble. If you run into any red tape, call me."

He replaced the receiver and wondered if he should talk to The Five Forty Five staff again.

Tack shoved through the door, the King's case file in his hands. He bypassed his desk and headed straight toward Murry.

Working for a neutral expression, Murry waited, knowing what was coming.

"Talked to that guy, James, about the bracelet. He identified it. Said it was from his safe." He set the file in front of Murry.

"Good. Connects Kimble to the theft. Not that it matters much, now that he's dead."

"Kinda puts you at a dead end, doesn't it?" Tack said. "I got Kimble, you got zip. Looks like I win the bet."

Despite the fact he'd handed Kimble over on a silver platter, Murry wasn't going to sound like a sore loser. He pulled out his checkbook. "What was your take on the guy?" he asked, hoping to change the subject.

"Arrogant asshole. Lives in a fucking castle."

"A castle?" He wrote in the date and the amount: $1,000.

"Might as well be one. It's up where those old movie stars used to build their little fortresses."

Murry knew the area. Prime real estate.

"Guy acted like I was an annoyance. Didn't seem all that concerned with getting his stuff back either. Was more interested in jawing about the Ice Pick cases."

The Ice Pick cases. That's all anyone wanted to talk about. Murry handed Tack the check.

"Rich bastard. Got everything. Looks down his nose at everyone." Tack waved the check. "Nice doing business, Murry."

Murry watched him leave, knowing that before the day was over, everyone in the station would see the check.

Billy walked in five minutes later. "Just heard. Tack didn't do anything to earn that, Murry. You shoulda never paid him."

"Hey, if I'd been smart, I would have kept my mouth shut in the first place."

Billy tapped the file on the King. "You looking for a loophole to get your money back?"

"No. Where you been?"

Billy's gaze skidded away. "Greene found the storage unit Kimble used. I went with him."

"Find any trophies?" Murry asked in as casual a tone as he could manage. The Kid should have run it by him first. He wondered just how much time Billy was spending with Greene, and if that meant the Kid had definitely turned his eyes to LAPD.

"Nope. Bunch of stolen items. Mostly from the last two hits. Proves you were right about Kimble."

Did that mean Billy would stay? "You come up with anything on his friends?"

"Zip." He set a small stack of papers on Murry's desk. "Typed up my notes. If there's something there, I'm not seeing it." His expression asked, what now?

Murry told him about the make-up and blond hair.

"Ramirez is going to Folsom, do some follow-up, just in case something got missed on their end. I'll get Greene and his guys to talk to the victims' families and friends again, see if anyone remembers an older, heavy-set blonde. You run a background check on all the King's victims. Maybe we'll get lucky."

Billy groaned. "How deep you want to dig?"

"Just the basics. If we don't catch another lead, it's a place to go."

"What's the point? It's gotta be someone from Kimble's past. Somebody he knew. Why don't I go back and talk to Mrs. Kimble and the brother again?"

Knowing Daniels would agree, Murry decided not to push the point. "Okay. Go." He'd do the background checks himself. He flipped open the King's case file and began listing the victims' names and missing items.

The vision of Éclair as Ice Pick's next victim crept into his mind and he shoved it down. That wasn't real. It was just fatigue. His mind playing tricks. It wasn't going to happen. Éclair was smart, careful, and a good shot. Besides, it was way too soon for Ice Pick to move again.

Momentarily convinced, he finished his list, shut the file, and reviewed his other notes, jotting down anything that stood out.

Light colored van?

Floor—how did killer know about wood floors?

Skin and blood under Olga's nails.

Ice picks in Kimble's car.

Black stocking in Kimble's house.

Old ice pick used on Olga.

Antique rug fiber found at Olga's.

Antique fiber . . . He stopped and flipped through the King's case file again. Nothing, nothing, nothing. Then he saw it.

Jackpot! Only one victim reported a missing rug—a missing *antique* rug. Conrad James III. First the bracelet, now the rug.

He punched in Billy's cellular. "Was there a rug in that storage unit?"

"I don't—Let me pull over and check my Palm." Murry waited, feeling a sense of urgency. Billy said, "Yep, yep there was. Why?"

"Forget Kimble's wife and brother. Go get the rug and take it to Bones to get a fiber sample. Ask him to see if it matches the fiber found at Olga's. And don't say a word to anyone."

"Greene'll have the place locked up," Billy protested.

"Not if you hurry. He's probably still writing up everything. Then he's got to get people out there to move it into impound."

"What do I tell him?"

"Tell him you think you left your Palm Pilot in the unit."

Billy hesitated. "You gonna tell me why I'm doing this?"

He quickly explained about Tack's comment, about the bracelet Kimble had stolen from James. If that rug fiber matches—"

"Geez, you think this James dude could be Ice Pick? That Kimble robbed him and that's how he got the picks?"

He hadn't thought that far ahead. "Jamison'll go ape-shit, if he hears about this. Let's see where it leads first. Call me as soon as Bones checks the fiber."

Murry flipped to the insurance information on James, punched in the number, identified himself to the secretary, and was put on hold. He needed to establish ownership—in case the fibers matched. Of course, it could still be argued that Kimble was Ice Pick and he'd robbed James's place, then killed Olga, thereby leaving the rug fiber.

"Detective Murry?" The voice on the other end of the phone sounded like British aristocracy. "I'm Miles Henderson. I'm in charge of Mr. James's claim. Have any of the items been recovered?"

"Found the bracelet. Possibly the rug. What can you tell me about it?"

"Hold on and I'll pull the file." He returned in seconds, and Murry could hear him flipping through pages. "Hmm. It's an Amristar carpet, circa 1870, approximately five meters by four meters, or, huh, fifteen feet by twelve feet. Purchase price was sixty thousand dollars. You found it?"

"Maybe." Murry scratched down the information, telling himself not to get too excited. "Do you know who he purchased it from and when?"

"Actually, it was purchased by his mother, Georgia. From a shop in California. Let me find a copy of the receipt."

His mother. Murry hoped the man could narrow it down to an actual store. He listened to Henderson breathe and imagined an overweight guy.

"Poor woman died a few years back," Henderson said. "Mr. James inherited everything." He cleared his throat. "Ah, here's the receipt." He read off the name and address of Nola Brookes's shop.

Bingo. That tied James's mother to the antique shop. His thoughts raced. What was it Brookes had said about the young priest? He looked like someone she'd met—maybe a relative of a client. Would she recognize Conrad James? Could he really be the one? If he could tie James to the antique store where Ice Pick's first victim worked, to the rug, and to Olga's funeral, he'd have enough for a warrant and a tissue sample to compare with what they found under Olga's fingernails. He thanked the man, then punched in Bones's number. "Has Billy dropped off the rug?"

"Just took a sample. I'll call you." *Click.*

Son-of-a-bitch. But something was still out there between him and the finish line, something nagging at him. He rang up Ye Olde Shoppe of Antiquities, but Nola Brookes wasn't there. Her granddaughter said she'd gone home ill.

Praying it wasn't anything serious, Murry called her at home. What if she didn't recognize James? What if she died before he talked to her?

She answered on the tenth ring, her voice faint. "Yes?"

"Ms. Brookes, this is Detective Murry. I'm sorry to disturb you when you're not feeling well, but I'm wondering what you can tell me about Georgia James?"

"Georgia?" A pause. "She died a couple of years ago . . . It was rather sad."

"What was?"

"How few people were at her funeral. I didn't know her that well, but she'd been coming to my shop for years. You probably wouldn't remember, but she made a string of awful films in the sixties, then dropped out of sight after her husband died. Used the name Georgia LaFleur, I believe."

Where had he heard that name before? He flipped through his notes, scanning until he found it. The reservation! He felt a surge of excitement. "Do you recall her son, Conrad?"

A pause and the sound of swallowing. "Excuse me. Dry throat." He heard her drink something before continuing. "Poor boy. She ignored him. Or so it seemed to me. The few times she brought him to the shop, she made him sit quietly by the door. Never seen a kid so still."

"When was the last time you saw him?"

"At the funeral. He was all grown up then . . . Why that's it!"

"What?"

"That's who the priest in the photo looked like. Georgia's boy." Her voice rose with excitement. "He was wearing a black suit and standing so somber-like. The priest had the same expression."

"Think they could be the same person?"

Hesitation. "Well . . . I suppose so."

Wham! Another nail. "Would you mind if I send someone over this evening, provided you're feeling better, to pick you up and bring you down here to make a statement?"

"Why? What's this about?"

"I can't say quite yet, Ms. Brookes, but it would be a big help to us if you'd make a statement."

She hesitated. "All right. Seven o'clock. I'll be ready."

Murry told her to expect Ray Ramirez and hung up. Another thought hit him and he called her back. "Did you ever sell an antique desk to Georgia James?"

A long pause. "Why yes. For her son. The year she died."

Murry worked to keep his voice bland. "Did it have an old-fashioned key?"

Another long pause had him tapping his fingers on his desk. "Yes, it did. Two keys actually."

Another possible link. Jamison wouldn't be happy with Greene if the key led to Conrad James, not when they'd had it all along.

Almost noon, he rang Billy for a progress report.

"Dropped off the rug a half hour ago. Bones is hemming and hawing but not saying much. You want me to keep hanging around?"

"No. Do a background check on James." Murry gave him the man's full name and address. "Do it quietly, but dig."

"What are you going to do?"

"Wait for Bones's call. If the fibers match, I'll go for a warrant."

"Murry, Kimble could have robbed James, then killed Olga."

"Kimble doesn't fit the profile. And the antique dealer identified the priest as James. He's our guy. I know it."

"Hold on a sec, Murry."

Murry listened to indistinct voices coming over the line, then Billy's excited, "They match!"

Things were falling into place. Finally. "Okay. Meet me at LAPD. I'll hit Jamison up for the warrant, while you check out James."

"You want what?" Jamison asked, his blue eyes questioning Murry's reasoning.

"A search warrant for Conrad James's residence and vehicle."

"Based on what?"

Murry hurriedly laid everything out, point-by-point, ending with, "The scrapings under Olga's nails didn't come from Kimble. We know they don't match Kevin Jones."

Jamison's steely gaze changed from skepticism to excitement. "Send some of your guys to stake out James's place. Make sure he's inside and doesn't disappear. We don't want *his* wife and brother, we want him. I'll talk to the judge."

Murry found Billy at Quintez's desk, the two of them tapping away on keyboards, Billy on his laptop, Quintez on her PC.

"Anything interesting?"

"Not yet."

Not what he wanted to hear. "Warrant's on the way. Sent some guys over to James's place. It's bound to be a long night; let's grab something to eat now."

"There's a Chinese place across the street," Quintez said, her fingers not missing a beat.

Billy rolled his eyes but said nothing.

"Look at this." Quintez squinted at her screen. "James was arrested once. Four years ago. No conviction."

Murry looked over her shoulder. "For what?"

"Looks like an assault charge. No weapon." Quintez picked up the phone. "You go ahead. I'll call Hollywood and see if someone remembers this guy. Order the Kung Pao Chicken for me, and I'll meet you there."

Billy looked torn. Murry knew how he felt, but Quintez could be on the phone awhile before she learned anything.

"I'll wait," Billy said.

Murry paused, noting the sparks between the two and wondering what happened to Gina. If the Kid wanted to play with fire . . . "And what should I order for you?" he asked, unable to restrain his sarcasm.

"Kung Pao Chicken sounds good to me."

Murry doubted if Billy had ever had it, shrugged, and headed across the street. The place was busy but not packed, and he sat near the front.

Five minutes later, Billy and Quintez strode in, their expressions like cats who'd eaten the family goldfish. "We got the low-down," Billy said. He pulled out Quintez's chair.

She flashed him a smile, then looked at Murry, her dark eyes all business. "A high-priced hooker accused James of trying to strangle her. James claimed they were playing a sex game and he hadn't intended any harm. I talked to the arresting officer. He said he thought James was weird. He also thought the prostitute might have made the accusation to get money out of him. Just before trial, she dropped the charges."

Billy leaned forward. "Guilty or not, he paid her off."

"Practicing his choking technique?" Murry wondered aloud.

"We think so," Billy said, his blue eyes casting out lines to Quintez.

Murry wondered if Gina had moved out. Throwing a pointed look at the Kid, he asked, "James have a girlfriend or wife?"

"He's single," Billy answered in unison with Quintez. If he caught Murry's oblique jibe, he hid it.

"Anyone living with him?" Murry asked.

"Don't know," Quintez said.

Billy was saved from another poke by the arrival of their food. Their waiter slid three steaming plates of Kung Pao chicken and vegetables, fried rice, and chow mein on the table, then left the bill and three fortune cookies. Murry's stomach rumbled like a hollow drum.

Billy tasted the chicken, swallowed, then gulped some water. "Hot," he gasped.

"Isn't it great?" Quintez said, before eating a bite.

"Yep, great." Billy jabbed his fork into the noodles and wound them up like he was eating spaghetti, looking grateful to have something besides the spicy chicken on his plate.

Murry hid a smile. He had barely swallowed his third bite when his pager buzzed. "Rock and roll."

Billy inhaled the last of his chow mein before shoving to his feet and dropping three tens on the table. "I've got it." He ignored the cookies.

"Thanks, Billy." Quintez snapped one open. "Hey, I'm going to be a star." She grinned. "Don't forget your fortune."

Billy snatched a cookie and dropped it into his pocket.

"Aren't you going to read it?" she asked as they crossed the street.

"Later," he said, his expression daring Murry to say one word.

Quintez's eyebrows rose in a questioning look as they entered Jamison's office, but she dropped the subject.

Jamison handed Murry the warrant. "Murry, we—" His

phone flashed before he could say more. He picked it up, listened, then hung up. "James is home. Farel called his number; a guy answered."

"Anybody see him go in?"

"No, but his car's in the garage. Farel looked through the window."

"Not a van?"

"No van," Jamison answered. "Could've dumped it."

"You want Greene on this?" Murry asked.

"Greene who? This is yours, Murry. You earned it."

Murry resisted the urge to look at Billy. He nodded to Quintez. "Let's go serve the warrant."

Chapter 26

Conrad spotted the detectives in the car across the street. Did they suspect him?

He reviewed all possible links and figured it had to be Kimble. Something the son-of-a-bitch had left behind. Still, they had no evidence. They couldn't know about his private exit through the side of the house, or the van in a garage three blocks away.

Pulling on gloves, he packed the picks, duct tape, and other necessary items in his backpack. From his office, he took all the newspaper clippings and stuffed them in a plastic bag. Wouldn't do to have them here if they searched the place. Lastly, he pulled out his trophies.

He buried his face in the crotch of Olga's leotard and inhaled a faint whisper of lavender. Barely anything left. He tried the others. *Nothing. Nothing.* Anxious to go, he dumped the leotard and the rest into the bag, hating the thought of having to destroy them.

After he finished with Mary.

The grandfather clock chimed 5:15. On the computer screen, he punched up the face he'd worn at Olga's funeral. The priest. Tapping keys, he quickly erased the beard and sideburns, shortened the hair, changed the color to auburn—his mother's color—and replaced the blue contact lenses in favor of his mother's pale green. Perfect.

She'd made ten rotten movies with ten different co-stars. They promised her everything and used her like a whore, and with every movie "Connie" paid the price. Oh yes, that was Connie's job. And now Conrad passed on the lessons and gave his own bit of glory to each of his lovers—his butterflies. And this time . . . this time it would all be on film.

He slipped on the cowboy outfit from movie number six. No six-guns though. Beneath the leather jacket, he wore the holster over his shoulder, his new stun gun within easy reach. He studied his reflection in the mirror, then glanced at the snapshot of Mary Éclair. He smiled and imitated a cowboy's drawl. "Happy Birthday, Miss Éclair, ma'am."

By the time he cracked the door that led to a path behind his neighbor's house, the sun had set and he was ready.

Chapter 27

Murry parked a block from James's place in a dark patch between street lights. James's estate rested on a hunk of land that had more foliage on it than a South American jungle. The windows, what he could see of them, were barred with black iron. Iron bent into the shape of wings. Butterfly wings.

Billy stared. "Looks like he shoulda hired a gardener ten years ago."

"He likes his privacy," Murry said. He walked down to Farel's car. "Anything happening?"

"Nothing."

Murry glanced toward the corner as headlights swept across the pavement and Evan Vermont's minivan rolled to a stop. "The techs are here. Where's Machado?"

"Behind the house at the base of the stairs."

Farel's phone trilled. He flipped it open and listened, his easy-going Michael Jordan features tightening into a scowl. "Got it." He looked at Murry. "Machado says he thinks he saw someone near the corner of the house, but it's a jungle back there. He wants back-up."

Murry nodded. "Go. We'll cover the front."

Farel was back in five minutes. "Didn't find anything. Machado's still at the back door."

"Good."

Vermont and the three techs climbed out of Evan's van and joined the group. Murry quickly explained the warrant, what he hoped to find, then led them up the palatial front steps.

Billy hit the buzzer three times. No answer. The security decal on the window read *Champion*. Murry pulled his cellular, called the company, identified himself, and informed them they were going in.

Billy sprang the lock with a crowbar and the door swung open. Guns drawn, he and Billy went in first, backs against the walls. "Mr. James?" Murry yelled. "This is the police. We've got a warrant for your arrest. Come out now and you won't get hurt."

Silence.

From the entry he could see the kitchen, the sunken living room, and halfway up the staircase. He gestured at Quintez and Billy and pointed toward the living room and kitchen. Quintez nodded and Billy followed her lead. Murry nodded at the techs to stay put, then took the staircase, straining to hear any noise. The place was quiet as a mausoleum.

He worked his way through a master bedroom bigger than his condo. Everything was neatnik perfect.

He checked the other bedrooms. Nothing. Dammit, they'd screwed up and lost him.

Billy and Quintez were waiting in the entry. "He's not here," Billy said. "But you should take a look at the basement." His voice transmitted excitement.

Murry turned at the sound of footsteps.

Tack came through the front door. "Thought you might need another dick on this one."

Help? What the hell was he up to? His gaze met Tack's, and Murry was surprised to see only sincerity. Glad to have an extra body, even Tack, Murry said, "Thanks. We were about to check out the basement. Vermont, why don't you and your guys start with the garage, work your way in from there?"

"Yo."

Murry turned to Billy. "What'd you find?"

"Lathe, bench, saws, drills, you name it, he has it."

Bingo. Murry followed the Kid down, Quintez, Tack, and Farel on his heels. At least ten degrees cooler, the basement held a thousand square feet of equipment.

Vermont stuck his head into the room. "Car's still in the garage, Murry. Engine's cold."

"Which means he left after Farel's call. Billy, does this guy have an office?"

"Next to the living room."

"Okay, you and Quintez check out his desk for names and phone numbers, call anyone listed, and see if they know where he is. Tell them we're following up on the robbery."

Murry listened to Quintez and Billy's retreating footsteps as he studied the basement layout. "We need to find some hard evidence."

Tack motioned Murry toward the work bench. "Safe's been drilled. Empty."

Murry blinked, and for a second could have sworn he saw ice picks inside the safe. Another blink and they disappeared. He found himself thinking aloud, like he'd done with Tack when they were partners. "Think Kimble drilled it, found the ice picks, and realized who James was?"

Tack shrugged. "Good a theory as any I can think of."

"It would explain the picks in Kimble's car," Murry said. "And it would explain Kimble's death. He got an ice pick through both eyes."

"You want me to search here?" Tack asked, his gaze scanning the area.

"Good idea." Murry doubted James would keep anything incriminating in the basement. It looked too sterile, everything vacuumed clean, the empty safe lying open as if to say, *no secrets here.* Too easy. "I'll tackle the bedrooms." If this guy's home was his castle, then his bedroom was the Keep.

In the master bedroom, he again wondered at the sparse furnishings. The room was big, four times the size of Murry's bedroom, but it had little personality. Besides a king-sized bed with a massive cherry wood headboard, the only other piece of furniture was an ornate cherry wood dresser. Above it hung ten neatly-arranged black-and-white photos of a woman he assumed to be James's mother. She was with a different man in several of the photos, looking starry-eyed, a young starlet who hadn't yet been ravaged by time or had her dreams ground into dust by the Hollywood machine. Other photos, not so glamorous and at least a decade later, were of her beside a much older man, her smile forced and the spark gone from her face. Nowhere did he see any family photos or any of her son. Looking at the array of pictures, he wondered what it must have been like growing up with someone who needed so much attention. Nola Brookes had said James was unnaturally quiet. Why? What had driven James to murder? Did it matter?

Éclair said he liked to analyze things too much. He shifted his thoughts back to the room. Besides the photographs, the only indication anyone lived there lay in the closet full of clothes. One suit cost more than his monthly paycheck. All were immaculate, with matching shirts and ties hung beside each jacket. The guy was organized.

He started going through the suit pockets first, finished with the closet, and went through the dresser. After thirty minutes, he'd found nothing unusual. He started on another bedroom, going through everything twice. Nothing.

He called down the stairs, "Hey, Billy, Farel, you find anything?"

"The key from White's key chain fits his desk," Billy called back. "But that won't convict him. Desk hardly looks used, and there's nothing incriminating. Need some help up there?"

"Sure," Murry answered.

"Living room's clean as a whistle," Farel yelled from the other side of the house. "He's got some godawful, ugly art on the walls though. My five-year-old could do better."

That godawful art was probably worth a million or two, Murry thought, but he didn't say so.

Billy took the last two bedrooms. Murry forced himself to go through the master bedroom and bathroom again, his frustration building. It was like the guy had gone through with lemon polish and spit-shined everything. In the hall, he nearly ran into Billy. The Kid's eyes were big, like he'd met *Ms. February* and she had a few warts. "You have to see this, Murry."

Murry followed him into the last bedroom. "Christ Almighty." Two entire walls were covered with butterflies, the multitude of winged bodies reflected in an opposing mirrored wall. Although the room was huge and filled with massive antique furniture, the furnishings were like a blip next to all those thousands of butterflies. The way the butterflies seemed to close in on him made him feel claustrophobic.

"How would you like to sleep in here?" Billy lifted one of the framed butterfly collections from the wall and peered at it. "Look at the wings." His face filled with disgust. "See the holes? They were pinned alive."

The Kid's face looked green and Murry knew they were both remembering Olga. Murry gave Billy a nod. "Good job, Kid."

He eyed the edge of the fourth wall, scanning the column of movie posters. "*A Cowboy's Heart*, starring Georgia LaFleur. James's mother. There's a bunch of photos of her in the master bedroom." It was odd how James had hung the three framed posters ceiling-to-floor. Why not put the posters in the other bedrooms and leave this one completely to his collection? Curious, he stepped closer and saw an alarmed keypad half-hidden by a large collection from Central America, the frame much wider than any of the others. To hide the keypad? He rapped on the wall, the sound hollow, and pulled down the posters.

"A door . . ." Billy's voice rose in excitement. "This must be how he got out without Farel seeing him."

Impatient, Murry said, "Get a sledgehammer."

Ten minutes later, they were at another dead end. The man had a secret passageway in and out of his house—but no trophies. Nothing to tie him to the murders.

Stepping into the hallway, he glanced back. The room was twice as big as any of the others, even the master bedroom. Between the dark furniture and the butterflies, every inch was covered. Why were the butterflies in this room and not the master? He studied the walls again. The butterflies made him uneasy. Maybe it was the way they reflected in the mirror on the other wall. Maybe it was because they were so damned creepy. He shrugged, about to turn away, when he noticed a TV remote on the dresser. But there was no TV.

He pointed it at the stereo system. Nothing. Then he noticed a remote beside the stereo. He picked it up, clicked it; classical music began to play. He turned off the music. Everything in the house was well-organized, everything in its place. He scanned the room again, sank down on the edge of the bed, and aimed the thing at every wall, hitting PLAY. Nothing happened. He tried it again, hitting POWER.

Nothing. He started over, hitting DISPLAY. First the wall with the closet. *Click.* Nothing.

Then the wall with the stereo. *Click.* Nothing.

Then the huge mirror. *Click.*

With a deep rumbling sound, the entire wall shifted sideways, unveiling a deep, vast, well-lit, walk-in closet.

On a motorized rail hung latex body suits of every possible shape.

"Shee-it!" Billy said.

Beyond the clothing stood a wall of shelves five deep. Rows of Styrofoam heads with everything from pencil-thin mustaches to thick handlebars, goatees, beards, every style and era you could think of, stared back at them. Contact lenses in a variety of colors lay in a display case in front of the heads. Plastic hands with fake nails from purple-black to dark red waved from his left. He did a double-take at the set of scarlet ones. Blood-colored with tiny black flowers. He looked from those to the latex body suit of a big bellied, big busted woman. *Madame Zena.* "Dammit, the fortune-teller. I should have guessed."

Billy ran the rail, moving the latex body suits toward the back, bringing forward a bunch of costumes. Bloody costumes. "This guy's a double fruitcake."

Murry eyed the dark splotches on the Civil War uniform. Then he eyed the movie posters, all starring James's mother. What kind of sick game was James acting out? Some kind of movie drama where he directed and controlled everything?

He turned his attention to the vanity table. The computer was still on, the screen saver a series of butterflies fluttering blissfully across the screen. He tapped the mouse. The face of Conrad James smiled smugly back at him. Only instead of being bald, like his DMV photo, he had a thick mane of auburn hair. The guy was a chameleon.

Murry rolled out the keyboard, intending to check the files. A photograph lay face-down on top. He turned it over and his hand went numb as though he'd been stung. The temperature in the room dropped twenty degrees. His mind felt sluggish with disbelief. It was the picture Billy had taken of him and Mary in front of Lance's twenty-foot Christmas tree. Where did James get it?

The more important question hit: Why did James have it?

"Murry?" He was vaguely aware of Billy stepping closer.

He had an abrupt vision of Mary on the gurney, dripping wet, bloody holes in her hands and feet . . . He tore out his cellular and punched in the morgue.

"You think—" Billy began.

Murry shook his head as Susan Newton answered. He forced himself to speak calmly. "It's Murry. I need to speak to Éclair. It's important."

"Don't you dare say you're going to cancel," Newton said.

"Cancel?"

Her tone suggested he had gone senile. "Your dinner reservation. Mary's birthday."

Oh, shit. "Let me talk to her."

"She's not here."

His throat felt like he'd choked down sandpaper. "Where is she?"

"She went home when I told her you were going to pick her up at six-thirty."

"Who told *you* I was picking her up?" He checked his watch: 5:50.

"Detective Kidman called and asked me to deliver a message from you."

"What, exactly, was the message?"

"That you'd made dinner reservations at Shandelay's and

you'd pick her up around six-thirty."

"When did she leave?"

"Fifteen, twenty minutes ago. What's wrong, Murry?"

But he was already running for the door. "Billy, come with me. Farel, get some guys over to Shandelay's." He punched in Mary's home number as he dashed for the stairs. Each unanswered ring left him feeling more and more helpless. All he could see were Mary's polished oak floors.

Chapter 28

Conrad parked his van a block away, just beyond a street light, and adjusted the remote video recorder. A perfect view of the hallway. *Absolutely perfect.*

He affected a casual walk over to Mary's door. He'd disarmed the motion lights the night before. He punched in the code and quietly stepped inside. Now all he had to do was wait. Soon, she would be home—to celebrate her final birthday. *With him.* Dear, dear Mary. She'd never have to know the pain of growing old, losing her beauty, being rejected. They would be lovers, and then he would paint her wings and set her free.

In the living room, he cued up the CD of *Lance Murry Live at the Met*, ready to go. Detective Arthur Murry would appreciate that little irony.

Entering Mary's bedroom, he took her Browning from the night stand, emptied the clip, then replaced it. He studied his reflection in the mirror over the dresser. Just another rough-and-ready cowboy in need of some lovin'. And afterwards, a stiff drink.

He stepped into the hall closet, set his pack at his feet, and closed the door to a crack, so he could see the hallway and bedroom.

Ten minutes later, he heard the click of the front door

deadbolt. The faint scent of perfume tingled his nostrils as she passed by. He heard the clunk of her shoes, saw a brief flash of skin as she removed her bra and panties, then the sound of water from the shower.

Cautiously, he crossed into her bedroom, made certain she was in the shower, then lit a stick of his mother's favorite incense—sandalwood. He blew on it softly until the scent permeated the hallway, then set it aside. Next, he took out the hammer and picks and placed them on the floor. He laid the special calligraphy brush on the opposite side, imagining how beautiful she'd look with her wings. His butterfly. Liberated from the cocoon of her body. First the pain, then the bliss.

He lit three candles, set them at the far end of the hall, dimmed the lights, then surveyed everything. Perfect for *A Cowboy's Heart*.

Moving quickly, he stepped behind the bathroom door, pulled the stun gun from his holster, and set it to the weakest setting. It would paralyze her for at least three minutes.

He didn't have to wait long.

The shower door clicked open and damp heat wafted toward him like a cloud. He inched to the edge of the doorway and glimpsed her with a towel pressed to her face. His heart was pounding so loud it was all he could hear.

Two quick steps and *zzzt*. She spasmed, started to fall, and he caught her under the arms. Touching her excited him, but seeing her green eyes wide with fear excited him more. He pulled her into the hallway and laid her in position, hands out at her sides, feet spread, then straddled her. "Smile for the camera, my love."

Her lips moved, her words slurred. "Know you . . . ?"

"Yes, we've met. Like your security system, ma'am?"

Like water closing over a drowning face, her eyes filled with panic.

He settled his weight on her thighs, leaned close to her ear, and whispered, "No one will come to your rescue. It's just me and you, Mary." Her cheek felt soft beneath his lips. He gave her a reverent kiss before sitting up. Beneath his palms, her skin quivered.

She had small, round breasts and he teased her nipples the way his mother had liked. She writhed, enticing him to caress her legs, to run his hands over her hips. A deep shudder rippled through her body. He could feel himself getting hard. He pressed his groin against hers, the friction through the denim driving him to rub harder, then to reach for the zipper.

He was getting ahead of the game. He eased up and whispered, "You're mine. You know that, don't you?" He reached for the hammer, then realized he'd forgotten the music. "Don't move, my sweet." Wanting to hurry, he forced himself to slow down and enjoy the moment. He adjusted the CD so that Lance Murry's voice lilted softly through the house. *Perfect.*

Leaving his boots by the stereo, he hurried back. The hall was empty.

He felt a moment of panic, then smiled to himself. He knew exactly where she'd go. Then he saw that one of his picks was missing. Naughty girl. He drew his stun gun and turned the power up a notch, then inched toward her bedroom.

Nine-millimeter in hand, she turned on him and, after only the briefest hesitation, pulled the trigger.

Click. Click. Click. Sheer terror showed in her eyes.

"It's empty," he said. "I've taken care of everything—just for you. Just for our time together. Relax. I'll set you free." He liked the way she measured the distance to the hall. She'd run, but she wouldn't make it.

She hurled the gun at him. He ducked. She had nearly

made it to the doorway when he caught her. She jabbed the back of his hand with the pick and he jumped back. She stabbed at him again, missed, and he zapped her.

She crumpled to the floor.

Blood dripped between his fingers as his hand began to throb. "Bitch." This time he dragged her into position less gently. No more delays.

Once he had the hammer, picks, and brush back in order, he slapped the duct tape over her mouth, then rolled the black stocking over her face. *Ready bitch?*

Straddling her, he pressed her hand against the oak floor, placed the pick against her palm, and raised his hammer triumphantly. *Now you know how it feels.* With one hard stroke, the pick went straight through her flesh and deep into the wood. *Perfect.*

Her eyes flew open, a scream lodged in her throat beneath the tape. She almost bucked him off. With her free hand she dug at his face, clawing his eye. He jerked his head back, grabbed her hand, and forced it to the floor, pain stinging his cheek. Again she bucked and nearly unseated him. Such strength and beauty. It was perfect that she'd stuck him, that their blood would mix. He groped for the pick and hammer, impatient to get her other hand out of the way, to make love to her before he finished pinning the rest of her and painting her wings. He was fully aroused and ready. So ready. God, he needed this, needed her.

Chapter 29

Murry listened to the unanswered rings with growing desperation. *Come on. Come on.* She always answered her cellular. It continued to ring, then switched to her voice mail. He disconnected and redialed.

He drove down Santa Monica Boulevard with the siren screaming, his mind screaming along with it.

Billy pulled his cellular. "I'll call for back-up."

"Right. No. No. Too many cars. Sirens. It'll blow it. Wait a few minutes. That'll give us time."

"Time to do what?"

"Save her." They were only seconds away, but it felt like hours. "Turn off the siren."

They rolled silently to the curb. Her well-lit street suddenly looked quiet and eerie, like something out of the "Twilight Zone." Her car was in the driveway. The lights were on in her bedroom, no sign of movement.

"Call Jamison and tell him we think Éclair's the next target and to send back-up. You cover the rear. I'm going in through the front."

"Doesn't she have a security system?"

"Fuck it. I'm going in."

Billy disappeared around the side of the house.

Murry took his key and turned it. The dead bolt slid back

without a sound.

Gun drawn, he eased inside. Lance's voice? His brother's CD was playing. For a split-second, he thought everything was normal after all, thought he'd be apologizing to Mary for calling the cops, thought that everything must be okay. He stepped into the hallway.

The world slowed down to a hellish crawl. He froze, his mind unwilling to believe the bizarre images his eyes were witnessing. The images slammed into his brain like bullets.

A cowboy in full regalia straddling a body, an ice pick in one hand, a hammer in the other.

The cowboy's wristwatch, white Arabic numbers on a black face, black alligator band.

A flash of memory—the guy in the three-thousand-dollar suit walking beside Tack—same wristwatch.

The pale, bare feet on either side of James's knees. The pick against one instep, the hammer coming down . . .

"No!" The yell tore from his throat as he squeezed the trigger of his Sig.

James's body jerked, and a red blossom appeared between his shoulder blades. The hammer clattered to the floor.

Murry squeezed again. Then again. The last shot took off the back of James's skull.

He heard Billy calling for an ambulance as he pulled the bastard off Mary's legs. Without a thought, he yanked the ice picks out of her hands. She tried to sit up. He scooped her into his arms and carried her to the bed. As carefully as he could, he peeled off the stocking and tape. Tears splashed down her cheeks as she turned her head and heaved.

He grabbed towels, the first-aid kit, and her robe. He dropped a towel over the bile, dampened the second one to wipe off the worst of the brain matter. All the while, she shook as if she were freezing to death. Gently, he helped her into the robe, then wrapped her hands. Hugging her to his chest, he felt her damp hair, smelled her lemon shampoo. But she was alive, not dead on a gurney. Alive. He felt her tremble. Her tears soaked his shirt. He rocked her and held her, uncertain who he was comforting most, her or himself.

"Murry, he—" she buried her face in his neck.

Chapter 30

Murry hated hospitals—the smell of disinfectant, the stark walls—but most of all he hated seeing someone he loved lying helpless. Careful to avoid all the tubes running in and out of her, he leaned over and kissed Éclair gently. Guilt hit him like a sledgehammer. He thought the word *raped* and hated it. "I talked to the doctor. You're going to be okay."

Her green eyes flashed with anger, her gaze skidding around the room like it wanted to land anywhere but on Murry. "Hands," she muttered hoarsely. They were covered in gauze. Then fear replaced the anger. She started to sob.

He was relieved when the nurse came in and added a sedative to her IV. A moment later Éclair's eyes closed and her breathing softened.

"She'll sleep for awhile," the nurse said before leaving the room. "I'll be back to check on her later."

"I'll be here," Murry said. He knew the Kid didn't like hospitals either, and was glad Billy was outside the door.

His phone buzzed and he almost ignored it, then had the feeling it was Lance.

His twin said in a worried voice, "Murry, are you all right? I had a bad dream. Woke me up."

Murry glanced at Éclair, then stepped out of the room. "Mary's been hurt. She's in the hospital, but she'll be okay."

266

He'd leave the rest for later—if he could talk about it. He wasn't sure he could.

The nurse at the end of the hall saw him talking on his phone and gestured at him to take it outside. He nodded okay.

"I'll be there in the morning," Lance said.

"Lance, you don't have to drop everything—"

"The hell I don't. I'll call you when I get in."

Once more Sir Lancelot was on his white charger, but for once Murry didn't mind. He flipped his phone shut, and the nurse lost her scowl. After clipping the phone back on his belt, he glanced at Billy.

The Kid chomped hard on his gum. "I couldn't quite make out what you yelled at James before you fired, but in my report I plan to put, 'Drop it, or you're dead meat.' Did I quote you correctly?"

Murry tore his gaze from a passing gurney, the occupant covered completely. "Ears like a bat, Kid."

"Thanks." The Kid shifted on his feet, his gaze flicking toward the door then back to Murry. "She's gonna be okay."

Murry nodded, telling himself it was true, but not quite believing it. Wounds like this changed people. Éclair was afraid, and she had a right to be. He cleared his throat and eyed his partner. "So, you going to LA?"

Billy leaned against the door jamb. "You look worried, Murry."

"Well, dammit, you're a good partner—and a friend."

"It crossed my mind a time or two. More action, lots more action, more overtime, Quintez. You know Greene had me bulldozed for awhile—but here's the deal, Murry. I've learned more from working with you on one case than I'll ever learn from a play-it-by-the-book guy like Greene. Besides, you seem to attract weird murders, and if I want weird, this is where I need to be."

He could feel the tightness in his chest relax. "Two weird cases in twenty years—both after I got you for a partner. Maybe it's you."

"No, it's you. You're the crystal ball guru, hands down." Billy patted his pockets, but instead of gum or a cancer stick, came up with a fortune cookie. He eyed it doubtfully. "Forgot about this sucker."

"Well?"

Wearing a suspicious expression, Billy cracked it, extracted the tiny slip of paper, and read. A slow grin broke over his face. "Well I'll be damned. Looks like my luck has changed." He handed the paper to Murry.

A good partner worth much gold.

About the Author

L. F. Crawford is the author of twelve novels, including bestsellers *Hat Trick* and *12 Jagged Steps*. She won the Eppie Award for Best Mystery Novel in 2000. Crawford lives with her husband and daughter in California. Her Web site is www.lfcrawford.com.